Books by Vella Munn

Feral Justice

Punish

Single Titles

Death Chant

Death Chant

ISBN # 978-1-78686-046-0

©Copyright Vella Munn 2016

Cover Art by Posh Gosh ©Copyright 2016

Interior text design by Claire Siemaszkiewicz

Totally Bound Publishing

DEATH CHANT

VELLA MUNN

Dedication

The premise and setting for Death Chant have lived with me ever since my husband and I joined dear friends in exploring Washington State's Olympic National Forest. That magical place spoke to all of us, so, Tallie and Bruce, this one's for you. And for their son, Lance, you will always live in my heart. Miss you so much.

Chapter One

"Peace and renewal. That is what Cha'lak'at'sit has always meant to the Chalat. The river was a gift from K'wati, who intended it to provide for our people. Whatever we decide now must be done with traditional Hoh belief in mind."

Jay Raven rubbed his aching right shoulder, doing his best to pay attention to his uncle. At thirty, Jay was in the best shape of his life, but that didn't mean he was Superman. "I was certain he'd say that," he whispered to his brother, who stood next to him on the banks of the Cha'lak'at'sit — or, as the non-Natives called it, the Hoh River — near where it fed into the Pacific Ocean in Western Washington. "Our uncle and the rest of the elders will always see everything in the context of the past."

Floyd jerked his head at the cedar canoe they'd pulled onto the gravel shore after bringing their uncle to where the Narrow Roaring Creek stretch began. "They're going to be at this for hours. At least we'll be moving with the river's flow when we head back."

"Fighting the current about did me in. Thanks for the help."

"No sweat, bro. I knew you couldn't get Uncle here on your own. I wish he'd sit down."

So did Jay, but Uncle Talio was doing what he believed he'd been born to do.

"Seeing so many of the Chalat here today fills me with gratitude." Uncle Talio moved in a semicircle, connecting with the over one hundred Hoh Native Americans who'd come for the meeting. "This shows that the decision we've been asked to make means a great deal to you." He shifted position, leaning more of his weight on his cane. "Before I read the request from Dr. Anthony Gilsdorf, I'll do my best to make sure everyone grasps the ramifications should we decide to have anything to do with the anthropologist."

It had rained last night and, judging by the sodden clouds, Jay figured another downpour wasn't far off. He'd grown up in and around Olympic National Forest. He didn't quite have webbed feet, but as he'd told the woman he'd naïvely thought he'd spend his life with, one reason he'd left the Northwest rainforest was so he wouldn't grow gills.

Leaving hadn't lasted long, but he'd changed during those years while the forest remained the same. A thousand years after his death, this wet realm would endure. Ancient moss-studded Sitka spruce and western hemlock would still rise above mats of vine maples and fern. Maybe he should let it absorb him as it had his uncle and other members of the small tribe.

Only he couldn't.

"Until whites ventured inland from the ocean," Uncle Talio continued, "the river and the land around it was home to us and the other tribes. But even then our ancient way of life had been threatened by the newcomers' diseases. Now what remains of the Chalat live near the mouth of the river we love, even as it slowly steals what little land we still have."

"Did he have to bring this up?" Floyd muttered. "That anthropologist's request has nothing to do with erosion."

Jay smelled booze on Floyd's breath, but Floyd wasn't drunk. As many times as he'd attempted to get Floyd sober, he recognized the signs.

When Uncle Talio was acting in his role as a tribal Old People, he tended to sound as if he barely understood English, but just because he'd grown up speaking Quinault didn't mean he was cut off from the twenty-first century. He simply preferred to live in the past.

Jay's shoulders weren't the only part of his body that ached. His back threatened to knot, and his knees were tender from supporting his weight the whole time Uncle Talio, Floyd and he had been in the canoe. As an Olympic National Park ranger, he was accustomed to spending his days on his feet, not struggling with the seldom-used but well-maintained canoe.

That's what he was, he reminded himself as Uncle Talio held up a deerskin decorated with the tribe's symbol of a stylized eagle and a salmon — a forest ranger. He was proud of who he was, he just didn't want his heritage to define everything.

Uncle Talio swayed but caught himself. Concerned, Jay made his way around the Hoh who'd been standing in front of him. He unfolded the lawn chair he'd brought along and braced it as his uncle sat down.

He became aware of the river grumbling and laughing behind him and the darkening skies. A distant rumble had him looking for lightning, but he didn't see anything. The land on either side of the river was open, but the forested mountains trapped the members of the small gathering. In some respects, he felt less claustrophobic when he was surrounded by thick vegetation than when he had a glimpse of space. It hadn't always been like this. He'd loved growing up with a temperate-zone rainforest for his playground.

Something to his right and down the riverbank a couple hundred feet caught his attention. He recognized a salmon carcass. The thunder continued, slowly getting louder. A toddler clung to her father's legs while the older Hoh nodded and occasionally exchanged glances. They were looking for signs that Thunderbird was in the forest. Thunderbird, yet another of the legends his uncle had shared with him while he was growing up.

For the better part of an hour, Uncle Talio alternated between the tribe's history and recent changes brought about because the government had agreed to let the Hoh purchase thirty-seven acres in the national park. The land was away from the river's flood zone, and new houses were being built there. Uncle Talio didn't mention that he'd remained in the house his father had built, a house Jay wanted to keep from falling down around his uncle's ears.

You could help, he silently told Floyd. *Stay sober long enough to get on the roof with me.*

He could hire his brother. Floyd could certainly use the money, but what if he used it to buy booze instead of paying the rent for the singlewide trailer in Forks? Floyd would wind up homeless, again.

Frustrated, he closed his eyes. Alcoholism was a disease. It wasn't as if Floyd wanted to be a drunk. Still —

"The request from the university professor was delivered to our director," Uncle Talio said. "Ned, would you please read the letter?"

A heavyset man with graying black hair and deep creases around his mouth and eyes positioned himself near Uncle Talio. Ned Hudson pushed his glasses higher on his nose, took several sheets of paper out of the large envelope he was carrying and unfolded them. Like Uncle Talio, Ned spoke softly. In contrast to Talio Raven, he never missed an opportunity to express his opinion.

"Have you decided how you're going to vote?" Floyd whispered.

Truth was, Jay didn't know enough about what Dr. Gilsdorf was proposing to have an opinion, but even if he did, he wasn't sure he'd express it. Decision-making should be left up to those who would be most impacted by it, not by an outsider.

"Dr. Anthony Gilsdorf is an anthropology professor in the California university system," Ned began. "He wants our cooperation and assistance while he researches the possibility that our ancestors, and the ancestors of other local tribes, established settlements at a distance from the waterways."

Sharp thunderclaps stopped Ned. When the sounds fell away, Ned started reading. Dr. Gilsdorf was in the process of submitting a grant application based on his premise that the recent discovery of bone and stone barbs from hunting weapons miles from the Hoh River was proof that ancient Native Americans had ventured far inland.

"In historic times," Ned read, "there were at least seven permanent settlements along the Hoh River. Locating and documenting those sites and others deep within the Olympic Forest is vital."

Floyd nudged him again. "You see what our uncle's doing?"

Jay studied Uncle Talio. The older man clutched the deerskin to his chest, with the symbols next to him. His eyes were closed, his mouth moving. The river continued its endless run behind him, and the murky clouds had stripped most of the color from his features. He looked not old so much as timeless, part of his environment. The wind had tangled his longish hair, making him appear a little wild. Just the same, Jay had no doubt his uncle, the man who'd raised him, was at peace.

Praying to his guardian spirit.

Jay looked up, half expecting to see Eagle overhead.

"I know what's on your mind," Floyd whispered. "How does it happen? Damn it, how…"

How could a sixty-something man communicate with a winged predator? Because Uncle Talio's belief went that deep. Because Eagle and Uncle Talio had connected in ways Jay would never experience.

It took Ned several minutes to get through the multi-page request. Dr. Gilsdorf stressed the public's right to understand indigenous populations and anthropology's responsibility to collect, analyze and share all possible information—with him taking the lead.

"We don't owe him anything," one of the older men muttered. "We don't dare have outsiders nosing around where they don't have a right."

Jay's stomach knotted. It didn't matter that he no longer lived and breathed his heritage—he was still a Hoh. If anything was sacred, it was Grandparents Cave.

"Here's Dr. Gilsdorf's pitch," Ned said. "The grant is limited to the professor's expenses for four months. Any assistance he receives from local Native Americans will have to be donated. Of course he hopes he's convinced us of the necessity for this *essential* project, but whether we do or don't, he'll be there. So there you have it." Ned shrugged. "We've had anthropologists and archeologists here before."

"But he's the first to intend to focus on the interior," a woman said.

"Tell him to stay the hell out of our business," Floyd grumbled.

"It isn't that easy," Ned replied. "We don't own the forest. The federal government does."

And I work for the government, Jay silently added.

"We have two options," Ned said. "Either we can pretend to cooperate or we turn down his request for assistance." He'd barely gotten the words out when thunder sounded.

"What about you, Jay?" Ned pulled his jacket against his neck. "If your supervisor orders you to work with him, you'd have to, right?"

"That won't happen. With all the budget cutbacks, I'm already working overtime." He rammed his hands in his back jeans pockets. It was starting to drizzle. Well-accustomed to western Washington's weather, he'd worn a rain jacket. What he wasn't looking forward to was getting Uncle Talio into the canoe and back home in a downpour.

Uncle Talio pointed his cane at Jay. "My nephew is searching for his truth. He walks in a world I don't. I can't tell him what to do any more than I can order my spirit to guide us in the right direction."

"What does your spirit say?" an elderly woman with gray braids asked. "You've been praying to it."

Uncle Talio stood. The auto accident had taken a toll on his physical body but hadn't diminished his intellect. "I'm not here to sway my people's decision. That's never been my way. If you want to grasp what thoughts my spirit has handed to me, I'll tell you, but you each have to make your own decision." He nodded at several members of his audience, Jay included.

"He isn't going to say we have to do everything possible to protect Grandparents Cave," Floyd whispered. "He'll never advocate for violence."

"I hope it won't come to that," Jay muttered. *But it might.*

"Everyone with Chalat blood has the ability to connect with his or her spirit," Uncle Talio continued. "Our grandparents and grandparents' grandparents lived their lives according to their spirits' wisdom."

Although Uncle Talio stopped talking, Jay knew he wasn't finished. His uncle wasn't determined to make up people's minds for them, but when he believed in something, he didn't let go.

"The spirits are with us today." Uncle Talio indicated the sky.

"It's just thunder," Floyd said. "He's going to turn this into a history lesson when we have an important decision to make. Are you as tired of the whole spirits thing as I am?"

He was. Floyd didn't live with Uncle Talio, which meant his brother didn't have the 'whole spirits thing' as Floyd called it constantly hanging over him.

The thunderclap sounded as if it was directly overhead and was so loud it hurt Jay's ears.

"T'ist'ilal." A look of peace came over Uncle Talio's features. "Thunderbird wants us to heed his wisdom as we make our decision."

Floyd shook his head. "Does Thunderbird flip coins?"

Maybe Floyd had had more to drink than Jay had thought, because cold sober his brother would never show disrespect around their uncle.

"Who is T'ist'ilal to us?" Uncle Talio asked. "Thunderbird is one of the great ones. He lived in a lair beneath the Blue Glacier and loved whale meat. When he was hungry, he flew down to the sea, swooped and grabbed a whale as if it weighed no more than a salmon."

"Yeah, that's right," Floyd muttered. "And if you buy that, I have a bridge to sell you."

"Sometimes," Uncle Talio continued, "the whale would struggle out of Thunderbird's grasp. When that happened, the whale fell to earth and died. It then changed into the great Whale Rocks near the ocean. Sometimes, Thunderbird grew tired from carrying the whale and set it down. The whale would thrash its tail, knocking down many trees."

"And," Ned said, "those actions helped form the land where the Hoh have always lived."

Thankfully, Floyd didn't say anything. No matter how many times Jay fought his uncle's efforts to pull the past into the present, he never fully succeeded. Maybe today's storm and the Thunderbird legend were simply coincidence, but what if there was something to it?

His ancestors believed Thunderbird, or T'ist'ilal, was one of the creators. The Hoh had been charged with protecting the land. However, forces beyond their control had spelled the end to their ancient way of life. These days the Hoh clung to a few acres. Grandparents Cave meant a great deal not just to the Hoh but every Northwest tribe. No one would let Dr. Gilsdorf get close to it.

Someone might resort to violence to keep that from happening.

Jay looked around for something to take his mind off the possibility. Uncle Talio was staring at him.

"Thunderbird does many things," the man said. "Is many things. We can't forget any of them."

Jay sucked in more wet air. "What can't we forget?"

"Thunderbird and Yakanon speak to each other of death," Uncle Talio said. "Many times like when one of them sees something that has died" — he pointed at the fish carcass — "their conversation remains between them, but sometimes Yakanon hears news in the wind about the death of a soulless one. Because only Thunderbird comprehends Yakanon, Thunderbird agrees to pass on Yakanon's message."

A few people were trying to protect themselves from the

downpour, but most stared at Jay.

Yakanon wasn't real! The spirit or force or whatever the Old People chose to label it was a fairy tale. Part of his ancestors' attempt to give order and reason to what they hadn't understood.

Ned laid his hand on Uncle Talio's shoulder. "Is that what you're hearing today?" Ned asked. "Yakanon, through Thunderbird, is warning of such a death?"

Uncle Talio stepped toward Jay. "I hear thunder and stand in a storm. Those things remind me of what I learned from my elders, and I feel compelled to pass on that wisdom. Whether someone believes as I do or walks his own way is up to him."

He tilted his head back. Rain washed his face. "If you believe this is simply a storm, that's your decision. But if you believe, as I do, that Yakanon is looking into the future, then you must ask yourself who doesn't have a soul."

Chapter Two

San Diego, California
Three months later...

Winter Barstow circled the UPS package on her coffee table.

"What have you been up to, Doc?" she muttered. Not that her mentor could hear her. Doc was working on his grant in Olympic National Forest, hundreds of miles to the north. She placed a hand on the package. It had been on her front porch when she'd arrived, which made her conclude that Doc — Dr. Anthony Gilsdorf — didn't place much value on its contents. But Doc wouldn't have sent her a gift on a whim. Whatever this was, it had meaning for him, meaning he wanted to share with her.

She went into the kitchen for a knife and then cut through the layers of tape. Inside the package sat a reinforced cardboard box. She untangled the flaps to reveal a small mountain of wadded newspaper.

A crawling sensation stopped her from removing the newspaper. Suddenly, she wished she could walk out of the room. And yet, at the same time, anticipation made her pulse race. She pressed her hand against her chest then tossed the paper aside. Closed her eyes and reached in. She touched wood.

Wood. Smooth, with intricately carved curves and angles. She opened her eyes, carefully freed the object from its cocoon, and lifted it with numb fingers. Her heart rate kicked up even more as she placed it on the table. Then she stepped back to study what her mentor, a man who'd given her life focus, had sent.

A large, intricately decorated mask.

Of a wolf.

Painted red, black and white, and with pointed ears, abalone eyes, long snout and sharp teeth — teeth capable of tearing and killing.

"How..." Childhood memories washed over her and her legs grew weak. Unlike the predator that had once been a vivid part of her dreams, the mask didn't look alive. Yet it took her back to when her dream wolf had been the one good thing about her world.

Either Sitka spruce or western hemlock had been used to form the base shape. Dried but intact hide stretched over the bridge of the nose, and tufts of brittle hair formed a dark halo. The teeth were bone fragments that had been glued or drilled into the jaws.

"Wolf symbolism," she managed, her hand now at her throat. Native American ceremonial. Surely stolen. "My God, Doc, what have you done?"

Doc was a university anthropology professor, currently on a grant-supported field project. A professional like him didn't remove artifacts from national parks. He didn't break the law.

And yet he had.

She pulled her gaze away from the mask and stared at the road beyond her living room window, as if to assure herself that no one could see what she'd just unveiled. Fortunately, living in a small rental in the desert east of San Diego gave her elbow room and relatively few neighbors.

The mask was real. But why would Doc violate the Native American Graves Protection and Repatriation Act getting it to her? The mask wasn't worth a one hundred thousand dollar fine and a year in prison.

She circled the table, studying the mask from all angles. There was something compelling about the cold, lifeless eyes, as well as the challenge shown in the flared nostrils and fierce open mouth. A master carver had created it, as evidenced by the lack of tool marks. Her educated guess was that it had come from either the Makah or Quileute tribes living along the Washington coast. Then she noted the black accenting the eyes. No. This was more likely Hoh.

Turning from the mask, she dug through the wrapping for a note, but she found nothing. Suddenly weary, she pulled her cell phone out of the backpack that served as her purse and sank into her recliner. She had a message.

It had better be from the man who'd given her equal parts encouragement and lectures about doing something with her life. According to the automated voice, he'd called this morning.

"Where are you?" Doc started. "Winter, this *has* to be between the two of us. You're the only one I can trust."

Trust? What was this about? She shivered.

"I need you up here as soon as possible. There's—I can barely bring myself to speak the words. I'm on to something beyond incredible. Something I believe is worth the risk I took. The danger."

"What are you saying?" she muttered.

"It'll change our lives. Place our stamp on everything anthropology stands for. Make Wilheim doubly sorry I got the grant instead of him. Call me. But first take a good long look at it. The mask dates back to early fur trading days."

She gasped. No, it couldn't. The elements would have destroyed it.

"Wilheim's going to give you hell when you tell him you're bailing on him, but I can't do this alone. I shouldn't say you owe me but, if that's what it takes, I'll play the card."

Praying he'd continue, she strained to listen, but all she heard was dead air. Feeling cold, she sat straighter and replayed the message. This time, she concentrated more on his emotion and less on the words. Fought to ignore the electrical charge racing through her. In the nearly ten years he'd been part of her life, he'd never sounded anywhere near this agitated. Doc was a tenured university professor, not some kid opening Christmas presents.

No, he wasn't Christmas morning excited. More like overwhelmed. Scared. Out of his element.

Scared? Damn it, she didn't want that for him.

Doc was right. She owed him a great deal. Alone in the world, yearning to belong, she'd snuck into his lecture hall. Instead of kicking her out, he'd seen through her emotional shields to the hungry-for-knowledge teen she'd been. Once he'd won her trust—no easy task—he'd helped her get several scholarships, a part-time job on campus, a roof over her head. A reason for existing.

She called him, but the phone went right to voicemail. Swayed by his cautions, she didn't leave a message.

When Doc had been preparing to leave, he'd made sure she had several ways of getting in touch with him, including the number for Potlatch, the employee-only park camp where he had his field office. She punched in the Potlatch number. As she waited for someone to answer, she debated how to best frame her reason for calling. Doc and she worked for the same California university system, albeit far from the same place in the pecking order. She could—

"Potlatch. Ranger Jay Raven speaking."

She couldn't remember Doc mentioning anyone named Raven. "I'm trying to reach Dr. Anthony Gilsdorf."

Silence. That was odd. Had they been disconnected? "Can you hear me?" she asked. "I'm trying—"

"I heard you."

Thrown off balance by the man's hostility, she struggled to concentrate. Jay Raven hadn't said whether he was acquainted with Doc, but what if he was and the relationship wasn't friendly? Doc had been disappointed by the local Native Americans' refusal to help him. Much as she wanted to tell the man everything Doc had done for her, now wasn't the time. It never would be.

"Is he there? I tried his cell phone but—"

"I haven't seen him for several days, maybe a week. Why don't you try later?"

"Wait," she blurted. "Don't hang up. When you saw him, where was it?"

The man hesitated, as if finally hearing the desperation in her tone. "Here. It might have been when he was talking to our budget officer, Michael Simpson."

"How do I get in touch with Mr. Simpson?"

"Who are you?"

Doc might not have told anyone there about their close relationship. Jay Raven would have no way of connecting her to the wolf mask—if he even was aware that it was missing. He couldn't track her.

Track her? Where had that thought come from? Damn it, she needed to get a handle on herself. Between the compelling artifact commanding her attention and her concern for Doc, she wasn't at her best.

"We're worried about him. He was supposed to check in this afternoon," she lied.

"Was he? Look, I don't have any more contact with him than necessary."

"Why not?"

"Maybe you aren't aware of this, but Dr. Gilsdorf's relationship with my people is somewhat strained."

"Your people?"

"The Hoh. We leave him pretty much alone. If he's gone missing—"

"He *has* gone missing." So she'd been right about the ranger's heritage.

"I'm afraid he has." His voice softened. "Dr. Gilsdorf had several meetings with the budget officer and park historian. They might be able to help."

"I'd appreciate the suggestion. Doc is staying at Potlatch, isn't he?"

"When he isn't camping in the forest."

Which was a lot of the time. "Would you mind leaving a note at his place for him to call me?"

"No, that's okay. Who should I tell him this is?"

"I'm Winter. Winter Barstow."

He paused. "Interesting name. I imagine you've been told that before."

"Yes, I have."

"My compliments to your parents."

Unfortunately, my parents had nothing to do with it. "I could say the same about yours. It's unique."

He chuckled. "Not many people are named after two different birds."

Listening to him, she realized she'd actually relaxed. Although she was still looking at the mask, it no longer dominated her thoughts. "You will tell him I called, won't you?"

"Of course." After giving her the numbers for the budget officer and historian, he hung up. Losing the connection left her feeling cut off from not just Doc, but so much of what mattered to him.

Jay Raven was Native American. That meant they had everything and yet nothing in common.

After hanging up, she noted that the sun was now below the horizon. The mask was being cloaked in shadows, prompting her to look away. She wished she knew what Jay Raven did. Undoubtedly he was charged with safeguarding the forest, but how did he and his coworkers go about it? Why had he chosen that career?

After yet another unsuccessful attempt to call or text Doc, she again acknowledged the mask's presence.

Silver eyes stared at her. The slightly open mouth could either represent a grin or a snarl. If it was as old as Doc had said it was, the mask had been created as part of ancient Native ceremonies.

Going by what she'd learned about the Northwestern tribes, someone, probably a proven hunter, had placed it over his head and mimicked a wolf's movements. Little children might have cowered before the fierce figure, but hopefully their parents would have assured them that the wolf dancer represented courage and survival. The hunter would stalk, threaten and mock attack.

How did wolves factor into Hoh spiritual beliefs? The tribe was small and had a lot in common with other tribes in the area. She wasn't aware of any study done on the subtle differences, if there were any. More to the point, the Hoh might not be willing to share their beliefs.

It shouldn't be here. If university staff learned what Doc had done, he'd be fired — unless someone like Dr. Wilheim decided the rare treasure would bring enough attention to the university to warrant defending a colleague under the cloak of research and discovery.

Dr. Wilheim defend Doc to the point of challenging the law? Wasn't going to happen.

She came closer then picked up the mask. Although heavy for its size, the incredibly well-preserved artifact seemed to have been designed to fit over her head. Holding the mask at arms' length, she walked into the bathroom, put it on the counter and stood in front of the mirror. Large black eyes, a somewhat broad nose, high cheekbones and thick, shoulder-length midnight hair reflected back at her. She'd studied herself countless times over the years, but the feeling that she was looking at a stranger remained.

Who was she?

Determined to shake off the unanswerable question, she started to reach for the mask but wound up unbuttoning the top two buttons on her blouse and pulling it away from her chest. Still staring at her reflection, she lightly stroked the small tattoo over her heart. It wasn't particularly remarkable — just the outline of a wolf's head with red eyes. It represented her reverence for a childhood obsession.

"Coincidence," she muttered. "Don't put anything into it."

Hesitant, she picked up the mask, lifted it over her head and settled it into place. Immediately she plunged into a world of weight and darkness and wood scent.

Claustrophobia washed through her, causing her heart to slam against her chest, but she fought her way past the fear. All these years on her own had taught her to face life squarely. No way would she let a little darkness get the better of her. If some superstitious Hoh could wear it for hours, she could put up with a few minutes. Then when she got a hold of Doc she could tell him — tell him what?

The question faded along with her awareness of where she was. She was no longer hot and thirsty. Instead, she swore she was breathing cool, damp air that smelled of vegetation both growing and decaying.

Two holes had been drilled into the base of the muzzle, allowing her to catch a glimpse of herself in the mirror. She saw nothing of Winter Barstow. That woman had been replaced by fierce ancient symbolism.

A howl echoed throughout the small room.

Chapter Three

Relatively speaking, summer was the dry season in the Northwest. Still, it was cloudy and the air coming in through Winter's open car window felt cool, reminding her of the eerie sensation that had overtaken her when she'd put on the wolf mask two days earlier. After hearing the howl — or suspecting she'd heard the howl — she'd packed up the mask, unwilling to put it on again. Once had been enough. Until and unless she got her emotions under control, she'd chalk the experience up to a touch of exhaustion, coupled with worry for Doc.

That, and memories of childhood dreams of walking alongside a powerful but gentle wolf.

A blanket of green existed as far as she could see. There were dark tree trunks, interlacing root systems of a lighter hue, fog sliding through everything, and gray overhead. Lush, rain-fed life dominated. Despite her interest in Northwest Native Americans, she'd never been to the state of Washington. Now, driving down a winding road, the environment seemed both alien and familiar.

No, not familiar. Darn it, was she ever going to stop looking for her roots and accept that she'd never be able to put the pieces of her past together?

Rounding a bend in the road, she noticed a collection of buildings and a US Forestry sign identifying *Potlatch*. She'd arrived. She parked in front of a small, weathered building marked *Office*. Delaying the move that would force her into that deep and inescapable world that existed, fog-shrouded, outside her car windows, she leaned forward and worked the kinks out of her neck and shoulders.

Although she'd left several email and text messages, Doc hadn't responded. When she'd called his son, he'd said he hadn't heard from him in the past few days, either, but hadn't expected to. She'd reached the budget manager, but he hadn't been able to shed any light on Doc's whereabouts. Finally, consumed with fear and worry despite her rationalization that cell phone reception was unreliable, particularly in the remote parts of the park, she realized she *had* to come to where he was. Something wasn't right — she could feel it in her bones. Maybe he'd gotten hurt or lost, but maybe someone had discovered what he'd done and decided to make him pay for it.

She'd driven nearly nonstop from San Diego. She had to find Doc. Nothing else, not even remaining employed, mattered.

Dr. Wilheim, who she'd had to call because his office had been locked the two times she'd dropped by, had been furious when she'd told him she needed to take some time off. He'd curtly pointed out that several out-of-town commitments had made it necessary for him to miss work earlier this week. He certainly hoped she'd attended to the tasks he'd given her. According to him, she was demonstrating the ultimate in irresponsibility. He'd gone so far as to tell her he was questioning his decision to grant her the rare entry-level university employment opportunity.

His reaction might have been different if she'd told him what she was doing and why, but she'd only shared her concern for Doc with her best friend, Carolyn Jensen. She'd been tempted to tell Carolyn about the mask, but in the end had decided to keep that to herself for now. As Carolyn had pointed out, Dr. Wilheim and Doc were academic rivals. Both had applied for the same grant. If Dr. Wilheim learned Doc was MIA, if he so much as suspected Doc had stolen —

No, Doc wasn't a thief. He'd simply used the mysterious mask as bait to get her to come here. Once she found him, they'd develop a plan for returning the mask to where it belonged without alerting authorities.

Before leaving San Diego, she'd refreshed herself about what the penalty was for violating the Native American Graves Protection and Repatriation Act. Whatever it took, she'd make sure Doc wasn't charged.

Her, either.

Looking up, she noticed that the office had been made of whole logs, a throwback to pioneer days. The foundation had cracked in numerous places. Water at the small settlement, Doc had informed her, came from a well, and underground electrical lines lessened outages during frequent storms. Covering more than nine hundred thousand acres, Olympic National Park included five commercial lodges and close to twenty public campgrounds, although Potlatch itself was off limits to visitors.

She stretched then eased her stiff body out of the vehicle, locked the doors and faced the forest. It seemed to be waiting for her, ready to pass judgment on her. Pausing, she listened, then realized she'd been hoping to hear a wolf, which wasn't going to happen because wolves no longer existed in the area.

She'd debated leaving the mask behind, but in the end had decided to bring it along, well hidden in the locked trunk. She couldn't begin to count the number of times she'd thought about the mask during her drive. She'd wondered what had been on the long-dead craftsman's mind as he'd worked on it. How much soul-deep spiritual belief had flowed from his heart through his fingers? The question she most wanted the answer to was whether he'd left something of himself in the work. Maybe that was what had been behind the howl she'd heard in her bathroom. An ancient Native American reaching through to the present.

To her.

You imagined the sound, she told herself. Just the same, she slid her hand under her shirt and stroked her tattoo. Doing so eased some of her tension.

After climbing the four steps leading to the office, she reached for the knob. Before she could turn it, the door opened. She stared up at a man dressed in Forest Service olive green, who was looking back inside, giving her time to study him. He wasn't particularly tall, probably not quite six feet. His shoulders were broad, his chest and arms substantial, belly flat and thighs thick.

Whatever life throws at me, his form said, *I can handle it.*

"I figured you'd say it isn't in the budget," the ranger said to whoever was inside, "but there's considerable social media talk about the trails' poor upkeep. People aren't going to come where they can't get around."

Deep-set coal-black eyes regarded her. His face was more round than oval, and his dusky skin looked as if it spent a lot of time being subjected to the environment. She noted thick, coarse, short black hair.

He looked down at her, making her feel small and vulnerable. Exposed. She grew frustrated with her reaction. This was simply a man. She looked at his name tag. Jay Raven.

She felt lightheaded and emotionally unbalanced.

"I'm sorry, but Potlatch isn't open to the public," he said.

"I'm here looking for Dr. Anthony Gilsdorf. He—"

Eyes widening and expression sobering, he held up a hand. His lips parted, but he didn't immediately speak. "You're Winter Barstow, right?"

Her heart stumbled through a beat at the sound of her name coming from him. "You remember."

"Of course. I'd never forget that name."

As his scrutiny continued, his gaze sweeping up and down her form, she became aware of herself as a woman, something she hadn't done for a long time. Her breasts tightened, and she was tempted to run her hands over her hips.

A tall, slightly overweight man with sagging jowls appeared behind Jay, ending whatever had been happening between them. "What's going on?" he asked.

"This is the woman I mentioned," Jay said without taking his attention off her. "Dr. Gilsdorf's colleague."

More than a colleague. There's a connection between Doc and me. One I wish I could trust you with. "I'm here because I've been unable to contact him. That concerns me."

The door opened, and the other man joined Jay and her on the porch. His tag read Michael Simpson. He held out his hand, and she took it. "After you gave her my name as a possible contact," he told Jay, "Ms. Barstow and I spoke briefly." He faced Winter. "Like I told her, I've been overloaded with work, so I haven't had time to see if he has been around."

"Dr. Gilsdorf mentioned budget cuts in the national parks," she said, responding to Michael's comment as a way of gaining a connection, although she'd rather be talking to Jay, studying him, listening to his voice. "The same thing is happening with higher education, where I work."

"And yet you were able to come here." Jay's expression sobered. "I assume that took some doing."

"It did."

As Jay continued to regard her, she wished she was privy to his thoughts. She hadn't expected him to welcome her with open arms, but was that resistance she was feeling? Maybe he didn't want her here.

"Dr. Gilsdorf told me he was disappointed his grant didn't allow him to bring you on-site," Michael said. "It sounded as if he values your expertise."

"I take that as a compliment. Neither of you knows where he is?"

Michael frowned. "I asked him to give me his schedule, but he refused."

"Refused?"

Michael shook his head. "He expected a certain amount of cooperation from locals and park staff. When he didn't get that, he obviously made the decision to work independently."

"Why did you want his schedule?"

"I'd hoped we could work out something that would benefit both him and the park's bottom line. Even though he didn't see the same possibilities I did, I wanted to keep the lines of communication going. If I had some idea how to get in touch with him—"

"It's more than that," Jay interrupted. "No one should go into the park without telling someone about their destination. I've been on searches that were more complicated than necessary because we didn't know where to look."

"I'm surprised he didn't take that into consideration."

"Obviously his agenda took priority." Michael pushed sparse, flyaway hair back from his temple. "Jay grew up here. Despite that, even he doesn't go out on his own without first reporting his destination."

Jay Raven's roots were in this forest. Most of the time, she tried not to imagine what a sense of belonging would feel like. Now she couldn't stop the thought. Glad he couldn't read her mind, she again focused on Jay. Talking to the budget officer hadn't taken away Jay's impact on her nervous system. He was sexy in a rough, maybe wild way. Unlike the academics she spent her days with, this man was defined by the environment.

"What about you?" she made herself ask. "When's the last time you saw Doc—Dr. Gilsdorf?"

"You asked me that when you called. It could be as much as a week. I prefer to avoid him."

Surprise rocked her. "Why don't you want anything to do with him?"

"It's just easier that way."

"Easier?"

His gaze lingered, strengthened, made her want to scream. "I'd rather not go into it. Has Dr. Gilsdorf told you about his relationship with the local tribes?"

She'd gone through the emails Doc had sent her over the last few weeks before leaving San Diego, looking for a clue as to why he'd sent her the wolf mask. Or why he'd gone off the grid. "It wasn't proving to be as fruitful as he'd hoped. One of his goals was to get his hands on as many personal

Native histories as possible. Apparently someone here had transcribed a number of oral interviews. He thought those would prove valuable."

Jay folded his arms over his chest. "That someone would be Booth Deavers, the park historian. The interviews were conducted a long time ago and pretty much forgotten until Deavers uncovered them. The tribes asked for them back, but he refused."

"Why did he do that?"

"So he could exploit them."

"In what way?"

Jay shook his head. "You'd have to ask him, but I'd say Booth is out for his own professional gain."

"The same could be said about Dr. Gilsdorf," Michael said. "Everyone's looking out for number one."

"Doc wouldn't do that," she insisted.

"Wouldn't he?" Michael's tone was caustic. "I made an honest attempt to give his agenda priority when I approached him about what I remain convinced could be a mutually beneficial relationship. Unfortunately, Dr. Gilsdorf made it clear he was answerable to the university and the foundation behind the grant, not the park."

That wasn't the man she admired. No way would Doc alienate those who were familiar with the area. In fact, he'd do everything possible to get along with everyone here. "What about Booth Deavers?" she asked Jay. "Do you know anything about Doc's relationship with him?"

"Sorry. Most of my time is spent in the forest. I stay out of personnel conflicts."

"That's easy for you to say." Michael gave Jay a dismissive glance. "You don't have to deal with Deavers. I do."

"What's the best way to get in touch with him?" she asked.

"He spends much of his time at the Lake Quinault Lodge, where he set up a combination library and museum."

"Thanks for the suggestion. Is there anyone else I should talk to? Maybe someone helped him learn his way around the forest."

When Michael drew himself upright, she sensed she'd rubbed him the wrong way. "We don't have the manpower to offer anything like a guide service."

She was wasting time talking. Besides, standing close to Jay Raven had her a little off balance. Confidence radiated off him. The man was surrounded by his heritage while she'd barely been able to scratch the surface of her hers.

"Which cabin is Doc staying in? There might be something there that—"

Michael jerked his head at Jay. "You take her there. I don't have the time." Not waiting for Jay to respond, Michael went back inside.

And it was just Jay Raven and her again. The two of them, surrounded by vegetation that had been growing for thousands of years. Vegetation capable of swallowing the most important person in her life. Maybe her, too. What else did the forest hold?

"I'm sorry. I didn't mean for him to dump responsibility for me on you," she finally thought to say.

"He deals with stress by being uptight. Don't take it personally." Jay started toward the steps.

"Wait." Before she realized what she was doing, she'd grabbed his forearm. Touched strength. "Do you have anything personal against Dr. Gilsdorf?"

Jay could have easily broken free. Instead, he stared at her hand. "I wouldn't say that. Our contact has been minimal. I wasn't there when he met with my uncle and the other elders, but Uncle Talio said Dr. Gilsdorf doesn't and never will understand."

"Understand what?"

Something changed about Jay's expression. It was almost as if he'd forgotten she was there. "I'm a Hoh. Most of the less than three hundred members want to retain their individuality and keep that individuality close to their hearts."

She'd just told herself to view Jay Raven simply as a forest ranger, but listening to him, that was no longer possible.

He was part of something anthropologists could never describe.

"He didn't seem to get that we're much more than subjects or research projects."

Didn't? Why had Jay Raven referred to Doc in the past tense? "You make it sound as if he's taking advantage —"

"He would if he could. At least, that's what the elders believe."

"What do you believe?"

"It doesn't matter."

"Why not?"

"Winter, whether or not the Hoh cooperate with Dr. Gilsdorf should be decided by those who have the most at stake. Those who see the land and the past as integral to what they are. Like many others, my uncle has spent his entire life here. He buried his wife, parents and niece — my mother — here."

Jay's expression sobered, telling her how painful the subject must be to him. Even though she wanted him to feel free to tell her more if he felt the need, daylight was already working against her. If she was going to stand a chance of finding Doc today, she had to get started.

She released Jay's forearm. "Is Doc's cabin close by?"

"Yeah." Jay headed down the steps. She followed suit. In addition to trying not to study the solid form ahead of her, she fought the impulse to look at her car with its precious and hopefully safe package in the trunk.

As they threaded their way down a narrow, graveled trail, she felt as if she were leaving what little civilization there was in the area. Cabins were tucked into small, barely cleared spaces, with considerable distance between each one, and she and Jay were the only two humans around. Even with what he'd said about his uncle's deep connection with the land, she suspected the same was true for him.

"I appreciate you doing this."

He didn't look back at her.

"Can I ask you something? What does Michael do?"

"He mostly tumbles numbers, fewer and fewer numbers these days. There's political pressure to make the parks self-supporting, which means he's expected to come up with ways of increasing revenue."

"And he thought working with Doc would help?" If that was true, wouldn't that put Michael and other park personnel at odds with the Natives? Did that mean Jay had to straddle the fence?

"You'll have to ask him."

As she tried to match his long stride, she puzzled over why she continued to feel compelled to learn what made Jay Raven tick. He'd made it clear he had little if anything to do with Doc, and Doc was where all her energy should be directed.

That, and attempting to make her peace with the wilderness that seemed to be reaching for her and separating her from the world she'd left behind.

Her world. Her career. The connections she'd made.

When would she return to them?

"All the budget cutbacks where parks are concerned," she said, "must make things stressful for you."

For long seconds, she thought he wasn't going to answer. She didn't blame him. After all, she had no right saying what she had. Maybe he'd leave her to search for Doc's cabin on her own. Maybe she should admit her people skills sucked, but then she'd have to explain why.

"It does, as I'm sure you can relate."

"I can, unfortunately."

His smile said he'd acknowledged something they had in common. She wondered what else might connect them. "I'm grateful this position came my way," he said. "Decent-paying jobs are scarce in this area, and I have responsibilities here that go beyond my career."

What responsibilities? Maybe a wife and children. He wasn't wearing a wedding ring. "So do I. That's why I came."

His nod gave her no indication of what he was thinking, and she missed what they'd briefly had. A couple of minutes

31

later, he approached a cabin with a sagging metal roof. He knocked on the door, then to her surprise, pushed against it and walked in.

"The locks on these things are a joke," he said.

The idea of Doc not being able to close himself off from the world concerned her. When Jay switched on the light, she took in her surroundings. The cabin consisted of a single room that served as bedroom, kitchen and living room. There was a tiny bathroom with a curtain instead of a door. A sleeping bag covered the twin bed. The dish drainer was full. What had been designed to serve as an eating table was covered with books and a stack of folders stamped *Olympic Park Library*. A laptop sat half buried under the books and folders.

She moved to the potbellied wood stove in the corner and touched the surface. The cabin and the stove were cool—Doc hadn't built a fire this morning. There was no sign of the backpack she'd given him as a going-away present.

"Is he often gone overnight?" she asked.

Jay jerked his head at the door. "I live on the Hoh reservation, but sometimes when I'm working overtime or on a project, I stay in one of the cabins here. I've seen Dr. Gilsdorf a few times in the evening."

"Did the two of you talk?"

"Not much. By the time I hit the cabin, all I wanted to do was get something to eat and fall asleep."

Her concern growing, she walked over to the bed and touched the sleeping bag. "He'd have taken this if he'd intended to be in the field for longer than a day."

"Yes, he would."

"Do you know where he's been going?"

"He didn't tell you?"

She was supposed to ask the questions, not him. "I've been working fifty-plus-hour weeks. Between that and the limits with cell phone reception, the answer is no."

He briefly closed his eyes. "The last I heard, he was around Ghost Totem Ridge."

Ghost. Jay's voice hanging on the word added to her unease.

"Why there?"

"It's near a valley that, judging by the number of old elk, deer and other animal bones found there, had been a popular hunting area." His eyes opened, but his gaze refused to meet hers.

"What about somewhere else? I don't want to charge to Ghost Totem only to discover I'm wasting my time."

He locked eyes with her. Something jumped inside her, a reminder that she was a woman and he was a man.

"I wish I could give you something more," he said, "but that's all I'm aware of."

She worked a lump out of her throat. "What's it like?"

"Beautiful." He whispered the word. "Ancient. My ancestors and other tribes camped in the area for centuries, but since that part of the mountain is one of the more popular areas for visitors, it's been trampled on a lot."

"I'm sorry."

"Yeah." Still looking at her, he nodded. "So am I."

He was making it nearly impossible to think. "Could parts of it be so rugged that most hikers don't venture into it?"

"Wild and impenetrable, you mean?"

She swallowed. "For all but the most physically fit." *Like you.*

"It's that, all right, and your professor isn't in the best shape."

Jay's comment served as the reminder she needed of why she was here. She mentally shook off his impact on her. "Is Ghost Totem far from here?"

He didn't hurry his reply. "Five miles. The trail starts at the parking area and is marked."

That sounded easy enough, but what if Doc had struck off cross-country? What if he'd had a heart attack or injured himself? Damn him for not telling anyone where he'd gone.

Of course, she wouldn't have met Jay Raven otherwise.

"My hiking boots and pack are in my car." There. That

was a practical and necessary statement.

"You're not going to take off now, are you?"

She needed to be on the move, to do something. Besides, being alone in the wilderness would give her the opportunity to try to make sense of why she was reacting to Jay like she was.

In addition, solitude might force her to come to grips with her reaction to the blanketing unknown. To open herself up to what, a wolf?

Only in her dreams.

"I'm an experienced hiker and camper. This spring, I hiked through much of the Chocolate and Palo Verde Mountains."

His smile touched a deep place in her. "Those aren't mountains, Ms. Barstow. They aren't the kind that swallow people. I lived in Southern California for a couple of years, so I'm aware of the difference."

"You're right. There's a huge difference between the climates. Do you ever want to go back?"

"Not really."

Right now, neither did she. She started toward the open door so she could get her hiking gear from her car. Before she reached it, however, an older man using a cane stepped into the room. His weathered skin, long gray braids and eagle feather necklace contrasted with his jeans and flannel shirt and made her think this was what Jay would look like in thirty years. Granted, Jay was considerably taller, but both of their features were Native American.

Like hers.

She studied not just the striking silent newcomer but also the change in Jay's demeanor. His full attention was now locked on the older man. She sensed both affection and wariness between them. Jay's gaze went from the man's face to his legs, then back to his face.

The newcomer pointed a leathery finger at her.

"Yakanon," he said. "Yakanon."

Her heart beat painfully. "What—"

"Take my message into you and listen to its wisdom."

Still unnerved, she flicked her gaze to Jay, but he was still staring at the newcomer. Shock transformed his features.

"Yakanon," the man repeated.

The word was both beautiful and unnerving, multilayered. "What?"

The older man started to lift his arm only to let it drop, as if he'd considered touching her. "Your soul does. Open yourself to its messages."

"Look, if you're thinking to scare me—"

"He isn't," Jay interrupted. "That isn't his way."

Maybe she shouldn't, but she believed the ranger. The older man started to rub his right thigh. She debated suggesting he sit down, but this wasn't her place. It belonged to Doc.

No matter how much she wanted to question the man she suspected was Jay's uncle, that would have to wait until she'd accomplished what she'd come here for. Even her soul would have to take a back seat to that.

* * * *

"Why did you say what you did?" Jay asked his uncle after closing the door behind them. Winter Barstow was jogging back. Earlier, he'd simply wished he didn't have to spend time around her, because, if he was being honest with himself, she spoke to the male in him. The last thing he wanted to do was be concerned for her, but he had no choice.

Uncle Talio shifted the cane to his other hand and wiped sweat off his forehead. That would be the only indication he'd reveal of how much getting here had taxed him.

"I felt compelled to," Talio said.

"Compelled? I need more than that." Jay crooked his arm so his uncle could take it. They started after Winter. "Saying 'Yakanon' isn't exactly the same as 'Hi, how are you?'"

"Do you remember what it means?"

On the verge of pointing out that he was no longer a child needing to be taught about his heritage, he nodded. "Yakanon mourns the death of the soulless one, and yet you told her to listen to her soul. What was that about?"

"That's for her to decide, if she has the courage to seek the truth."

Not for the first time, his uncle was talking in riddles. "You brought up Yakanon that day out on Cha'lak'at'sit, when everyone had gathered to decide about Dr. Gilsdorf's request. Wasn't that enough?"

"I wish but, no, it isn't. My spirit rules my words."

Even though he didn't want to, and long experience had left him with no doubt that it wouldn't do him any good, Jay couldn't help but study the trees for a raven. He saw nothing. Felt nothing.

"Eagle told me where to look for her," Uncle Talio said. "He was aware of her existence before she arrived."

He didn't tell Uncle Talio that he envied the man's belief system, because that would open a box that needed to remain closed. Life would be simpler if his so-called spirit guided him like Eagle did his uncle, but Raven had never been more than a young man's misguided belief that something had happened during his spirit quest.

"Why would Eagle care?" he asked.

"She's Native American."

As if that explained everything. "Just because she is doesn't mean she'd have any idea what you were talking about when you mentioned Yakanon. And even if she did, death talk is the last thing she'd want to hear right now."

"I didn't want to have to come here today." Talio indicated the leg he'd nearly lost in the automobile accident that had brought Jay back to Washington. And what might keep him here for as long as his uncle lived.

"I wish you hadn't."

Uncle Talio fixed somber eyes on him. "Someone needed to hear Yakanon's message. All I knew was where I needed to go to say the word."

"To Dr. Gilsdorf's cabin? Maybe he's who the message is about?"

"I cannot say. Jay, it might be for you."

With his uncle's words, the old wound opened up. He hated the idea of being soulless, but it might be true. After all, he'd turned his back on a core part of his heritage.

Chapter Four

The western hemisphere's largest virgin temperate rainforest had a rhythm. Trees so tall and thick and dark she could barely comprehend the hundreds of years it had taken to create them closed around Winter. The trail to Ghost Totem was marked, but that didn't stop the shadows from surrounding her. Her attention strayed to the wall of green to her left.

Massive trees grew so close together that even if there had been no mist or clouds, the sun would have made little impact. The scent of loam, dampness and decay made the air heavy. Brush hid the ground, and great, moss-covered boulders littered the area to her right.

Green. Deep and dank. Vivid beyond belief.

As an experienced hiker, she'd automatically brought along her backpack with sleeping bag, water, granola bars and a jacket, but the idea of spending the night out there was disconcerting.

Although she'd researched the area, only now did she truly appreciate not just its mass, but its pulse and beat. Maybe its spirituality.

She couldn't say she loved this place. The land was wilder than she'd imagined and spoke to her on a level she couldn't ignore or deny.

The deep, faint whisper that was the forest's voice rose as a gust of wind chased overhead, then faded into almost nothing. Why had the old Native American said what he had? She couldn't figure out if he'd been speaking to her or Jay. Maybe he'd been warning or blaming her for something, but, if so, he should have spelled it out. Now that it was too late, she wished she hadn't taken off. Given a little more time, the older man might have explained.

Shaking off her thoughts, she attempted to orient herself, but plant life pressed in on all sides. Thank goodness for the well-trodden trail. Needing to assure herself that she existed separate from her surroundings, she touched the base of a cedar so tall she couldn't see its top, its thick bark covered in lichen. When she pushed her nail past the vibrant growth, she encountered rock-like resistance.

Some of the giants were three hundred feet tall and a thousand years old. In their own complex way, they lived and breathed. Maybe they even held memory deep in their cores — memory waiting for her to tap.

She'd never pondered the possibility while hiking in Southern California.

A muted and unexpected sound cut a path through her half-thoughts. Poised on her toes, she strained to hear. She hadn't encountered anyone the whole time she'd been walking.

Unease licked up her spine. Could someone be singing? No, not singing, because there was no rhythm or melody to that faintest of whispers. Rather, it was as if the forest was about to create music.

A faint buzzing caught her attention. She should be able to dismiss a swarm of insects. Just the same, she'd spent enough time alone in the wilderness that she'd never discount anything.

Leaving the trail, she scrambled onto the remnants of a downed tree. She longed to take in her surroundings, but the mass of brush and trees made that difficult. Even on the tree stump, her field of vision was compromised. At least up she was able to determine that the sound came from her left. After leaving the tree carcass, she hiked a little farther. If there was a hornet's nest out there, she needed to locate it. Before she could put her decision into action, however, the wilderness seemed to start breathing.

It had become something alive.

Unnerved, she touched the utility knife at her waist and called out a loud, "Hello."

No one answered, but the buzzing continued. After a half-dozen sliding steps in the direction it was coming from, she was all but certain she heard flies. Not hornets. They might have been attracted to animal excrement, but would even a bear's scat draw that many? Bear? And her with a small knife. Her second thought, the one that slowed her even more, was that a dead animal was responsible. This afternoon, she didn't want to be hit with proof of the end to life's cycle.

Jaw clenched, she pushed her way into and then past a thick grove of ferns. That was when she saw him. Or rather, that was when she saw the blood and flies. Acceptance took a few more seconds.

Doc.

Dr. Anthony Gilsdorf lay on his back, his body twisted so his face was toward her. One scratched and cut hand was clamped over a gaping wound in his throat, as if he'd been choking himself. At first, she thought—prayed—he was looking at her, but he wasn't.

Dried blood soaked his clothing and the ground around him. The right side of his head had been smashed in. A long horizontal gash split his left cheek apart. His eyes had no sheen of life. Ants trailed over his face.

"Doc!"

The wilderness swallowed her cry, held it for too many heartbeats, then threw it off into the wind. She felt alone and yet surrounded.

Finally, fighting waves of horror, disbelief and revulsion, she came closer. Came to a halt. Widened her stance. Then she forced herself to kneel beside Doc and furiously fanned the air until the flies darted away. They hung over her, eager to return.

Oh, please, not Doc. Not him!

Her face grew hot. In contrast, her fingers felt frozen. A thudding in her temples became a violently beaten drum, the pounding making her sick. Her stomach contents lodged in her throat.

Ignoring what she'd learned from TV programs about not touching crime scenes, she pried Doc's too-stiff hands off his throat. The mangled carotid artery was exposed and drained.

"Doc, no-no-no-no," she crooned stupidly. She brought his frozen fingers near her mouth and breathed on them. "I'm here. You're... You aren't alone anymore. I'm here. Please. Oh, God."

Her mouth felt dry, her muscles both numb and on fire. She lost the ability to move and couldn't get her eyes to focus. This wasn't a nightmare. There'd be no awakening to daylight and sanity. Some monstrous excuse for a human being had done this obscene thing to the most important person in her life. Because this was no animal kill. No, those cuts had been made with a knife. This was murder.

She stood on quivering legs and looked all around. She cursed the trees that blocked out the sun, then pulled her knife out of its sheath and gripped it in both hands. Doc's dry blood stained her fingers in chilling contrast to the knife's silver handle. She swayed and quickly locked her knees in place.

Giving in to the need, she threw back her head and drew in air until her lungs protested. Then, vision once again clear but control lost, she let loose a sound somewhere between a sob and a scream. Her heart cracked and bled.

Once again, she filled her lungs and released what she could of her agony. This time, the sound came out more howl than cry. It belonged not to a human being, but to something horribly wounded.

On the brink of shattering.

Her throat burned, prompting her to rub it. Reality returned as the sounds she'd made faded away. She wasn't an animal, not anymore.

She couldn't do anything for Doc. No one could. She could keep the flies and ants off him, but, eventually, they'd return. Before long, nothing would remain of the man she loved and admired. He'd become part of the wilderness.

He'd been murdered. The horrible wounds, plus his soiled and torn shirt, told her how desperately he'd fought for life.

Had he known his killer? Maybe it was someone he'd antagonized. Maybe he'd come across something he shouldn't have.

The effort of taking a backward step exhausted her. Her heart feeling as if it had been jammed into her throat, she strained to listen, but the wind refused to be silent, and the damnable flies were again landing.

Nerves edged around her subconscious again. Judging by the dried blood and state of decay, Doc had been dead for what could be days. She was standing in a place of death.

Alone in the wilderness.

Leaving Doc to the elements, she spun around so she could start back and alert the authorities, but she'd only taken a single step when the need to say some kind of goodbye overwhelmed her. She whirled around. Already, Doc was half-hidden by his surroundings. She was losing him, had already lost him, needed to make her peace with reality.

She again knelt beside him and attempted to close his eyes, but his lids were too stiff. A killer was out here, someone with utter disdain for her mentor's life, a man or woman with reasons and motives and —

The wind brought a soft yet deep-throated howl to her, stopping her in mid-thought. Wolf. She'd never seen a wolf in its natural state, but the creatures had always fascinated her. Her dreams about the predators when she was a child had somehow sustained her. Given her something to believe in.

But she was no longer that small girl. Still, for a heartbeat, she accepted the ageless cry and again made it part of her.

A wolf when she understood there were none left in the Olympic National Forest?

She placed a hand over her heart. The fingers gripping her knife threatened to cramp, but she didn't dare release her hold.

Deep and clean, the howl again sped through the forest.

Despite everything, she felt herself being drawn to the sound as if she was tethered to the unseen and impossible animal. She wanted to run, to plunge so deep into the forest that it became her. Instead, she stood frozen in place.

The afternoon air felt cold on her arms and face. A twig broke under her boot. She smashed fragile spore capsules growing from a carpet of moss.

The back of her neck prickled. Every nerve and muscle taut, she scanned her surroundings. For a long time, she saw only the forest. And then —

Eyes. Yellow and hot, bracketed by black, watching her from a riot of growth.

"No!" Shocked by her outcry, she forced herself to be silent. No human had eyes like that. She wasn't looking at Doc's killer.

Or was she?

The burning orbs belonged to a wolf. She could now see the outline of a powerful body, large head and small, alert ears. A deep rumble came from the depths of that immense chest.

A wolf. Primitive. A creature that had once thrived here but had been hunted to extinction.

She detected no fear in that magnificent, impossible body. And no aggression, either. Rather, it simply studied her, blinking, pointing its dark muzzle at her, taking in her scent.

Her legs wanted to run while her heart begged her to stay. Swaying a little, she struggled to make sense of what was happening. She wouldn't, of course, but she longed to approach the creature, to touch it, to make it part of her.

When it started toward her, she told herself it had read her thoughts and was going to grant her wish. At the same time, survival instinct warned her to run, not that she could escape a predator.

Step by step, the distance between them shrank. Then, when only some fifty feet separated them, the wolf spun to the left and disappeared into the wilderness.

Don't leave me! Please, come back.

Chapter Five

Winter's throat was sore from calling out. Her lungs ached from the high-altitude run, and the bouncing backpack had rubbed her shoulders raw by the time she'd covered a quarter of the distance back to Potlatch. She'd repeatedly tried to get through on her cell phone. The maze of branches and tree limbs framing the path had scratched her arms and face. The cool air helped a little, but she was drenched in sweat.

Her life would have been much different if it hadn't been for Doc. He'd insisted she gave him too much credit and that eventually she would have found herself, but how could she when there'd been nothing to find? That's what happens when a child has no idea who her parents are. That child goes many years looking for a sense of belonging.

Then, at least in her case, she connects with someone.

Murder. A killer. Motive — there had to be one. There was always a motive for murder.

Winter continued sporadically calling for help as she headed down the path. If one of the rangers was out, they'd have a radio unit and could call in the local law enforcement to come to the murder scene.

Finally, she heard a man's voice respond to her calls. A figure separated itself from the vegetation. A shadowed man was heading toward her. Despite the uneven ground, his strides were sure. She had time to note his uniform and sturdy frame before she recognized him.

Jay Raven.

What was he doing here?

He stopped when about six feet separated them. Whatever

his reaction to seeing her, he kept it to himself. When he acknowledged her weapon with a nod, she put the knife away. In contrast to his calm demeanor, her shock and grief must've been written in every line of her body.

"What happened?" he asked. "You see a bear?"

"No." She swallowed. "He's dead."

"Who are you talking about? Dr. Gilsdorf?"

"Yes."

Except for his slowly shaking head, his body was still. "You're sure?"

What was he thinking? And why did his eyes remind her of the wolf's? They weren't alike—except for their intensity. "He was murdered."

"Murdered. Damn." Jay pressed his fingers against the sides of his head as if dealing with a headache. His jaw tightened and relaxed, tightened and relaxed. "Are you all right?"

Relief flooded her at the thought that he cared about what she was going through. At the same time, she'd give anything to read his mind. "Physically, yes. Emotionally, not so much."

"Of course. You can't expect anything different. Take it one minute at a time. That's all you can get through."

Her gratitude grew because he was saying exactly what she needed to hear.

"Where is he?" Jay asked.

Still studying him, she pointed back the way she'd come. "Off the trail to Ghost Totem." *Near where I saw a wolf.* "I couldn't get through to nine-one-one."

He pulled a UHF radio out of its carrying case but didn't engage the communication tool. She might've been wrong, but was he debating hugging her? Offering physical comfort? "You were the only one there?"

"Yes. I haven't seen anyone for—please, we have to tell someone."

"I will, but I don't want to until I have more details to pass on."

What more did he need to hear? She extended her hand. "Show me how to get in touch with your supervisor or the police. I'll tell them. It's going to get dark and…"

He kept the radio away from her while placing his free hand on her shoulder. "You don't have to do it all by yourself. Let me do my part."

The touch had only lasted a second, but it helped reassure her. Besides, along with her strength, she was losing her sense of urgency. No matter what anyone did, their actions wouldn't help Doc.

Her head drooped. "All right. What do you need?"

He stepped closer. Maybe he sensed how near she was to the edge. "For starters, tell me what brought you to Olympic. The truth."

All thoughts she had that she'd found a sympathetic ear ended. "I told you. When I couldn't get in touch with Doc —"

"You abandoned your fifty-plus-hour a week job, jumped in a car, and hurried up here." He leaned away from her. Just the same, she sensed that wasn't what he wanted to do. "There's something you're not telling me."

The mask and everything it stands for. "If there is, it has nothing to do with right now. He was murdered. You're a park employee. It's your responsibility to do something."

"Yes." His chest slowly rose. "It is."

Caught between trying to make sense of his mood and the memory of the weight and warmth that had briefly rested on her shoulder, she reminded herself she was in no condition to determine what someone was thinking. "I'm sorry I reacted as I did. It just seems strange that you're asking me about my motives. You — you don't suspect I —"

"No, of course not." He again placed his hand on her shoulder. "You've left me with no doubt how you feel about him. How far have you run since you spotted the body?"

She clenched her fists to keep from covering his hand with hers. She'd never needed a touch more. "I'm not sure. Maybe a mile."

"And you're positive you were alone?"

Just a wolf. "I passed a couple of groups going the opposite way not long after I left Potlatch on my way out, but no one since then."

He nodded. "I wish I didn't have to put you through this, but how did you find him?"

Fighting tears brought on by the latest example of his compassion, she told him about hearing flies. "He was about thirty, maybe forty feet off the trail. If not for the sound, I wouldn't have seen..."

He patted her shoulder then took a backward step. "You have good hearing."

Stay near me. "I guess. I can't—it still seems unreal."

"Trauma does that."

Realizing he was waiting for her, she again fought the impulse to cling to him. He continued to stand close, dominating her, really. This was a man who took responsibility seriously. In addition, who and what he was lived deep inside him. Unlike her.

Don't go there today!

"What now?" she asked.

"I want to make sure I tell them as much as possible. You took off right after finding him?"

"Yes. All I could concentrate on was getting help." Until she'd seen the wolf. Then she'd run not just for Doc, but for herself.

He held up his radio. "I'll make the call, but, until they know where the body is located, there's not much anyone can do."

Oh, God. "Which means I have to take you there."

He slowly nodded. "I'm sorry. I wish it didn't have to be this way."

"So do I." She pressed a hand to her forehead. "All right."

Jay reached behind him and adjusted his pack, the gesture expanding his chest and making him look even more formidable. At the same time, the everyday gesture made it possible for her to regain a little of her equilibrium.

"Maybe you don't want to be alone with me, considering what I said about Dr. Gilsdorf."

"This isn't about you or me. I never thought something like this would happen." *Or to hear and see a wolf – something that takes me back to my childhood.* "There's so much I have to accept."

She listened as he made his call. In terse, brief terms, he explained that a visitor to Olympia had come across Dr. Anthony Gilsdorf's body. It appeared the anthropologist had been murdered.

"Yeah," Jay said into the radio, "tell them it's near Ghost Totem. I'll relay what I learn through you once I have more details." He paused. "No, I don't see any reason for that yet."

"What isn't going to happen yet?" she asked when he was finished.

"Making preparations to remove the body. The crime scene investigation has to come first."

"The police are going to get involved, aren't they?"

"If you're asking about state, county or city agencies, the answer is no. National parks have their own law enforcement officers who are also rangers. They're stationed at different regions, so they can't all get there at the same time."

"Oh. Are you trained to do that kind of thing?"

He shook his head. "I want to get the training, but I haven't been a ranger for long. Maybe I can, in a year or so."

She wished he'd tell her what he'd done before that. And comprehend why who and what he was mattered to her.

As she led them back up the trail, all too aware of Jay Raven behind her, she struggled to remain separate from the thick, green world surrounding them. The forest shouldn't make so much of an impact. She should be focused on what would happen once she showed Jay where she'd found Doc's body, the things she'd have to do, the people she'd have to tell.

Instead, she surrendered as the wilderness pushed at her, slid along her flesh and entered her lungs. She tasted, tested and accepted.

The wolf was out there. Watching.

Why hadn't she said anything to Jay about it?

* * * *

A spider was making its way over Doc's chest. Out of the corner of her eye, Winter caught a glimpse of movement as a crow took flight from a nearby stump. Despite her vow to be strong, she couldn't take those last few steps.

The man who'd come as close to a father figure as she'd ever had looked lonely and discarded. His flesh, bone and muscle were no longer needed. The world was done with Doc, and he was done with the world.

"Hopefully, I've made this clear," Jay said, "but I wish you didn't have to go through this. I've experienced personal loss — my parents are dead — so I have a good idea how difficult it is. If there were any other way — "

"There isn't." Later, maybe, he'd tell her about his parents' deaths, and she'd offer the sympathy he'd been handing her.

"You're a strong woman."

"I don't have a choice."

Leaving her to deal with her emotions, Jay positioned himself near Doc's head. He crouched and studied the various wounds. She couldn't read his expression. As his silent observation continued, she decided that whatever Jay felt for Doc, grief wasn't among his emotions.

"Why?" he muttered.

"Why what?"

"Did they cut him so many times?"

She shuddered. "They?"

"Or he. Probably he. The cuts look deep. That took a lot of strength. My guess, there was a lot of hatred behind the attack."

He stood and faced her, his features somber in the shadows. She was struck by how much a part of his surroundings he was, as if he might fade into the forest. Maybe the wolf was waiting for him. Part of him.

No, she chided herself. That wasn't it at all. Her imagination was getting away from her. Despite her desire to do so, she wouldn't tell Jay about the wolf. "What are you thinking?" she asked.

Instead of answering, Jay slowly walked around Doc, keeping distance between himself and the body.

Leaving what had been a living human being not long ago, Jay rejoined her. "Someone really wanted him dead."

Yes, someone had. She just wished Jay hadn't brought that up. "Do you have any idea who it might be?"

"That's what I need to discuss with investigators," he spoke softly.

Was he thinking of someone in particular? "Why didn't you want him in Olympic?"

His mouth tightened. "I'm protective of what used to be Native American territory. Look, I didn't want him here, but I didn't want him dead. No one deserves to be treated like that."

His low tone touched her as the soft breeze had earlier, bringing her to the brink of tears. She forcefully stopped them. "Thank you for saying that."

He nodded. "Like I said, I've lost people I care a great deal about, nearly lost others. It's difficult."

He removed his pack and propped it against a rock. Watching him, she was struck by how strong he looked now that he was unburdened. How much a man. Strange that she should be aware of that tonight.

Maybe not so strange, because grief sometimes turned people primitive.

"I have to get back in touch with the dispatcher," he said. "Get things going. Before I do, I need you to grasp something. It's almost evening. Whoever comes will have to do it on foot and won't come until first light. That means your professor and I will remain here until morning. You can leave now if you want, but you'll have to hike most of the trail in the dark. I'd like to loan you my headlamp, but I'm going to need it." He paused. "My suggestion is that you stay here."

"Here?" *You, me, Doc's body, the wilderness, the wolf?*

"I'm considering your safety. Besides…"

"Besides what?"

"You've been through hell today. You shouldn't be alone."

Chapter Six

Winter Barstow wasn't a small woman, but, despite her hiking clothes, she struck him as innately feminine. She was in good physical condition with long lashes, large shining eyes and more than a hint of breasts beneath the practical top.

No matter how many times he'd looked at her since they'd run into each other on the trail, every time felt new.

The forest embraced her. Maybe that explained why he felt as he did.

"For the record," he told her as she repositioned herself on the log she was sitting on, "I was following you."

"You were? Why?"

Winter sounded unnerved but not hysterical. Her ability to control herself was, in part, what had prompted him to explain. As for the other reason, now that his calls were over and the sun had set, there wasn't much to do except talk.

He brushed loose bark from a log opposite her and sat down. "You said you hadn't been able to contact Dr. Gilsdorf for a while. I decided I didn't want you to be alone in case—it happened anyway. I'm sorry."

"I appreciate your concern," she murmured. "Who is the older man who briefly spoke to me at Potlatch?"

"My uncle Talio."

"I figured it was something like that. It was as if he wasn't surprised to see me."

"I didn't ask him."

Her expression in the lamplight said she wasn't sure whether she should believe him. Not that he blamed her.

He'd wanted to provide her with an explanation for his presence on the trail before she had to ask. He should have given the whole scenario more thought. Truth was, he wouldn't be here if Uncle Talio hadn't mentioned Yakanon.

If his desire to learn more about Winter hadn't been so strong.

"I shouldn't have hurried off like I did, but—what was the word he said?"

"Yakanon."

"Do you know what it means? I don't remember coming across it in my studies, but—"

"You don't really want to talk about that now, do you?"

"I guess not."

Thank goodness she felt that way. The last thing she needed was to have more thrown at her.

Don't forget that, he reminded himself. She was going through hell, and he owed it to her to make things easier for her somehow.

"Do you mind telling me what happened to your uncle?"

Night usually quieted him. He'd rather spend the dark hours surrounded by the forest than anywhere else. Tonight he felt unsettled. However, his mood couldn't hold a candle to what she was experiencing.

Lamplight was good to her, he concluded. It highlighted her thick, long, dark hair and lean body. Reminded him of how long he'd been sleeping alone.

"He was on his way to Forks to see my brother last winter when a drunk hit his vehicle head-on."

"It sounds as if he's lucky to be alive."

"He is. They had to fly him to Seattle for surgery on his hip and leg."

"What about the person who hit him?"

Jay stared into the night. "He broke a rib, that's all. A damn single rib."

"I don't blame you for being bitter."

Was that how he'd come across? "My brother's an alcoholic. I'm aware of what it takes to fight the disease, but when the man who raised my brother and me nearly dies because of an alcoholic…"

"You love him."

"There isn't much I wouldn't do for him."

"It sounds like a wonderful relationship."

Her mouth trembled. He had no doubt she felt the same way about Dr. Gilsdorf. They'd spread their sleeping bags on a relatively flat area out of sight of the body. Because there wasn't that much level space, their bags were close together. Maybe having to sleep—if she could—next to a near stranger made her uncomfortable, but maybe his presence would help. A forest night complete with sounds she'd probably never heard was a far cry from sleeping in her own bed, wherever that was. The moon was only a sliver, and trees hid most of the stars. As a result, she'd become more voice than reality.

Did she have a husband, a lover? So far, she hadn't said anything about who was in her life or been concerned about getting a message to a loved one. He supposed he could attempt to draw that information out of her, but he'd rather her tell him.

Listen to her voice.

As silence stretched over them, he studied her as she sat cross-legged on her sleeping bag. She'd taken off her shoes and was massaging her right instep. He couldn't help wondering what it would feel like to have her foot in his lap and his fingers easing away her discomfort.

"Your animosity toward Doc—does your uncle feel the same way?"

"Uncle Talio is a tribal elder. Being a Hoh defines him at the deepest level. Anything that impacts his people impacts him."

"What about you? Does it define you the same way?"

Maybe he was wrong, but he thought he caught a melancholy tone in her voice. "Not as much as my uncle wishes it did."

"Generation gap?"

"It's more than that." He couldn't remember the last time he'd talked to anyone about his relationship, with not just his uncle, but with who he was. It had to be their isolation and death's reality that had him wanting to tell her more. "Uncle Talio has never lived anywhere else. He barely comprehends that there's more to the world than Northwest Washington."

"And Doc intruded on what the local tribes consider their territory — at least that's how they saw it. Maybe one of them resented him enough to —"

"That isn't my people's way." *Unless someone believed Grandparents Cave was threatened.*

"You said your brother is an alcoholic. Does that mean he's an outcast? What about others who don't fit into the romanticized mold?"

Why was she pushing? "The Hoh held a meeting after Dr. Gilsdorf made his request for assistance. Like the other tribes, they decided not to. End of discussion."

She was briefly silent. "He told me that, but he had no idea why."

Because more was at stake than Doc could possibly have comprehended. More than Winter could comprehend, either. They weren't Hoh.

"Doc was murdered," she said softly. "You can't blame me for needing to know who did that to him."

"That's law enforcement's job."

"And I should, what, simply bury him and go on with my life?"

If he'd been in her position, he would be asking the same questions. The thing was, when he'd told her his people weren't violent, it wasn't strictly the truth. When drunk, Floyd had put more than one fist through a wall. Several of the younger Hoh had threatened to storm Washington D.C. when it had taken Congress so long to deed the tribe a measly thirty-seven acres because erosion was destroying what land they had. Congress had finally granted their request, but there was still resentment on the part of some tribal members. The relationship between the Northwest Natives and Park authorities was complicated and sometimes adversarial. Some Natives saw Dr. Gilsdorf as just another bureaucrat.

"I don't get Native Americans' animosity toward Doc. He was an anthropologist doing his job."

"That's your take on it." He made no attempt to keep his disagreement out of his voice. "But there's another side to the issue."

She didn't respond for so long, he wondered if she intended silence to serve. Darn it, she'd been through hell today. He should be focused on comforting her, not whatever was happening.

"What's the other side?" she asked.

"Some educators see the world as a lab. To an anthropologist, the cultures he studies aren't the same as living, breathing people."

"Now there's a generalization if I've ever heard one."

Imagining her with fire in her eyes had him sitting up straighter. He didn't want to hurt her, but he might not have a choice. One thing, talking might keep her from focusing on the nearby body and encroaching wilderness.

"What did he hope to accomplish?"

"Something he'll never be able to." Tears thickened her words. "All right. I need to do this. Anthropologists and historians have long assumed that Northwest Native Americans lived on the coast and thrived from what the ocean and other waterways provided. Artifacts such as canoes and their houses bear that out, but being close to the sea also made the natives vulnerable to their enemies."

"Because their enemies know where to look for them."

"Exactly."

She sounded excited, which reminded him she wasn't that different from Dr. Gilsdorf.

"After his wife died," she said, "Doc threw himself into his work. I'm not sure what initially prompted him to decide to take another look at conventional wisdom with regards to the Northwest tribes, but, once he did, it became an obsession."

Did she feel the same way? If she saw the past as nothing more than something to be studied, he'd spend as little time as possible with her.

Hopefully she was worthy of his, what, his attraction?

"Doc formulated the theory that Northwest tribes occasionally moved inland. He believed it entailed more than hunting camps. If he was right, entire villages relocated many miles east of the shoreline and at a distance from the rivers. They did so both for safety reasons and because fishing is seasonal. When the fish weren't running, hunters went after the plentiful game in the forest. They took their families with them."

More than just their families. But that wasn't something a Hoh would ever tell an outsider. "Was he just obsessed, or did the drive for job security factor in?"

She didn't immediately answer, and when she did, her tone was terse. "The university only has two tenured anthropology professors. Doc was one of them, so, no, he wasn't afraid for his job."

"What about his reputation? Leaving a legacy?"

"That factored in. Can you blame him?"

"No." He meant it.

"Regardless of how you and the rest of your tribe feel about what he was doing, the bottom line is he'd convinced the grant committee to provide him with the funds necessary to prove his hypothesis."

"Or disprove it."

She sighed. "Yes. Another professor—Dr. Wilheim, my immediate supervisor—presented the grant committee with basically the same hypothesis."

"It doesn't seem strange to you that they'd reach identical conclusions?"

"Their offices are side by side. They run—ran—in the same circles and shared the same interests. I'm sure they'd discussed the possibilities."

"So we wound up with two competing professors after the same status and money. Put you in an awkward position, didn't it?"

"Sometimes. I tried not to let it."

"Do you have any idea what's going to happen now?"

"As far as the research is concerned? I have to talk to the grant committee."

"Maybe Dr. Wilheim will take over."

"Maybe."

Unless he was reading her wrong, that was the last thing she wanted to see happen.

"There's a good chance he'll try," she said at length. "He was furious when Doc got the grant."

"How furious?"

She looked up from massaging her foot. "What are you saying?"

"You know him. I don't."

"I'm not sure I do. He doesn't see me as an equal."

"Pompous?"

"He has a powerful ego."

"Stay out of his way."

She didn't respond, which gave him too much time to ask himself why he'd warned her. He wasn't a detective. It wasn't his job to figure out who'd attacked Dr. Gilsdorf, or why.

As for Winter Barstow, she wasn't his responsibility. Between taking care of his uncle and trying to keep his brother out of the bottom of a bottle, to say nothing of earning a living, he had enough on his plate. Tonight, he'd do what he could to keep the young woman from falling apart. Tomorrow, he'd go back to being a park ranger.

"Can I ask you something?" she said. "If you had the final say, would you have let Doc work to prove his theory? Maybe you would have told him not to come."

"It doesn't matter. I don't—"

"You're Native American, so don't tell me it doesn't matter to you."

"I care about my people's quality of life. That's as far as it goes."

"Is it?"

"You don't believe me?"

He heard her take a shaky breath. "I envy you," she whispered. "At least you know who you are. Where you came from. Who you belong to. If you don't embrace your heritage, I feel sorry for you."

Until now, he'd thought of her as a woman being buffeted by an emotional wind, her every mood and word painted by her loss. She'd started to reveal something about herself, but he didn't know how to draw it out of her. Or if he should.

"I'll tell you what I tell my uncle," he deliberately bit out his words. "I'm a national park employee. Doing my job is my priority."

"That's all?"

"It's enough." It wasn't.

* * * *

Her bare feet made a slapping sound as she ran down the empty trail. Her lungs burned, and her heart pounded, but she couldn't slow down. Bony arms and legs pumped while long black hair trailed out behind her. Every time she looked up, she saw the same thing — desert.

Fear toyed with her. She didn't want to be alone. If only someone would take her into his or her arms, cradle her and tell her she was loved.

But she'd never heard the words.

After what seemed like forever, her legs caught fire. Her instep cramped, forcing her to stop. She pushed sweat-wet hair away from her eyes and looked around.

Where were the sand, cactus and lizards that had always been there? The air wasn't dry and hot. Instead, it tasted cool and damp.

Confused but not alarmed, she took hold of her arms. They were still child-skinny. She had no breasts or hips.

"Where am I?" Her voice was high. Like that of a child.

No one answered, but then she was alone – always alone.

Her heart still raced, and her lungs hurt. She'd run all she could tonight. It was time to face – what?

Trees. Ferns. Bushes. Steep hills. And, in the distance, a curving, curling creek.

"Where am I?"

Not alone after all. A wolf was here.

Tears burned her eyes and cheeks. Her hands shook as she extended them toward the dark form.

"Wolf. You're here."

The predator came closer, opened its mouth and gently held her fingers with long, sharp fangs.

"You found me."

Wolf never spoke. In all the times he'd visited her, he had yet to send a single message. It didn't matter, because she understood.

Wolf didn't want her to be alone.

"I missed you. You've been gone so long, I thought – Where are we?"

"Winter, wake up."

A man's voice. Despite the hands on her shoulders, gently shaking her, Winter fought to stay in the familiar place. "You found me," she whispered.

The fingers tightened. "What are you talking about? Winter, you're having a dream."

Winter. Cold night air settled along her neck and throat. Between that and Jay crouching over her, she reluctantly pulled herself out of the dream and embraced the reality his form represented. Still half asleep, she gave silent thanks for the return of what she'd thought she'd lost in childhood.

Wolf was back.

Maybe aware of what was happening to her tonight, to Jay.

"Maybe I shouldn't have woken you." Jay's hands stayed on her. Warmed her. "But your dream sounded like it was pretty vivid. I was afraid it would turn into a nightmare."

Nightmare? She nearly told him that was the last thing that would happen. Wolf brought love. A sense of belonging.

Then memories of what had happened a few hours ago swamped her. She placed her hand over Jay's. The bit of human warmth helped. She couldn't let go. "I'm sorry. I didn't mean to wake you."

"You didn't." He laced his fingers through hers.

As more and more consciousness returned, her awareness of Jay Raven's presence increased. Despite the dim lighting, the moon and stars revealed dark hair and features as well as a white undershirt stretched over muscles. Cold as it was, she wished she had something around her shoulders. At least her lower body was warm. Hoping he couldn't see what she was doing, she glanced at his legs. He was wearing what appeared to be sweat pants. Tonight, this man in casual sleepwear was the only human in her world.

"Do you want to talk about it?" he asked.

"I'm not sure."

"Because it's fading?"

"Not really."

She wasn't sure how she felt when he released her hand and scooted back so she could sit up. Cold. Alone.

"It's an old dream," she told him. "One I haven't had since I was a child." She reached under her nightshirt's neckline and spread the fingers his hand had warmed over her tattoo. "I'm surprised I had it tonight."

"Surprised in a good way?"

She was tempted to tell him about it, but this was so personal. "I'm all right."

"Try to get some sleep."

"I'm not sure I can."

"I thought you might say that." He returned to his sleeping bag. "Would you like to talk?"

"I don't want to keep you awake."

"Don't worry about it. I was only dozing."

"You're sure you don't mind?"

"I'd rather you talk than keep things bottled up inside."

The night wasn't bright enough for her to make out his expression, but maybe she didn't need it thanks to his words. She wished he'd stayed at her side. At the same time, she needed distance if she was going to be able to concentrate on something other than him. "What am I going to do with Doc's belongings? I need to ask Pearson—"

"Pearson?"

"Doc's only child." An unwanted thought lodged a moan in her throat. "I have to tell him his father was murdered."

"You could let law enforcement. Don't ask too much of yourself."

Thanks for saying that. "It's all right. I owe Doc that much."

"It sounds to me as if you believe you owe him a lot."

She was wrong about wanting to talk to Jay. It wasn't as if she intended to keep her past a deep, dark secret, but it needed to stay like that until she could plan her explanation of what had brought her to this place in her life.

Besides, come morning, she and Jay might go their separate ways.

She sidestepped his comment. "Do you often spend the night out here alone?"

"Sometimes."

"And it doesn't bother you?"

"I grew up here."

In other words, he belonged. When her chest started to ache, she realized she was rubbing her tattoo. Sometimes, she all but forgot about it, but it had been on her mind since Doc had sent her the wolf mask.

"Have you been to Olympic before?" Jay asked.

Grateful for the change of subject, she explained that she hadn't, but that during her senior year of college, she'd joined other upperclassmen in a trip to the Makah Cultural and Research Center in Neah Bay, Washington. Seeing some of the fifty thousand artifacts that had been preserved as a result of an ancient mudslide at the whaling village Ozette had been an amazing experience.

"I felt the same way when my uncle took Floyd and

me there so we could get a sense of what Native life had been like back then. Despite the mudslide, everything from fishing nets to bark hats was intact. It wasn't the first mudslide, so my question is why did they stay there?"

Jay and she were on the same wavelength. But she didn't tell him about her heightened sense of awareness the whole time she'd been in Neah Bay or the dreams of a wolf that had come every night.

"Tradition, probably." She shrugged. "Maybe they believed their spirits and gods wanted them to live there."

"That's something we'll never know."

Unless Jay, even though he wasn't a Makah, comprehended more than he was letting on. Part of what had driven Doc was his belief that Northwest Natives had kept their history alive by passing it on. He was also convinced that the Natives deliberately kept some of their stories and traditions from outsiders. Natives considered their relationships with their spirit guides sacred and private, so it made sense that they felt the same way about their roots.

Where had the wolf mask come from? Given its pristine condition, it must have been in the possession of someone experienced in caring for it. Jay had mentioned the park historian. Maybe the man knew something about where a Hoh artifact might have come from, but how could she poke around without raising his suspicions?

What if the mask had been in a private citizen's possession or Doc had come across it while in the forest?

The forest? Was that possible?

"Why don't you lie down?" Jay asked.

"My mind's like a hamster running in one of those wheels. There's nothing to do right now except think."

"You're right."

For a short while, she'd forgotten that Jay stood between her and isolation. Now she debated asking why he'd become a ranger and what he'd done before that, but he might want an explanation of what had brought her to this point in her life, and she wasn't ready to go there. It was better if they remained strangers in the night—except they weren't. At least on a superficial level, they shared the same ethnicity.

Too much pondering. Too much of everything.

At first, she thought the wind was responsible for the sound. Then it became stronger, and she sat upright. The long, quiet howl wrapped itself around her. It stood in stark contrast to the sharp sound she'd heard when she'd put on the wolf mask, and carried none of the threat the one earlier today had.

There was something exquisite about it, maybe a gift from this wild place.

"What are you doing?" Jay asked.

"Listen."

The howl rose and fell. By turn, it reminded her of a misty morning and a drumbeat. Ignoring the cold, she scrambled out of her sleeping bag and stood. She stared in the direction the sound seemed to be coming from. If she was certain of the source, she'd head toward it. Ignore all possibility of danger. Fully embrace the mystical appeal.

"You hear something?" he asked.

"You don't?"

"An owl a few minutes ago. Something, a rodent probably, is gnawing."

"A wolf. Listen."

Despite the lack of a response from Jay, she concentrated on the almost lilting sound. As a teenager, she'd convinced the managers of a wildlife preserve to let her volunteer for them. There'd been nothing glamorous about what she did, which mostly consisted of cleaning out enclosures. She hadn't told anyone that her main reason had been so she could study the three wolves that lived there. Even though the wolves hadn't wanted anything to do with her, she'd fallen in love with the remote creatures. She'd learned as much as she could about them, including how they communicated. Not once had the trio vocalized nonstop like this one was doing. Also, the preserve wolves' yips hadn't made the hairs on the back of her neck stand up like now.

"You believe you hear a wolf?"

"You don't?"

"No."

Jay's tone pulled her from the unseen creature. He'd stood. She couldn't see his expression. Unless she was mistaken, he'd fisted his hands. His legs were widely spread, his spine rigid, head cocked.

Their conversation hadn't disturbed the wolf. If anything, its howls were lasting longer and seemed to be coming from deeper in its chest.

"This isn't the first time today," she admitted, almost unwilling to mar the sound with her own voice. "Earlier, right after I found Doc's body."

"No," he muttered. "Did you see anything?"

The mournful howl spun around her. "I can't believe — Are you sure — ?"

"You're still hearing it? There's only one wolf?"

It wasn't possible. He had to hear what she was. "Yes." She pressed a chilled hand to her forehead. "Don't make fun of me, Jay. I can't handle it."

"I'm not."

Watching Jay step around his sleeping bag and head for her shifted her focus from the howl to the shadowy ranger. When he was only a couple of feet away, he extended his arms. Not questioning what she was doing, she did the same. After lacing his fingers through hers, he drew her to his side.

She wanted to say something, to tell him about what she'd seen earlier and insist he acknowledge they were experiencing the same thing, but she couldn't. Olympic National Park at night was different from what she'd seen when she'd first entered it. It seemed to be sucking her into the cloistered space. Much longer and she'd no longer feel separate from it. Only Jay's presence might keep that from happening.

"You're certain you've only been to this part of the country once?" he asked.

"As far as I know. Why?"

Judging by how he was tightening and lessening his hold, she wasn't sure he was aware of what he was doing.

"What do you mean, as far as you know?"

"It doesn't matter," she told him, although it did.

"How much have you studied our people's spiritual beliefs?"

Our. A lifetime of feeling held apart from what her nationality represented threatened to overwhelm her. She blinked back tears she prayed he couldn't see.

"As much as possible. What ancient Native Americans felt and believed couldn't be charted like their tools, weapons and housing. Early explorers wrote about what they saw. We'll never know how much tribal members were willing to share about their spirituality."

"I grew up seeing myself first and foremost as a Hoh. I was a teenager before I began to grasp that there was more to life than what I'd experienced."

She wasn't sure what point, if any, Jay was trying to make. "From earliest times," he said, "the Northwest tribes relied on their spirit helpers so they could survive a sometimes dangerous existence. Because men did most of the hunting and fighting, a close relationship with their spirit guides was essential. My uncle never makes important decisions without asking his spirit for guidance. Almost every Hoh of his generation does."

The howling had faded away while Jay was talking, but even if it hadn't, what Jay was telling her was more important. As a child, she'd believed that her wolf dreams served as proof that Wolf was her protector. Then she'd grown up, and the dreams had stopped. She'd moved beyond imaginary friends.

How then could she explain today's wolf?

"How about you?" she finally thought to ask. "Do you share your uncle's belief?"

"I'm glad he has what he does." His hold on her hand tightened until she had to fight the urge to pull free. "I'm going to throw something out. You can call me crazy, but I believe you need to hear this."

Jay Raven felt vulnerable. She sensed his reluctance to expose himself in every inch of the body so close to hers. "I thought you might call me crazy," she told him. "Maybe there's no wolf out there. Maybe I thought I heard something because I've been kicked in the gut."

"No." He pulled her around so they stood face to face. She still couldn't make out his features. "Tonight, Wolf exists for you. That's all that matters."

"The way you said *wolf*... Are you saying it's more than flesh and blood?"

He let go of her and rested his hands on her shoulders. "What do you think?"

Chapter Seven

Instead of continuing his explanation that the wolf—Wolf—was supernatural, Jay headed to where Doc's body lay. She didn't want to focus on what he was doing, but that was easier than comprehending what he'd handed her with a few words. Jay had said Wolf existed.

Pieces of her dream swirled around her until she was convinced the change from desert to forest represented her journey here. Just before Jay had woken her, the wolf of her childhood had found her, only it was no longer part of a lonely girl's fantasy. It had become Wolf.

Where are you taking me? Where are we going?

Wolf hadn't answered.

The man sharing the night with her turned off his flashlight. "He's all right," he said.

"Thank you for doing that."

"You're welcome."

Jay Raven was caring and compassionate. Whatever else he might be, she'd never forget that. "What was growing up on a reservation like?" she asked as he went back to his sleeping bag. She'd consider Wolf when she felt stronger. "Where did you go to school?"

"Early on, my mother taught Floyd and me at home. The bus ride into Forks was about an hour each direction. Then, when our parents died, we went to live with Uncle Talio. Despite how important tradition is to him, he decided we needed to go to public school."

"Integrate?"

"It wasn't that big a deal. A lot of the students are Native American."

"What happened to your parents?"

His sleeping bag made a rustling sound. She wasn't sure but thought he was propped up on an elbow looking at her.

"Pneumonia. Both of them."

"Oh. I'm so sorry."

"It didn't have to happen." He sounded bitter. "If they'd gotten decent medical care—unless you've lived on the reservation, you can't grasp how inadequate certain services are there. It was worse years ago. We get the services of a doctor, dentist and nurse practitioner one day a week at the health station in Queets. There's a health center in Taholah. Neither of those places qualify as a town. My parents couldn't afford to go the hospital in Forks. By the time the rest of the family realized how sick they were, it was too late."

Had Jay watched his parents die? Maybe he'd taken take care of them. Just considering how helpless he must have felt made her heart go out to him.

"I love my uncle," he said. "I'm doing what I can. He isn't getting the physical therapy he could if he lived closer to civilization." He laughed, without warmth. "They say kids are stubborn, but they don't have anything on the older generation. Are your grandparents alive?"

I don't know. My parents, either. "What was the best part about being raised by your uncle?" she asked, hoping to shift the topic a little.

"The ceremonies," he said without hesitation. "Everyone made a big deal out of them. My brother and I would sit on logs around the campfire with the other kids while the elders conducted the rituals. Floyd got restless, but as soon as the drumming started, I lost myself in the sound and what it stood for. I understood it was more than entertainment. It was special."

She'd attended Native American spiritual ceremonies but had always felt like an outsider. As a result of her education, she'd come to see Native life as something to quantify and qualify, conclusions arrived at, oral histories dissected.

The more she concentrated on documenting what ancient Native life had once been like, the less she had to face how little she understood about her place in it.

Now, as Jay spoke of dancers dressed as deer, elk, mountain lions, grizzlies and wolves, she imagined she could smell the wet forest and wood smoke that were part of those ceremonies. Drumming vibrated through her. Prayers chanted by spiritual leaders gave men and women the strength and courage to face an uncertain future. Imagining an infant's cry, she watched as the little one's mother offered her breast to him. Dark-skinned children that existed in her mind squirmed only to be quieted by grandmothers. The dress she'd worn for the occasion was made of softened cedar bark and rustled every time she changed position.

"The dancers carried lances, knives, and bows and arrows for the spirits to bless," Jay continued. "A dancer might fall silent or wander into the forest because his spirit had taken hold of him."

"Do you have a spirit? I'm sorry. I shouldn't have asked."

He sucked in a loud breath. "Most outsiders consider them part of an ignorant people's superstition."

"I wouldn't do that. Not after — after Wolf."

"Wolf. Yes, Wolf. But before?"

What do you want from me? "I'm an academician. It's my job to document as much of a culture as possible."

"But not to live it."

Belatedly, she realized what Jay was getting at. Their day jobs kept them grounded in the modern world, but he had been brought up surrounded by his heritage. The past was part of his today. At least, it had been when he was a child.

In stark contrast to his rich upbringing, she'd had nothing.

Maybe Wolf read her thoughts and had decided to push her to the edge. That was what she pondered as another haunting howl began. Her flesh felt scraped. She sighed.

"Wolf again?"

"Yes." This time, she didn't ask whether he heard it.

"Are you afraid of it?"

"No. Everything I learned about wolf spirits—many of the tribes saw them as hunters. I've never hunted or wanted to."

"Here we also see them as guardians."

"I didn't know that."

"Maybe that's because it isn't in your textbooks."

She'd unwittingly backed herself into a corner, revealed some of her holes. "I get it. You're saying there's a hell of a difference between studying a culture and living it."

"What I'm saying is you can't take what my people are and shove that into a text. Considering your ethnicity, I'd think you'd grasp that."

I'm nothing. Don't you get it? I'm nothing. "I'm trying."

"Dr. Gilsdorf wanted to put us under a microscope, plug what we stood for into a neat cubbyhole."

"I can't believe he'd do that. Even if he did, I'm not him."

"No, you aren't."

Neither of them spoke. She didn't want to fight with the man who stood between her and the wonder of tonight. She wished he could hear Wolf.

"Please, if you don't mind, I'd like to learn more about what Wolf means to the Hoh. Wolf—he wants to tell me something. I can't figure it out on my own."

"My uncle can explain it better," he said after a too-long silence. "What I heard growing up was that a hunter who has a wolf spirit will live a long and successful life. If his village is attacked, his weapons will find their mark. When I went on my spirit journey, I prayed Wolf would embrace me."

The first time she'd seen Jay Raven, she'd seen a modern man, a product of today. It was no longer that simple.

"I walked, prayed and fasted for three days and nights. On the morning of the fourth day, I woke to see a raven standing a few feet away."

"Thank you for telling me that."

"I'm surprised I did."

She'd thought tonight would be about her, that she wouldn't be able to rise above her grief, but Jay had given her a piece of his heart, and she felt blessed. Overwhelmed. "Raven... What...became part of you?"

"No." Jay paused. "I was a teenager at the time. Uncle Talio warned that I was too young and a spirit wouldn't embrace me until I'd proven myself as a man. I was doing the teenage rebellion thing, wanting to show how tough I was. At the same time, I needed something to believe in. It was just a raven, my namesake, not a spirit."

Are you sure? "Did you go on another search?"

"Yes, not that it made a difference."

"I'm sorry."

"Yeah, well. I'm surprised my uncle didn't kick me out. All that youthful rebellion — I wanted to hang out with my friends, not attend rituals. You did the same thing, right?"

"Right." Only for her, surviving while living on the streets had taken priority.

"After high school, I looked at my options and came to the conclusion I wouldn't have any if I stayed here."

"How did your uncle feel about that?"

"He wasn't happy, but by then Floyd had discovered alcohol, and dealing with that took a lot of his time and emotions. Besides, Uncle Talio had considered himself an adult when he was the same age so he understood where I was coming from. I started logging, moved to Forks and lived there for a couple of years. It didn't take me long to realize logging was dangerous, but without an education, my options were limited."

"You have a degree?"

"A bachelor's in biology. I went to college in Seattle then transferred to the University of Oregon because I thought I was in love."

Jay had a right to be in love. Why, then, didn't she want to hear that? "Oh."

"Haven't we all? Are you married?"

She'd never come close, because the idea of sharing her

sheets and life with another person scared her. Having sex was great, but it just wasn't enough of a trade-off for the lack of privacy. "No. Are you?"

"I was. It didn't last."

"Children?"

"No."

But he wanted to be a father. His tone gave him away. She'd gotten pregnant once, only to miscarry when she was three months along. The pain of that loss still hurt.

"It's a good thing you're here," she said. "I couldn't leave Doc. But being alone — that would have been difficult."

"Fortunately, it didn't get to that point."

She was still debating what to say when he again got out of his sleeping bag and stood. "Are you still hearing Wolf?" he asked.

How could she have forgotten? She concentrated but heard only the forest's night sounds. "No. Where does a spirit go when it isn't — I don't know what I'm talking about."

Instead of responding, Jay slipped into the forest. He wasn't heading in the direction of Doc's body.

He'd left her, and she was alone. Tangled in a million thoughts and emotions.

* * * *

Jay didn't go far. Because he was barefoot, he stopped as soon as the woods surrounded him. Fingers clenched, he stared up at the stars. Even with a ravaged body not far away, the dark didn't bother him. Visitors had sometimes asked whether being alone in Olympic ever spooked him. In the beginning, he'd explained about his upbringing, but these days, he simply shrugged and indicated his radio.

He'd had no intention of telling Winter about his vision quest. Granted, he'd barely touched on his less than successful attempt to connect with a spirit guide, but it still surprised him. What he hadn't admitted was that

Raven, if the bird had been his spirit, hadn't stayed around. Several months later, he'd gone out on another vision quest which had been even less successful. Since returning to Olympic, he'd known better than to set himself up for more disappointment.

Spirit helpers existed for those, like his uncle, whose lives revolved around tradition and heritage, not modern men like himself.

Then how the hell did he explain Winter's experience with Wolf?

Maybe he'd been looking at this wrong. Grandparents Cave was about a half mile away. Instead of Wolf connecting with Winter, the spirit hoped to frighten her so she'd never want to return to the area.

Weary of asking questions without answers, he retraced his steps. Winter was standing near her sleeping bag, a slight form surrounded by the wilderness.

She nodded but didn't speak.

"I wasn't going anywhere," he said.

"Not without your shoes."

He chuckled. "You're right, not without my shoes. Were you looking for Wolf?"

"Don't ask. Come morning, I might convince myself none of that happened."

I don't think so. "Speaking of morning, have you thought about what you're going to do?"

"No."

"You should."

"I guess." She settled cross-legged on top of her sleeping bag. "Who's coming here? How are murder investigations in the park handled?"

"I don't recall if there's ever been another. We have a number of law enforcement- trained rangers, including a couple who could be considered detectives."

"Guess I need to talk to them. Tell them what I saw."

She hadn't seen anything he hadn't, but she was right. Whether she wanted to or not, she was going to be a vital part of the investigation. Eventually, her role would be over, and she'd go back to where she'd come from and resume her life.

"You mentioned you wanted to tell Dr. Gilsdorf's son, but you can let someone here contact the university."

"I need to personally talk to Dr. Wilheim."

"You believe he might take Dr. Gilsdorf's place?"

"I'm sure he'll insist on it."

He wondered if it had occurred to her that the Natives might use Dr. Gilsdorf's murder as ammunition in trying to get the study shut down. When Dr. Gilsdorf had initially contacted the Hoh and other tribes, no one had been particularly concerned that he could accomplish anything without assistance. That mindset had changed once they'd realized the professor was concentrating on the Ghost Totem Ridge area.

Maybe one or more tribal members had done more than resent Dr. Gilsdorf's presence. Maybe that person or persons had put an end to the threat he presented.

Chapter Eight

Jay was dressed when Winter sat up as it was getting light. Her back protested what she'd put it through, so she stretched. That done, she put on her shoes and headed into the forest to deal with nature. Fog hugged the ground and gave the surroundings a misty quality. The few clouds didn't detract from the clean blue sky.

She was nearly back to where she and Jay had spent the night, when his voice reached her. She couldn't make out what he was saying but guessed he was talking to whoever would be joining them.

Doc was dead. Murdered.

Wishing she could recapture her sense of peace, she rejoined Jay. He acknowledged her while continuing his PTT conversation.

"I've been to a couple of his sessions," he said. "He struck me as someone who thinks before he decides. Yeah, I figured he couldn't. Of course I'll be here."

"Who were you talking about?" she asked when he was done. Her stomach rumbled, but hunger wasn't enough to distract her from Jay. Maybe it was having spent the night next to him. Perhaps she'd moved beyond yesterday's disbelief and horror.

Whatever the reason, she saw him as more than a ranger. He was a man, steady and competent, part of something she'd always wanted to feel connected to.

Masculine.

"Christian Turney. He's the ranger who will be in charge of the investigation."

"Is he good?" Looking up at Jay made her feel—surely

not feminine.

Yes, feminine, she admitted. A woman in the presence of a man who appealed to her.

"I respect him. He's in charge of law enforcement in the park. He also runs occasional workshops on how to deal with drunks, vandals, that kind of thing. Last year, there was a rash of vehicle break-ins while people were out hiking. Thanks to him, we caught the two women responsible."

"Who else will be working with him?"

"It sounds as if the majority of the park's law-enforcement-trained rangers are coming. So are Michael and Booth."

"Why?"

He shrugged. "The best I can come up with is they've both had dealings with Dr. Gilsdorf."

She didn't understand why the two felt they had to hike here. "Some of the material at Doc's cabin belonged to the library. I wonder what's going to become of it."

"My guess, Booth will demand to have it back. In fact, I'm surprised he let Dr. Gilsdorf borrow it."

She pressed her hand to her forehead. Poor Doc. "What was it, jealousy? Booth resented having to share?"

"You'll have to ask him. Michael took it upon himself to call the university."

"Already? Who did he talk to?"

"Apparently, he reached Dr. Wilheim. It sounds as if the professor intends to get on scene as soon as he can book a flight. Maybe he's already in the air."

Having to face her no-nonsense superior was the last thing she needed today—next to looking at Doc's body again, that was.

"Maybe you won't have to deal with him. If you can talk to Christian right away, you could leave."

"I'm not going anywhere."

He faced her. There was something defensive about his stance, as if he wanted to protect her.

"There's so much…" She couldn't remember what she'd been going to say.

Jay returned the communication device to his belt and settled his hands over her shoulders. "If your determination to stay has to do with Wolf—"

She couldn't stop herself from leaning into him. "In part, but that isn't all. As soon as Doc started talking about what he wanted to accomplish here, I was on board. I hoped the grant would be enough so I could join him. Not being able to was a big disappointment."

"Because it would have meant a step up your career ladder?"

"That factored in." Was that disapproval in his gaze? "The chance to be part of something that revolves around Native Americans is what excites me." She held out her arm and pushed back the sleeve, exposing skin as dark as his in an attempt to make her point.

He brushed her forearm with his fingers, igniting her flesh. "Point taken. Winter, I don't want you saying anything about Wolf."

"That's the last thing I'd do." She couldn't stop staring at where he'd touched her. Would she ever tell him about the role wolf make-believe had played during her chaotic childhood, or last night's vivid dream, or show him her tattoo?

* * * *

Even though their presence made Doc's murder achingly real, Winter was relieved when the first two rangers arrived. They'd brought water, granola bars and dried fruit, which Jay and she promptly ate. The newcomers set about going through the nearby bushes. Although they didn't say anything, she concluded they were looking for the murder weapon and shoeprints. Within an hour, two additional rangers who'd come from a greater distance joined them. They took turns stationing themselves near the body and keeping insects away. Pictures were taken, but no one touched Doc.

"I wish you could leave," Jay said. "Surely Christian can wait to talk to you."

His consideration made her eyes burn. The best she could do was mutter a thank you. He took her arm and led her away from the others. He'd pulled out his phone when one of the rangers approached, waving a notepad at him.

"I'll be back as soon as I can," Jay told her as he and the ranger started walking away. Even with several people around, she felt cut off, alone.

What was she supposed to do? If only she were back in her desert rental, going through the routine of her life, doing what Dr. Wilheim told her to do, telling herself that her small circle of friends was enough.

No, she couldn't return to what she'd had before coming to Olympic. That part of her life was over, irrevocably changed by murder.

And by Wolf.

Are you out there? Can you read my thoughts? Are you aware of what I need?

* * * *

Winter had been leaning against a tree while the officers, including Jay, conducted their investigation of the crime scene when she heard labored breathing. As the newcomers came into view, she recognized Michael Simpson and guessed the tall, solidly built man with him was Booth Deavers. She could be wrong, but they didn't seem to be happy around each other. Of course, they were dreading what they were about to see, unless—

You aren't a detective. Don't try to think like one.

Jay had been out of sight in the wilderness, but he joined her as the newcomers arrived. She concluded he'd been watching her as much as he'd been helping look for evidence. He stood a few feet away from her, his silent presence both comforting and distracting.

Booth didn't resemble the stereotypical librarian. She

guessed him to be a good fifteen years younger than Michael, who she figured was in his mid-fifties. Booth had on a name brand jacket, black dress slacks and nearly new tennis shoes, which created a disjointed effect. He certainly hadn't dressed for a long hike. Despite what sweat had done to it, she concluded he'd recently had his hair cut, although styled was more like it.

As Jay made the introductions, Booth stuck out his broad hand. He gripped her fingers tight enough to mash them.

"Michael told me you found—" Booth interrupted himself, cleared his throat, then continued in a different direction. "I'm certain you're aware that Dr. Gilsdorf was delighted with my collection of oral histories. I felt honored when he commented on my efforts to make the collection as extensive as it is. Needless to say, before entrusting the collection to him, I requested assurance that it would receive the care it needed and deserved. We'd only recently finalized the agreement when—"

"Not now," Jay interjected. "That doesn't matter today."

Booth glared at Jay. "Why don't you let the young lady and me determine the timeliness of this conversation? Ms. Barstow, isn't it? On our way here, Michael shared what he knows of your association with Dr. Gilsdorf. Am I correct in my assumption that you had a hand in preparing the documentation he presented to the grant committee? If so, you did a thorough job."

Doc had always had an aversion to those he believed were in awe of academicians. Booth seemed to be determined to impress her. If Doc were here, the two of them would have a hard time not laughing.

"My involvement was minimal." That wasn't quite the truth, but she didn't want to say more. "I'm surprised you made the hike."

"Why wouldn't I? I'm intimately involved in the park's educational resources and potential, as was the late Dr. Gilsdorf."

How would Booth react if she told him his overblown

speech was adding to her headache?

"Dr. Gilsdorf is more than *late*," Jay said. "He's a murder victim."

Before Booth could reply, Michael, who'd been silent up until now, grabbed Jay's arm. "I didn't inform the media. Please tell me you or the other rangers haven't, either."

Jay pulled his arm free. "Having the press around is the last thing I want."

Booth snorted. "Michael, I could have told you this situation is safe with Jay for a while longer. Our Native American ranger would like nothing more than to bar not just the media but all outsiders from the park."

Jay's jaw tightened. "That's not true. Besides, we can't keep this to ourselves. Maybe the press has been listening to our scanners. Hopefully, we'll be able to finish our investigation here before they show up."

Michael shook his head, drawing her attention to the bags under his eyes and lack of color. Was he ill? But he couldn't have made the hike if he was physically sick.

"It's going to be a nightmare," he muttered. "Until the killer has been caught, people are going to be afraid to come to Olympic. Revenue will fall."

Who cared about finances? A decent man had been killed. That's what mattered.

"Don't get ahead of yourself," Jay told Michael.

Color bloomed on Michael's pale cheeks. "Don't tell me not to worry. You're not the one charged with making sure the park operates in the black. I am."

Anger was the last thing she'd expected from the budget officer. She was the one having trouble keeping her temper under control. Shouldn't someone in his position have a calm, deliberate demeanor? The reminder that she'd never be able to ask Doc his opinion of Michael or anyone else struck her like a physical blow.

Turning from the men, she looked around but couldn't escape today's awful reality. At least she could put distance between herself and the uncomfortable conversation. She headed toward a number of waist-high ferns, stopping when she sensed someone behind her. Hoping it was Jay, she looked over her shoulder. Instead, Booth stood a few feet away.

"You and I need to talk," he said. "Alone."

Was he going to confess he'd killed Doc? Shaking off the unnerving and crazy thought, she nodded and headed into the trees, Booth next to her. The smell of his sweat warred with his strong cologne. She wanted nothing to do with him but had no choice.

"I granted Dr. Gilsdorf access to the library when I wasn't there," he said. "I later discovered he'd taken more material than he'd led me to believe he was going to. The last time I saw him—I'm not sure when that was—I asked him for a list of everything he had in his possession. He apologized."

"What does this have to do with me?"

"Perhaps nothing." Booth smiled. "It's quite possible you'll leave as soon as the investigators have finished with you." His smile died. "However, if you don't, I'm hoping we can work together."

"I hope so, too."

"I'll cut to the chase, Ms. Barstow. On my way here, I debated saying anything about the project." He frowned. "Is that the right word, project?"

"Are you talking about the grant study?"

"Exactly. The timing is terrible because none of us can say what's going to happen going forward. I don't share Michael's pessimism about the murder investigation's impact on the park, but Dr. Gilsdorf's enthusiasm was infectious. I'm excited about possibilities, however remote, for turning parts of Olympic into a living history lesson."

"That wasn't quite Doc's goal."

"We had several conversations about that. We didn't exactly agree to disagree. What we did was make considerable strides toward acknowledging each other's points of view."

She tried to remember if Doc had ever said anything

about Booth Deavers, but she couldn't recall.

"I'm hoping," he said, "to soon have the opportunity to talk to you about how you would structure the study *if* it becomes your responsibility."

"I see it more as an opportunity than a responsibility, but I'm not in a position to say what's going to happen."

He cocked his head. "You're in a better position than you're giving yourself credit for. If nothing else, you'll get the sympathy vote."

She wondered if he was encouraging her to use sex appeal. The idea made her shiver. She'd never used her body that way and was debating saying so when she realized Jay and Michael were coming toward them.

"What are you doing?" Michael demanded of Booth, while Jay simply stared at her.

Booth chuckled. "We're simply having a conversation, aren't we, Winter? Don't mind Michael. He found so much fault with Dr. Gilsdorf that he's still working at putting it behind him."

"You found fault?" Winter asked Michael. "Why?"

Michael looked everywhere but at her. "It wasn't that at all. Yes, I would have preferred a more open relationship, but the professor was determined to do things his way. I respected that."

"Right," Booth snapped. "A heads-up, Ms. Barstow. Michael will say whatever he believes people want to hear."

"Are you interested in listening to this?" Jay asked. "Because you don't have to."

As grateful as she was to Jay, the time would soon come when she'd have to talk to Booth and Michael. If she was going to finish what Doc had begun, she needed more information about those he'd had to deal with.

Finish what he'd begun?

That was a decision she had to make, soon.

Chapter Nine

Less than an hour later, Jay and she were on their way back to Potlatch with him leading the way on the narrow trail. When Jay had reached Christian via PTT, the lead investigator had agreed with Jay that she didn't need to stay at Ghost Totem after all. The two had also concurred that she shouldn't make the return hike on her own, and since Jay wasn't a law enforcement officer, it made sense for him to accompany her.

"Did Christian say anything about a possible suspect?" she asked soon after they got started down the trail. "Maybe he heard about some crazy person hanging around the park. Maybe Doc was in the wrong place at the wrong time."

"No crazies. At least, none that we're aware of."

"We aren't certain Doc was specifically targeted."

"No, we aren't."

She didn't ask him to speculate beyond that, and, to her relief, he let the subject die. After a silence of several minutes, he called her attention to the sound of woodpeckers. Soon after, he pointed out fresh elk scat. He told her that, as children, Floyd and he had tracked mountain beavers, black bears, deer and elk. They'd even searched for cougars and twice had spotted martens.

Listening to him, she drew comparisons between what she saw as his perfect upbringing and the succession of foster homes she'd experienced. Maybe he hadn't had much in material possessions, but he'd had what she'd wanted most. How could he have walked away from it?

But he'd returned.

Between hanging on to Jay's stories, the sound of his

voice, and gratitude because she wasn't alone, she couldn't say how long they'd been walking when he stopped and looked back at her.

"Winter?"

She started and blinked. "What?"

"We're nearly back. You can try your cell phone now." He pointed at a nearby tree stump. "That look okay to you?"

For too long, his words didn't make sense, but then she realized he was reminding her that it was time to get in touch with the outside world. Because Michael had informed the university that one of its senior professors had been murdered, she didn't have to talk to them. That left her with only one call to make.

Doc's son had given her his number a long time ago because, as Pearson put it, Doc wasn't as young as he'd once been. If something happened to Doc, Pearson wanted her to be able to get in touch with him.

"I'm sorry," she repeated for at least the third time when she reached him. Jay had stepped away, allowing her to concentrate. "You shouldn't learn this way. He loved you so much, was so proud of his only child."

"Yes, he was." Pearson's voice broke. "But it helps to hear you say that."

Pearson was a good person. Not only was he happily married with two young daughters, he was on the city council, planted a large garden every spring and was respected for his barbecuing ability.

Now, as Pearson blew his nose, she desperately wished she could put her arms around him. "Where are you? I hope you aren't alone."

"I'm at work but not for long. I'm going to go home."

"Good. Hug those girls for me, will you?"

"I might never let go of them today. This is hell for you. I can't think what else to say."

"Neither can I."

She kept the phone against her ear, but Pearson remained silent. A breeze caressed the trees, and one squirrel chased another around a nearby trunk. Jay provided the sole human presence. Exhaustion dragged her shoulders down, and she could barely hold up her head. Neither could she take her mind or attention off Jay.

When she looked at him, he did the same. Compassion flowed from him. He understood what she was feeling, was privy to her deepest emotions.

How would he react if she sagged against him? Would he support her?

"Winter?" Pearson cleared his throat. "I'm not going to say this well, but Dad was certainly murdered? There's no doubt of it?"

"None." Her eyes burned from tears she couldn't shed. She hadn't spelled out what had been done to his father. Later, once she'd reconciled herself to the reality, she'd tell him everything. "I can't say whether the investigators will want to talk to you."

"Give them this number. I'll help in any way I can. The last time Dad and I talked, I hogged the conversation. His oldest granddaughter is turning into a hell of a basketball player, and I was hoping he'd have time to come watch her. There was…"

Concentrating on Pearson was becoming difficult. Jay's gaze was a mix of compassion, tension and something else. She appreciated the compassion but didn't understand the other emotions. Maybe he was looking forward to not having to be around her.

"Winter?" Pearson asked. "Right after Dad and I talked last, I told my wife I couldn't remember him ever sounding so excited. I asked if he believed he was going accomplish what he'd hoped to by going to Olympic. He said it was turning out to be better than he'd dreamed possible."

She stared at Jay. "Did he explain what he was talking about?"

"I'm not sure."

"What do you mean?"

"He asked how long I thought wood and hair would last

in a forest."

The wolf mask! "That's all?"

"No, it isn't. I was a little pissed at him. Does that mean anything to you?"

"I'm sorry." She had to work at getting the lie out. "It doesn't."

"I wish my last conversation with my father had been different." Pearson cleared his throat and repeated, "He was so excited."

And that could have led directly to his death.

Jay waited until Winter had put her cell phone away before taking hold of her shoulders so she had no choice but to face him. Despite what they'd been through, they were virtually strangers. He had no right touching her, but maybe this was the only way he could get her to focus on him.

"We need to talk about what Dr. Gilsdorf's son said."

"You heard?"

"Yeah. Gilsdorf brought up how long wood and hair might last in a cool, humid climate. What was that about?"

She briefly closed her eyes. "Doc was talking to his son, not me."

"But he might have said the same thing to you. Did he?"

"What is this about? I want to learn who killed Doc and why. That's all that matters to me."

She was sidestepping something. Well, hell, so was he. He also had to deal with her slight, warm body and dark glittering eyes.

"Listen to me. Dr. Gilsdorf talked to you about the lack of cooperation he was getting from the local tribes, right?"

She nodded.

"We've been hurt before, starting with when the first explorers showed up with diseases we had no defenses against. We've lost most of the land our ancestors' bones are buried on."

"You're blaming Doc for what happened hundreds of

years ago?"

She was right, that wasn't the point. Damn it, he couldn't say what he wanted to, after all. Yes, she was a woman in shock, but she was also an anthropologist, and that made her dangerous.

"Of course not," he said. "Michael admitted Dr. Gilsdorf rubbed him the wrong way. The professor had the same impact on my people."

"*Your* people?" Her lip started to tremble. She closed her teeth around it. "Earlier, you acknowledged that I'm Native American. Now, you seem to be deliberately putting distance between—"

"No. I didn't mean that."

"Then what?"

Tell her something. "You heard Wolf. You *heard* a spirit guide. I need to tell my uncle, let him decide…"

"Whether he and the other Hoh will help me continue Doc's work?"

His heart suddenly pounded so it alarmed him. "You've made up your mind about that?"

She took several deep breaths. "I'm pretty emotional right now. I don't trust myself to make an informed decision about anything. Jay?"

"What?" He let go of her. Stared into her black eyes.

"I want to show you something."

"All right."

She backed away, shrugged out of her backpack and pulled down on the left side of her shirt's neckline. He wondered if she was aware that she'd exposed a little of her bra. Then it didn't matter because he realized what she was showing him.

A small tattoo of a wolf's head.

"I got this when I was twelve."

His heart started pounding again. "Twelve? Your parents gave permission for—"

"I didn't have parents, Jay. And, no, I didn't ask the people I was living with if it was all right. The man who did it didn't care about my age, just that I paid him in cash. Do — do you think Wolf knows about the tattoo?"

"Maybe."

Chapter Ten

A sigh of relief nearly escaped Winter as Jay and she reached Potlatch. She now regretted showing him the tattoo and saying what she had about not having parents. In only a few words she'd exposed two deeply personal things to a man she'd recently met. Granted, she hadn't given him details, but she'd be surprised if he didn't want them.

She couldn't do anything about his curiosity. That didn't mean she owed him more than she'd given him.

He touched her sleeve. "Is there someone you want to talk to about what happened?"

Who? "I'm numb."

"That's probably good, but I'm surprised you haven't made other calls."

Her head throbbed. "I'm sure my coworkers know. News like that gets around."

"What about friends, relatives, a lover?"

In addition to Carolyn, there were several women she hiked with, two other new hires she met for Friday night drinks, the sixty-something widow who was her closest neighbor. She'd already told Jay all she intended to about her lack of a family. As for a lover, she hadn't dated in the better part of a year.

"I'm all right." She worked up a semblance of a smile. "Don't worry about me."

"But I do."

"I appreciate your concern." She couldn't look him in the eyes. Between the words and quiet tone, she had to fight tears. Damn it, years ago she'd learned to keep her emotions hidden. The lessons should be ingrained. "Right now, I feel as if I'm wrapped in cotton."

"That won't last."

"I know."

She thought he might touch her again, and when he didn't, she was torn between relief and disappointment. When she spotted the path leading to Doc's cabin, she started down it. Jay followed close behind.

Still walking, she looked over her shoulder at him. "I didn't thank you for making it possible for me to leave where…everything was closing in on me."

He indicated the sky-hiding trees. "This isn't exactly an open space so I understand what you're talking about. What do you want to do now?"

"I keep replaying what Booth said about needing back the library material. I won't touch anything in the cabin, but I'd like to take another look at what Doc had borrowed."

"I'm glad you realize law enforcement needs to go through the cabin's contents. Saves me from pointing out the obvious."

Beyond the warped door now only a few feet away lay much of what had been important to Doc. A fresh wave of disbelief overtook her. Why was it so difficult to acknowledge the word *murder*?

"Are you sure you're up to this?" Jay asked.

"I don't have a choice. I need to assure Pearson that his father's personal belongings are safe."

"I'll stay with you until you get it over with."

Supported by his words, she squared her shoulders and, as Jay had done yesterday, pushed against the door. It swung open. At first, she couldn't see anything of the interior, but then her eyes adjusted to the dim lighting.

Empty. Not completely, but close. She stared, simply stared as she struggled to wrap her mind around what she was seeing. It was all too much. First, Doc had been killed, and now—

"What the hell?"

Jay's shock echoed hers. She wiped suddenly sweaty

palms on her jeans. Someone had walked into Doc's domain, picked up his belongings and stolen everything of importance. He or she had left Doc's sleeping bag, the cereal on the counter and his clothes, but precious little else. The books, the papers — gone. Nothing remained of what he'd borrowed from the park library, but that didn't bother her nearly as much as the empty space where his laptop had been. The hairs on the back of her neck stood up.

"Jay?" It hurt to talk. "Maybe law enforcement rangers — but I don't get it. Why would they clear out his place so soon?"

"It wasn't rangers."

It took Jay's words for reality to sink in. Maybe whoever had killed her mentor had taken everything connected to his grant work. Maybe the theft was the work of an opportunist. The Hoh and other Natives hadn't wanted Doc around. It could have been any one or more of them. Maybe she was letting her initial reaction to Booth's bluster get to her, but, at this point, she couldn't dismiss anyone — including Michael, who impressed her as primarily looking out for himself.

Booth or Michael, killers?

"Don't touch anything," Jay said. "I need to call Christian."

Of course he did. A crime had been committed. It was as simple as that. And it had happened less than twenty-four hours ago.

Jay placed his hands on her shoulders. Her sense of having being violated eased a little, and she leaned back toward him.

"We need to get out of here," he said. "Can you walk?"

"Yes. Thank you for asking." His touch made it possible for her to fight the urge to run for safety. The slippers she'd given Doc last Christmas peeking out from under his bed were so ordinary.

"Why?" she muttered when Jay and she were back on the path. Shadows surrounded them. The guilty party could be watching. "What were they looking for?"

"Your guess is as good as mine."

Her lips went numb, and she made no attempt to continue the conversation. He stared down at her for too long, then withdrew his radio from his belt and activated it.

"Christian," he said in response to a faint hello. "It's Jay Raven. Where are you? Already? You made good time. Look, we've got a problem at Potlatch."

She listened, and yet she didn't, as Jay spelled out what they'd discovered. He'd handle everything, say what needed to be said, answer the investigator's questions. All she had to do was start feeling again. Only she didn't want to.

"Christian is with the others at—you know where he is," Jay told her after completing his conversation. "He isn't sure when he can get down here but is sending a couple rangers this way. In the meantime, he charged me with making sure no one goes inside."

"It doesn't matter," she whispered. "The damage has been done. Doc's laptop is gone. I'm certain his notes on what he's been doing here are in there, to say nothing of his lecture and reference materials going back years." She closed her eyes in an attempt to get through what she needed to tell Jay. "That's also where he keeps pictures of his grandchildren." No matter that Doc was dead, she'd spoken of him in the present tense. Maybe he'd always remain alive in her mind.

"Are you saying everything he'd been compiling about this area's history was in one place?"

She opened her eyes. Instead of the criticism she half-expected to see in his expression, she noted a slight sagging to his shoulders and took that as proof of how tired he was. Unlike her, however, he had reserves of strength to draw on. She couldn't imagine him being afraid.

"Unfortunately, yes." How long had it taken her to respond? "He loves—*loved*—that old laptop. He called it his personal workhorse. It has tons of memory. All his class notes are in it."

"What about backup?"

"Oh, I'm sure he did that." Damn it, she had to concentrate. Function. "I asked him about that. He said not to worry."

Jay looked at the closed cabin door. "Whoever it was didn't miss anything. I didn't see any of those memory stick things. He couldn't have used a remote storage service, because there's no Internet reception within the forest."

"He told me that."

She hadn't opened any drawers or gone through Doc's personal belongings, which meant maybe the thief hadn't found Doc's backup.

She looked at Jay, not wanting any of this to be happening.

"You've been thrown a new curve," he said. "Are you sure there isn't someone you can call?"

"It's all right." She forced a laugh. "I've heard of thieves who break in while people are at the funeral, but this—"

"Is that what you believe happened?"

"Right now I can't answer. Point me in the direction of a shower and something to eat, and I'll be..." She'd been going to say she'd be good as new, but that was a lie. Just the idea of being alone made her uneasy when she seldom felt that way. "A shower first."

"I get the sense you don't want to talk about this, but I'm going to ask anyway. Are your parents dead? What about siblings?"

Suddenly, her pack felt as if it weighed a hundred pounds. Even more disconcerting, she was getting lightheaded. "I don't know."

"You what?"

She started to shrug, then swayed. The questions had come out of left field and were more than she could deal with right now.

When he stepped behind her, she couldn't muster the strength to determine what he had in mind. When he pulled the pack off her shoulders, she sighed in relief.

"It's all right if you cry. You don't have to prove anything to me."

Didn't she? Seeking the answer, she spun around and watched as he shrugged out of his own pack. They had been through so much since they'd met. Granted, only she'd had to deal with the emotional component, but he'd been part of everything. He'd seen her raw and emotionally naked. In some ways, he got her better than she did herself right now.

"I don't know how to cry." Tears burned her eyes, built, but didn't release.

He held out his hands. "I don't believe you."

"I have a hell of a defense mechanism."

"Which you need why?"

Why couldn't she keep her mouth shut around him? "Don't play shrink on me. It won't work."

"This isn't a battle, Winter. I want to help."

Help. Even Doc hadn't attempted to reach beyond the barrier she'd erected around herself. Now she wanted to tell someone about the holes in her. She placed her hands in his. He drew her close. Lowered his head.

She lifted hers. Touched her mouth to his.

Hopefully no one was around, but even if someone had been, it wouldn't have changed things. Moments ago, responsibility and grief had weighed on her. Now, she became weightless, floated above mortal concerns.

Her body felt as if it were flowing into this strong, competent, compassionate and physical man. The lines between their separate selves were being sanded away, barriers breaking down. Wrapping her arms around Jay's waist, she pressed herself against him. He was so tall that continuing the kiss had her off balance, but that was all right. He'd keep her safe.

"Damn," he muttered.

When he made no move to draw away, she held on even tighter.

"Winter."

She reluctantly pushed back. When she was free, she stood staring up at him, with her arms heavy at her sides and disbelief enveloping her. What had she done?

Not just her, both of them.

"You need more than a shower and something to eat," he said on the tail of an awkward silence, "but those things are a start. It'll help you get your emotional equilibrium back."

He was right, of course. More than right—he'd become her lifeline. She hated feeling so vulnerable right now, and yet there wasn't much she could do about it until a little time had passed.

"I'm tired of hurting," she admitted, as if that explained her eagerness to press her mouth, her body against him.

"Of course you are. When my parents died—it was bad."

"It had to be."

"But I got past it," he said. "So will you."

She rested her right hand over where the wolf tattoo lay. "I want to make sense of why Doc was killed and his cabin ransacked. I can't help the investigation if I can't get past how Doc's murder impacts me."

"So you're staying."

Staying. Letting the forest envelop me. Listening and longing for another howl. Asking myself if I belong here. Maybe finally feeling whole. Connected. "For now."

"Is helping law enforcement the only reason?"

She focused on Doc's cabin. "No."

"That's what I thought you'd say, and I get your commitment to your friend, but it might not be safe." He drew her hand away from the tattoo and placed her palm against his ribs. "There's a killer out there. Maybe the same person ransacked Dr. Gilsdorf's cabin."

Her hand rose and fell with his breathing. Close. Warm and alive. "Are you trying to scare me?"

"No. Of course not, but you shouldn't stay where you might be in danger."

Because I have the wolf mask? The thought broke the spell, prompting her to pull free and back away. As soon as she did, she regretted her action. "I appreciate your concern, and I need to consider that possibility, but I'm dealing with more than just what happened to Doc."

"Wolf."

"Yes, Wolf."

His expression became darker. "I can't tell you how to handle that. I wish I could, but — Winter, Christian needs to talk to you, which means you have to spend at least tonight here."

Near you. "Yes."

"You'll need a place to stay. I might have a solution. There's a cabin not far from the one I use. For years, it was reserved for summer staff, but with the cutbacks... Anyway, there's a shower in it."

"You're sure it'll be all right that I stay there?"

"I'll have to clear things with Michael, but I doubt if he'll object."

"Why Michael?"

"He wanted to rent them out. So far, only Dr. Gilsdorf had been willing to pay what he's asking."

"I guess I could pay for a few nights."

"Don't offer. Remember, Michael wanted to work out a mutually beneficial relationship with Dr. Gilsdorf. As long as he suspects you might pick up where Doc left off, my guess is he'll do everything he can to get on your good side."

"You believe that?"

"His job is to bring as much revenue as possible to the park. Having anthropologists here...seemed like he was hoping Dr. Gilsdorf's study would translate into increased public interest in the park." Jay's mouth tightened. "Instead, he'll have to convince potential visitors that they aren't putting their lives in danger coming here. He'd like nothing better than to point to your presence as proof that a murder hasn't changed anything."

"So he'll want to put a positive spin on what happened to Doc?"

"Yeah. Look, I suggest you play along as best you can. He's been pretty volatile since the new fiscal year started. I've seen him go off a couple of times."

"He loses his temper?"

"It's happened."

"Do you think he could have—?"

"Don't get ahead of yourself. I'll mention Michael's short fuse to Christian, but it's a stretch to believe he'd go from being frustrated with Dr. Gilsdorf to killing him."

"Someone did."

His nostrils flared. "Yeah. Like I said, I'll talk to Christian, but I just can't see Michael…the amount of savagery—" He shook his head. "I'm sorry. I shouldn't have said that."

"Not talking about what we saw won't change anything."

"You're right," he said softly. "I'm not doing you any good by trying to protect you."

Hearing you say that does me a great deal of good.

"So you're clear on where things stand with Michael?" he asked.

"I believe so." She started to ask where this cabin with hopefully hot water was when she remembered something. "Booth is going to be upset when he learns about the robbery. Some of that material might be irreplaceable."

"Let Booth worry about that. How about we go to your car and get your belongings?"

Her car, where the wolf mask lay beneath items Jay was offering to carry. Feeling trapped, she looked around. Instead of providing an escape route, however, the forest closed in on her.

"That's all right." She rushed her words. "There isn't much. Besides, don't you have to stay near Doc's cabin? Just point me in the right direction, and I'll—"

"Don't push me away."

"I need time alone." She ran her fingers through her hair. "To make some decisions." *To put distance between myself and your impact on me.*

"All right."

She was trying to decide whether he approved when she heard a faint thumping sound. Talio was walking toward them. Despite his dependence on the cane, he carried himself with pride. Jay hurried to his uncle and offered his arm. Talio shook him off.

"You're stubborn," Jay said.

Talio's smile softened his features. "Of course I am."

"I take it dispatch was able to get through to you," Jay said as they joined her. "I asked them to tell you what happened."

"It helped explain..."

Knowing Jay had made a special effort to tell his uncle about Doc's murder set her on edge. Shouldn't the investigators be in charge of that kind of thing?

"Explain what?" Jay asked.

"The dark energy I've been feeling."

Dark energy? *What are you talking about?*

"How long have you been feeling that?" Jay asked.

When Talio shot a look her way, she wondered if he was warning Jay not to say anything more. Damn it, they were three Native Americans. Shouldn't that stand for something, a kinship maybe?

Of course not. She wasn't one of them.

"For weeks," Talio said. "It keeps getting darker."

"Why didn't you tell me?"

"Would you have believed me?"

Maybe she was wrong, but she thought she caught a look of pain before Jay blinked it away.

"I'll leave the two of you to talk," she said.

Talio held up his free hand. "No, not yet. Listen to me."

It had been getting cloudy, but, all at once, the gray sky didn't seem as oppressive as it had been. "All right."

Talio's stare intensified until nothing else mattered. "You heard Wolf. Saw the spirit."

"Did Jay tell you—"

"No, he didn't."

Instead of shock, she felt a strange acceptance. She studied the man with the weathered face and gray at his temples.

"I am aware of many things. Before yesterday, I would have never mentioned Wolf to someone who maybe has never walked on this land, but—"

"What do you mean *maybe*?" Blood pulsed through her temples. "Do you believe I might have been here before?"

"Do you?"

"Maybe. Maybe not," she whispered.

"And that causes you pain. Let it come, because that pain will open you to what makes this place special."

It took all her strength not to wrap her arms around this man who was saying what her heart desperately needed to hear.

"How do you know about what she heard and saw?" Jay asked.

Looking sad, Talio shook his head. "You shouldn't have to ask me. Did you see it?"

"No."

Jay had spoken so softly she barely caught the word. Studying both men, she realized she wasn't the only one in pain today.

"I'm sorry you didn't." Talio touched Jay's shoulder. "Maybe in time—"

"Maybe." Jay cleared his throat. "What about Wolf?"

"You believe she experienced the spirit? You have no doubt?"

The longer Jay stood there, the more exposed she felt.

"No doubt," he said at length.

"Thank you," she whispered. If she could trust her legs to do what she needed of them, she would be standing next to Jay, maybe linking her hands with his. Placing his fingers over her tattoo.

"Winter," Talio said, "I need you to open your mind to what I'm going to say, to simply accept. Can you do that?"

Trembling, she nodded.

"I hope so." He pointed his cane at a section of log that marked the trail. "But first, I want to sit down."

As he made his slow way to the log, she fought the desire to embrace him. Part of what she was feeling was because she missed Doc, but it was more than that. If she had a grandfather, she'd want him to be like this older Hoh. Wise and gentle. Accepting. When Jay sat near his uncle, she joined them, sitting on Talio's opposite side because that was easier on her nervous system than being close to Jay.

"I'm not sure how much my nephew has told you about our life here," Talio began. "There's more to it than outsiders will ever grasp. Even before you arrived, I sensed you would be different."

"Before?"

Talio stretched out his right leg and started rubbing his thigh. "Yes."

The wolf mask? Shock nearly pushed her to her feet. Could Talio have heard the same howl she had when she'd put on the mask? No! She'd been hundreds of miles away.

"Wolf spirit speaks only to those he trusts and feels one with," Talio continued. "A few days before you arrived, Wolf warned that things I have long taken for granted were changing. The spirits were already uneasy and had been since Dr. Gilsdorf arrived."

No! Don't say that.

"I've been asking my spirit to explain what was bothering me, but he didn't." He again rubbed his leg. "Some of it is my doing. Between recovering from the accident and worrying about my nephews, I've been unable to turn my mind and heart over to Eagle."

Going by how Talio was speaking, she half-believed the three of them had slipped into the past to when superstition and primitive beliefs had guided the area's Natives.

"Our spirits are complex. Real to those with open hearts and minds. That is why those like your anthropologist friend will never fully comprehend our ways. They call what exists for us 'Native American superstition'."

"You're saying anthropologists are wrong?"

He chuckled. "About many things. Thunderbird told me to contact you. He put a word in my mouth for you to try to grasp. Days before that, Wolf spoke of change and danger."

Danger to whom? "Where were you when Wolf, ah,

communicated with me?"

Talio gave her his full attention. "You are asking if I was near Ghost Totem Ridge."

"Were you?"

He pressed on his thigh with the heel of his hand. "I haven't gone there since this happened, but that doesn't mean I didn't experience what you did."

Jay groaned. "You really want to do this, Uncle? You trust her that much?"

"Trust? It goes beyond that. Not saying anything won't change what happened." Talio placed his hand behind his knee and lifted his leg so he could adjust its position. "Winter, yesterday my spirit opened my eyes, ears and heart so I could be one with Wolf. I clear my mind of everything else and let impressions take over. That happens sometimes."

"What did you experience?"

"Wolf. But not just him."

As shaken as she was, she again wanted to embrace the older man.

"In ways beyond my ability to explain," he went on, "I was there yesterday when you found Dr. Gilsdorf's body. I heard you cry out and watched as you attempted to close his eyes."

"Did you do that?" Jay asked her.

She'd nearly forgotten Jay was with them. Even now, she couldn't separate herself from what Talio had just described.

"Yes," she whispered. "I was so scared, sick with grief, but I didn't want to leave him like that. He—I thought he'd be more peaceful if he didn't have to look at his body." She stood and faced Talio. "What else did you see?"

If anything, Talio's eyes were even darker than Jay's. "Flies. That's what drew you to the body."

Nodding, she clamped her hand over her mouth.

"Many people would have immediately run, but you didn't," Talio continued. "The vegetation in that area is so thick, you probably would have walked past him if not for the flies — unless Dr. Gilsdorf's spirit reached out to you."

"I can't answer that. But hearing Wolf howl didn't surprise me that much."

"Why not? Maybe yesterday isn't the first time you've heard him."

Afraid she'd tell this wise man about the wolf mask, she clenched her teeth. What if he already knew?

"The howl isn't the only otherworldly thing that happened up there," she said, hoping to deflect the conversation.

Talio's face contorted as he stood. "You also saw Wolf."

Yes. "It was beautiful. Amazing."

"Were you afraid then?"

This wise Hoh would push for honesty from her as long as she allowed it. "I was dealing with so many emotions. Just the same, I felt complete."

"Maybe you were."

Talio's questioning tone had her looking at him again. "Maybe." She was tempted to tell him about her long-running connection with the predator.

Talio closed his eyes. When he started to lean toward him, Jay straightened him. "I'm letting my spirit in," Talio muttered, eyes still closed. "Opening my mind to more of its wisdom. You experienced Wolf one more time, later, when you and my nephew were together."

Jay muttered.

"She exposed her soul to something without explanation while you stood there. Ah, Jay, you're missing so much."

And it's killing him.

Wondering if she was right, she studied Jay. He wanted to keep his emotions locked up, but his uncle had penetrated the barrier.

"I'm sorry," Talio said. "I need to let you live your life instead of wanting to guide you as I believe is best." He opened his eyes. "Thanks to Jay, I was able to return to the house I was born in. He believes he owes me something for raising him, but my debt to him is as great, if not more."

Her chin trembled. "What the two of you have is special."

Jay nodded and briefly hugged his uncle. Watching them, she couldn't remember why she'd wanted to get away a few minutes ago. Both men were complex and multilayered. If she remained around them, maybe in time they'd reveal their cores.

She didn't only want that, she needed it.

"Winter," Talio said. "You believe you're here for one thing, but you need to open your mind and heart to more."

"What do you mean?"

Talio's expression softened. "The spirits are restless. Angry and anxious. When I try to look into the future, I see you. You're like mist—solitary and searching."

"Mist?" Jay repeated. "You told me a lack of clarity can be a sign that someone's life is in danger."

Too much! I can't absorb any more.

Talio smiled. "Mist can also mean a person isn't sure where to walk."

"You're scaring me." Shocked by what she'd revealed, she clamped a hand over her mouth.

"Fear is part of the journey." Talio straightened his leg, only to wince and rub it again. "In your heart, you know it's time to reach beyond what you've always been."

Chills broke out all over her. She wanted to race into the forest. At the same time, she needed to stay and continue this conversation. "I have no idea who I am."

Talio swept his hand over their surroundings. "Look for yourself. You'll never have peace unless you do."

Chapter Eleven

"Can you spend the night with him?" Jay asked his brother when he reached Floyd.

"Tonight?"

"Yes, tonight. I don't like the idea of him being alone. He's looking kind of shaky."

"Where are you?" Floyd asked. "I thought—I heard about what happened at Ghost Totem. Seger said he heard you called the murder in, so I figured that's where you were."

Seger owned the Forks bar that was his brother's favorite. Right now, Jay didn't have the energy necessary to deal with Floyd's sobriety, or lack thereof.

"I did, but I'm back at Potlatch." He stopped looking at where his uncle's pickup had been kicking up dust and stared in the direction of the cabin he'd directed Winter toward. "I need to stay here for—I'm not sure how long, but it's going to be a while. What have you heard?"

"Not much. I was holding off calling because I thought you'd be out of range."

Out of habit, Jay listened for more than the sound of Floyd's voice. He heard music and masculine voices. Wasn't it early in the day for Seger's bar to have that much activity? Maybe news of a murder in the park had brought the regulars in to gossip. As for why Floyd wasn't working—damn it, he'd better not have lost another job.

"Who was the broad who found the body?"

She's not a broad. Holding his temper in check, he briefly described Winter's relationship to Dr. Gilsdorf and a little about what had brought her to Olympic. He didn't say anything about what Uncle Talio had told Winter, because

Floyd was even less interested in what they called 'the woo-woo stuff' than he was—had been.

Instead of asking about the condition of the body like Jay thought his brother would do, Floyd agreed to head for their uncle's place before it got dark.

"You're sure you'll be in shape to drive?"

"Don't start, damn it. You aren't my keeper." Floyd got short-tempered when he was drinking.

"Look," he said as calmly as he could, "I don't want to fight with you. I've been through a lot lately."

"I'm sorry. Sorry as hell. You saw—everything?"

"It was easier for me than for Winter."

"Winter? Oh yeah, the broad who—"

"Don't call her that."

"Okay, okay. She freak out, did she?"

"She held it together better than I would have if someone I loved had been sliced like that. She's a strong woman."

"What's happening now? They're going to be investigating, trying to figure out who did it?"

That went without saying. He was surprised Floyd had brought it up.

"I don't believe you've met Christian Turney. He's been working in the park for about ten years and has had extensive law enforcement training. He's in charge of the investigation. I'll talk to him once he's done at the murder scene."

"What can you tell him? You weren't there when—"

After Floyd cut off his statement, Jay heard him order a beer. Damn. Not good. "How many have you had? Make this your last one." *If you can.*

"Don't baby me. If I'm responsible enough for folks to want me on the tribal council, I can decide how much to drink."

"Who wants you on the council? I didn't think you were interested."

"That's because you spend all your time in the park or working to keep Uncle Talio's place from falling down around him. I've been speaking my mind about how we should have never let that anthropologist come here."

For several seconds, all Jay could do was stare toward where Winter had gone. "I didn't think that mattered to you."

"It didn't at first, but the more I thought about it, the more pissed off I got. We've been pushed around for so long. Now here comes someone who might jeopardize what means so much to us. My friends are saying it was dangerous letting him explore around Ghost Totem Ridge because, well, I don't have to explain why."

No, you don't. "He won't be anywhere anymore," he pointed out.

"That's one good thing that came out of someone taking a knife to him."

Jay hadn't said anything about what weapon had been used, but he had mentioned that Dr. Gilsdorf had been sliced. Floyd had simply put one and one together.

Closing his eyes, he mentally cursed himself for briefly thinking like a detective. Dr. Gilsdorf had antagonized a number of people. His brother was far from on top of that list. Floyd as a suspect wouldn't have occurred to him if he hadn't been on the receiving end of Floyd's short fuse.

When they were boys, he'd discovered he could push his younger brother's buttons to the point that Floyd started throwing punches. Jay had usually come out on the winning end of their arguments, which infuriated Floyd even more. Then Uncle Talio had sat him down and told him that deliberately making his brother lose his temper wasn't the Hoh way. If Jay wanted to grow up worthy of his bloodline, he needed to start acting responsibly.

It had only taken that one lecture. Jay stopped goading Floyd, and they'd become best friends—at least, they'd been close until Jay had taken off to explore the world and Floyd had started reaching for a bottle.

"Floyd, I need to ask you something. Are you aware of anyone who might be so resentful of what the professor was doing that he'd want to actually *kill* him?"

Silence stretched out, making Jay uneasy. Was his brother trying to frame his response? A killing wasn't something anyone would brag about.

"Not a Hoh. Ah, I haven't said anything to you about this because you work for the federal government but…"

"What haven't you told me?"

"The reason I'm considering getting on the tribal council — it's mostly older men."

"Yes."

"Who take forever to make a decision and are stuck so far in the past they can't find their way out."

"What do you hope to accomplish?"

"Something. Anything. Dr. Gilsdorf didn't put the screws to you, did he?"

Much as he liked having a conversation with his brother, this wasn't what he'd prefer. "What are you talking about?"

"Nothing. Forget I— All right. A few weeks ago, he said he was trying to get those grant people to fork over enough money so he could hire a Native to help him at Ghost Totem."

"No Native would do that. At least, I hope they wouldn't."

"But if he offered enough money—"

"Yeah." Jay shook his head. "I hear what you're saying. Money talks."

Floyd sighed then sighed again. "Dr. Gilsdorf is dead, but someone else might take over. We have to keep strangers away from where they have no business being."

Before one of them finds Grandparents Cave. "Murder isn't the answer."

When again his brother didn't immediately respond, Jay wondered if the amount of beer he'd put away had slowed his ability to process.

"Our uncle believes the spirits will tell us what to do, but that isn't enough. We have damn little. We *have* to hold onto what's precious."

"I agree, so what—"

"Maybe we start by getting the council to insist the courts get involved."

"That might take a long time."

"There's a lot of wilderness out there. A person could get lost. Never be found again."

"Don't go there."

Floyd snorted. "Why not? That would solve everything."

Minutes later, Jay stood staring at but not seeing the dark green wall all around. He hadn't said anything to his uncle, because he hadn't wanted to make it real, but Floyd was becoming more and more unpredictable. It wasn't just his short fuse. Floyd now insisted that anyone who didn't believe as he did was wrong. Jay didn't buy that his brother was serious about wanting to become part of the tribe's governing body, and even if he was, there weren't any current openings. On the other hand, Floyd could be persuasive, especially with the young men he hung around with. What if Floyd had convinced one of his friends that Dr. Gilsdorf posed a danger to Ghost Totem, or even worse, what if a liquored up Floyd had decided to do the job himself?

No! His brother wasn't capable of murder.

Was he?

His head pounded, and when he pressed on his forehead, the gesture took him back to when Winter had done the same thing.

Was she in danger?

Probably not. At present, she was simply a visitor who'd found the anthropologist's body.

A visitor who wanted to continue what Dr. Gilsdorf had started.

Who could endanger Grandparents Cave.

Whose sweet lips and soft body made him forget everything else.

* * * *

The shower stall was so small Winter had difficulty turning around in it, but getting clean felt wonderful. Her ability to relax came in part because the wolf mask was safe in her trunk. Thankfully, Jay's sense of responsibility with regards to standing guard over Doc's cabin had taken priority over helping her unpack.

Jay and she had kissed. She'd held onto him, felt his warmth invade her, come alive during those brief but precious seconds. She refused to analyze the why. Accepted. Put the experience into a protected corner of her mind.

Her cabin was larger than the one Doc had been staying in, but the difference didn't ease her memories of what his had looked like. She was both relieved to have Jay out of her sight and more unsettled than she wanted to admit. She had to decide what to do next. Taking over for Doc was more than an intimidating prospect. She'd only been working for the university for a few months. Granted, she'd worked with Doc while he had been formulating his proposal, but that didn't count for much.

"Your obsession goes beyond Doc's project," she told the empty room. "All these years of being obsessed with wolves, and now—now what?"

Her hand on the tattoo, she let the thought in. How could she leave where Wolf *lived*?

"So how do I make it possible for me to stay here?"

She didn't have the answer, but the longer she thought about what had taken place between the spirit—yes, that was what Wolf was—and herself, the stronger her need to stay in Olympic became.

She had Dr. Wilheim's cell phone number but didn't want to talk to him. He'd say a few things about how horrible it was that Doc was dead, but he wouldn't really mean it. The timing wasn't right for asking him if he'd advocate for her with the grant people, but maybe in a few days—what?

Feeling as if she'd come up against a brick wall, she shook her head. She had to tell Doc's son Pearson about the robbery, but it might be better to wait until she'd talked to law enforcement.

Robbery? She wasn't convinced it was as simple as some opportunist taking advantage of the compromised lock.

Mentally replaying what had taken place prompted her to pull out her laptop. She pushed back in a musty-smelling recliner and started jotting down everything she remembered of what she'd seen at Ghost Totem so she could give the investigator all possible details. Reliving her first sight of what was left of Doc made her sick to her stomach, but she forced herself to continue.

She'd been in a grand total of two fights in her life. Both had taken place while she was living in a state-run group home. One had been with a boy who'd teased her about her Native American features. She probably would have lost it if staff hadn't pulled them apart. The second time, she'd opened the door to her room to discover a girl going through her meager belongings. As had happened with the boy, anger had ruled her. By the time someone had intervened, the other girl had a bloody nose, and her cheek was scratched. They'd both lost privileges.

Scratches were nothing compared to what someone had done to Doc.

Once she'd exhausted her memory, she picked up her cell phone and punched the number for her good friend Carolyn. Her university coworker answered after the first ring.

"I should have called you," Carolyn said by way of hello. "But then I thought maybe I should wait until you had a chance to get in touch. He's really dead? Murdered?"

Keeping her explanation as condensed as possible, Winter told Carolyn what had happened. Carolyn started to explain that rumors were running rampant and she'd do her best to temper them with the facts, but Winter interrupted her.

"I need you to do something for me. I might want to get a hold of whoever administered the grant. Could you get me some names and numbers?"

"You want to get the funding transferred to you?"

"Yes."

"Good luck. Of course you might have to compete with Dr. Wilheim. Speaking of, he flew up there last month during the break."

Winter sat upright. "He never said anything to me."

"One of the grad students saw him at the airport. Wilheim pretended he didn't see him. The student noted which flight Wilheim got on. You take care, all right? There's some crazy shit going on there."

After saying goodbye, Winter stood and paced. Why hadn't Doc told her about Dr. Wilheim's visit?

"I can't ask you," she muttered. "I'll never be able to ask you anything again."

Her legs ached from all the walking she'd done, but the recliner's musty smell put her off. Besides, she preferred to be closer to the window where the light was better. As soon as she sat in one of the two kitchen chairs, she questioned her decision. Her view was less than reassuring. Instead of the path and its relative connection with civilization, all she could see were trees. Massive, oppressive trees capable of hiding a human being. Someone could be watching.

Someone who'd murdered once and might again.

Briskly shaking her numb hands, she got up and headed for the front door. She hadn't been concerned for her personal safety when Jay was around—Jay, with his large and competent body. Maybe she should go to Doc's cabin so she could ask if there'd been any updates from those investigating Doc's murder. The investigators could have found a clue the killer had left behind and were planning to make an arrest.

Angry with herself for getting freaked out, she pressed her hands together to stop their shaking. She'd been twelve or thirteen the first time she'd slept on the streets. At first, she'd been scared, but between the comforting presence of a baseball bat and her keen senses, she'd made her peace with the night. Not once had she been robbed—not that she'd had much—or raped. Doc had called her a survivor, something he'd failed at.

"No one gives a damn what you do," she reminded herself. "There's no reason for anyone to want to kill you."

She'd explore Potlatch. Do something with her restless energy until she could talk to the investigator. Maybe she'd run into Jay, which would give her the opportunity to properly thank him for everything he'd done for her. Just because he didn't approve of what Doc had been doing didn't mean they couldn't, what, get along? No, it was more complicated than that.

More personal.

Her hand went to her lips, and she stroked where Jay's mouth had been. She wasn't sure which of them had made the first move.

Still lost in the memory, she stepped outside. She didn't expect to find Jay waiting for her, but that didn't stop her from being disappointed when she realized he wasn't around. In the short amount of time they'd been together, he'd slipped under her skin. Coming back from Ghost Totem, she'd been acutely aware of the strong presence walking ahead of her. Before that, she'd been in too much turmoil to think of him as a man, but now that she had, she didn't know how to stop, or if she wanted to.

Where had Doc found the wolf mask?

The question caught her unawares. Pushed thoughts of Jay to the back of her mind.

Needing answers about the mask had played a sizeable role in why she'd come to Olympic. Before the nightmare of finding Doc's body, she'd been looking forward to hearing how it had gotten into his hands. She might have asked if it had affected him like it had her.

Then again, maybe she wouldn't have.

Did Jay know where the mask had come from? And if he did, would he tell her? Maybe he'd accuse Doc of—no, he couldn't!

Why not? It wasn't as if Doc had any right to it.

Her wandering took her close to the office. She was

debating whether to remain near it or go somewhere else when she spotted several men trudging toward the parking area. As her gaze settled on the black bag they were carrying, nothing else mattered.

Barely stifling a moan, she wrapped her arms around her waist.

"I'm sorry you had to see this," a familiar male voice said from behind her.

She whirled around. "What are you doing here?" she asked Jay.

He frowned. "You sound as if you don't want to see me."

"It isn't—I don't know what I want." She tightened her hold on her waist.

"That's understandable." His expression softened. "Christian called to give me a heads up about when to expect them. I was hoping you were still in that cabin."

"I couldn't. The walls were closing in on me."

"More than the forest does?"

Realizing he'd noted her uneasy awareness of her surroundings made her feel even more vulnerable. "I'm getting used to the forest. Maybe Wolf is helping."

His expression became introspective, maybe envious. "If he is, I'm glad for you."

Even though having Jay there helped more than she wanted to admit, she focused on the laboring men and their burden. A solid hand settled on her shoulder. "You don't have to watch this."

Warmth spread throughout her, making talking difficult. "Yes, I do. It's the only way I'm going to be able to make everything real."

"You don't hide from reality," he said as he drew her back against his chest and looped an arm around her. Instead of feeling trapped, gratitude for his strength and caring nearly overwhelmed her. Even the question of whether he'd still want anything to do with her if he learned Doc had taken— stolen—an artifact did nothing to lessen his impact on her.

"I need to talk to Christian again," he said after a short

silence. "Find out if there's anything else he wants me to do."

"What about— What's going to happen to Doc?" She couldn't bring herself to say the word 'body'.

"Do you want me to ask?"

She nodded then shook her head. "I need to do this."

"Don't push yourself."

Jay was being so good to her. It took everything in her not to let him support her. She again reminded herself that their fragile relationship would shatter if he learned she had something she had no right to and that probably meant a great deal to his tribe. Regardless of her connection to the mask, she had no intention of keeping it, but how could she get it into the right hands without destroying Doc's reputation?

Before she had a chance to learn whether it provided a link to her past.

So much to concentrate on. So much to absorb.

She hated it when the men lowered the body bag to the ground near the stairs to the office. No matter that it wasn't practical for them to take Doc inside, she wanted him to be treated better than that.

Wolf. I need you.

"Have you called his son again?" Jay asked from behind her.

Irrationally hoping Wolf had heard her, she struggled to concentrate on Jay's question while not being distracted by his body. "I'm waiting until I've talked to the investigator. It's going to kill Pearson learning what happened to his dad's belongings."

"You'll handle it."

She made no attempt to say anything, only watched as the law enforcement officers gathered around a lean man of medium height wearing a long-sleeved dark green shirt and jeans. She guessed this was Christian Turney. Much as she hated needing to have anything to do with him, she respected him. Like Jay, he appeared in tune with his world.

"Damn," Jay muttered.

"What?"

"Booth is with them. If you don't want to talk to him, I'll tell him to leave you the hell alone."

Chapter Twelve

The park historian had separated himself from the group and was heading their way. Judging by how he walked, he was dealing with blisters. Concerned Booth might misinterpret her closeness to Jay as more than him offering sympathy, she straightened and stepped away.

It was better like this.

"Do you think he knows?" she asked Jay. "About what happened to Doc's cabin."

"I told Christian, so I wouldn't be surprised—unless he had something to do with the theft. In which case, that was old news."

"It that possible?"

"He'd want back what was in there."

"He wouldn't be that obvious, would he?"

"Maybe. Maybe not."

As she mulled over their exchange, she wondered if she and Jay should discuss possible suspects not just for the break-in but for Doc's killing. However, not only was she ignorant about how investigations were handled in the real world, she didn't dare forget that many Natives hadn't wanted Doc there. She couldn't ask Jay if he suspected his friends or relatives. That would destroy their fragile— whatever it was.

Booth gave her a weary smile. "You look better than I thought you would. I applaud your stamina. Of course you're younger than me." His smile fading, he acknowledged Jay. "I couldn't help but wonder if the night the two of you spent together might lead to something physical."

"Don't," Jay said. "I was comforting her, that's all."

All?

"I'm glad you're here for *support*."

Jay stared at the man.

"You weren't involved in opposing Dr. Gilsdorf like some of your tribe members were," Booth continued, "but I'd be surprised if you didn't agree with them. With him dead" — Booth shuddered — "you must be wondering what's going to happen to his project."

"Everything's on hold."

"But maybe not for long," she said.

Booth focused on her. "Have you talked to Dr. Wilheim?"

"You know him?"

"Oh, yes. I met with him every time he was here."

Every? It looks as if there's a lot I don't know about my boss.

"That's one reason I decided to come back as soon as I could." Booth patted a front pocket, drawing her attention to a bulge in the shape of a cell phone. "I thought Dr. Wilheim might have left a message, but he didn't. Have the two of you talked?" He lowered his gaze then looked at her again. "Unless I'm asking something you can't tell me."

"I believe he's on his way here."

"Good, good."

Something about Booth's tone made her wonder if he really meant that.

"Have you seen Dr. Gilsdorf's cabin since you got back?" Booth asked. "Is it really as bad as I heard?"

"A great deal was taken," she said. "Unfortunately, it looks like most of the library material is missing."

With an effort, Booth straightened. "Is it?" His gaze shifted to Jay. "I may regret saying this, but I'm exhausted. The first thing I thought when Christian told me was that the Natives must have done it."

"Why?" Jay demanded.

"Motive and opportunity." He nodded at Winter. "No one knows more than I do about the contents of those old oral histories. I've been concerned that tribal members would want them back. That would be a real shame, because they shed new light on the past and should be available to the public." He smiled. "Several articles about my efforts to preserve those records have been published in library publications. NPR twice interviewed me." Another smile lifted his tired features.

"I've been accused of using them for my personal gain, which is ridiculous. Dr. Gilsdorf was fascinated by the histories, which initially thrilled me and is why I gave him unrestricted access. I just wish he'd been more forthcoming about whether he found them useful."

"Does that have anything to do with you suspecting local Native Americans?" Jay asked.

Booth rubbed his stubble. "Good question. It's possible he told some Native Americans about what he'd found in the records. It might've been his way of drumming up their support." Booth shrugged and lifted his hands, palms up. "That could have backfired, made the Natives determined to get their hands on the histories."

Was it really theft if the Natives took back what represented their cultures? "There's going to be an investigation into the theft," she said. "Until that's completed, it's premature to point fingers."

Booth nodded. "You're right. What concerns me is that the files might be destroyed."

"Aren't there copies?"

"Yes," he muttered. "But if the tribes go to court to obtain custody of everything—I've heard the Hoh council is looking into using an injunction to force Dr. Gilsdorf to stop."

"An injunction?" She stumbled over the word. "The Hoh are suing to—"

"I'm not sure if it has gotten beyond the talking point, and I might be jumping to conclusions. Maybe the Natives had nothing to do with the robbery."

"Let's take this a step further," Jay said. "Are you also saying one or more of my people might have killed Dr.

Gilsdorf?"

No! She wanted to scream but couldn't. Just because she'd studied the Native Americans of the Northwest didn't mean she understood them. How could she believe she did when she didn't know herself?

"Don't put words in my mouth," Booth retorted.

"You and I aren't detectives," Jay told Booth through clenched teeth. "Let law enforcement do their job."

"I don't care," she told the two men when that wasn't the truth. "Right now, there's only one thing I can focus on." She pointed at the body bag.

"You're right." Booth's words dragged. He started to extend his hand toward her, only to pull back. "I held it together pretty well up until now, but I've never been around violence. I shouldn't have said anything. The last thing I want to do is make this any worse for you."

The way Jay kept staring at Booth, she gathered he wasn't buying Booth's apology, if that's what it was. As for her, she'd spoken the truth when she'd said she couldn't deal with any more. "I'm taking this one second at a time."

Booth sighed and licked his chapped lips. "I need to do the same thing. First things first is getting out of these boots."

He took a step. Before he could take another, raised voices cut through the forest sounds. Looking toward where they were coming from, she saw Michael standing toe to toe with Christian. Michael's hands were fisted.

"He's going off," Jay said. "I wondered if this was going to happen."

"Me too," Booth muttered.

"This is unacceptable," Michael said loud enough for every word to carry. "You're asking the impossible. I won't allow it."

She couldn't hear Christian's response, but his tone and stance made it clear he didn't share Michael's anger. If anything, Christian was attempting to calm and reassure the other man.

"Don't play me for a fool," Michael snapped. "I'm aware

of how the government works. Hell, I'm part of it. You're going to run roughshod over the park, make up your own rules and expect me to let that happen."

The other law enforcement officers had stepped back from Michael and Christian, but their body language left no doubt they were ready to step in if necessary.

"What is he talking about?" she asked.

"I have a pretty good idea," Booth answered. "Same as you, right, Jay? Christian just reminded Michael that law enforcement is in charge, and Michael doesn't like it."

Michael was still arguing, but at least he'd stopped yelling. Winter was willing to cut him some slack. After all, like Booth, he'd been on his feet most of the day. He'd had to look at a savaged body when he probably was as ill-prepared as she'd been. What she didn't get was why he'd taken it upon himself to notify the university of Doc's death.

"I saw this coming," Booth said. "All the time we were walking back, he kept on about how worried he was that the park would be shut down. I told him I didn't see that happening, but I might as well have been talking to a wall."

As Booth limped away, Winter focused on Jay. The way he watched the still-heated discussion put her in mind of a guard dog. He bore only a casual resemblance to the man who'd recently stood respectfully next to his uncle.

"Why is Michael so upset?" she asked. "He knows there has to be an investigation."

"Because he's scared."

"For his job? No one's going to fire him for something that's beyond his control."

"He was hired to increase revenue. That's hanging over his head. I have to hand it to him. He came up with a couple of programs that brought a few more people in while the programs were ongoing, but the gains he made will be reversed if the doors are locked."

"Whoever hired him would understand that, wouldn't they?"

"It doesn't sound as if he believes that. I'm not sure Michael knows why he's afraid."

In a way, she understood Jay's explanation. Those times were behind her, but she still remembered the fear that had gripped her every time she had no idea where she was going to spend the night. She'd slept outside enough that the lack of a roof had stopped bothering her. It was the isolation, the loneliness, wondering if it would ever end. Having no one to turn to.

Except for the remnants of her childhood belief in Wolf.

"Winter," Jay said, "I want to be part of this discussion. Go to my cabin and get something to eat."

Memories of homelessness evaporated with his words. "You're sure you don't mind?"

He ran his knuckles over the side of her neck, causing goosebumps and more to explode all over her. "Our relationship's a complicated one, but that doesn't mean I don't want to get something to eat."

Take care of me. "Thank you."

"I'll see you as soon as I can."

Between Jay's words and touch, long seconds passed before she got moving. Once she was on the path with the forest whispering whatever trees and wind whispered, she chalked her reaction to Jay up to the rabbit's hole she'd fallen into, starting when she'd opened the box Doc had sent her. She had a sex drive, of course, but she'd never come close to losing her mind because some male said he wanted her.

Jay hadn't said anything of a sexual nature. Just because they'd shared a brief kiss and he'd put his arms around her and touched the side of her neck —

Can you read my thoughts, Wolf? If so, please straighten them out.

* * * *

In some respects, the cabin Jay used was indistinguishable

123

from the two others she'd seen since coming here, in that it had been built at the same time from the same mold and subjected to the same harsh weather. The difference lay in the personal stamp he'd placed on it. Several wilderness posters had been taped to the walls. Instead of a sleeping bag, real bedding, complete with a dark brown spread, covered the single bed. He might have bought the efficient wood stove. The small kitchen was well stocked with a full-sized refrigerator, cast-iron skillets, heavy-duty pans, pottery dishes, and a supply of fruits, vegetables, whole grain bread and meat. Jay was a bachelor, but he obviously believed in a healthy diet.

Everything about being in his domain spoke to her. She wished he'd explain why he'd chosen the poster of a mountain creek flanked by deep snow or the awe-inspiring one of a bull elk, its head and massive rack lifted. Did anyone ever share the narrow bed with him?

Stop thinking like that.

A little later, as she ate a ham and cheese sandwich complete with tomatoes, lettuce and onions, her head cleared. She was still tired but no longer felt as if she was going down for the count. Even her grief had become less all-consuming.

While preparing her meal, she'd wondered if Jay would come in, but he hadn't. She wished he would so she'd know whether to return to her cabin or connect with Christian. One thing she was certain of, she didn't want to see the bag holding Doc's body again. She'd finished eating and was wiping off the counter when her cell phone rang. Hoping it was Jay, she grabbed the phone. The number displayed belonged to Carolyn.

"Do you have something to write on?" Carolyn asked. "I have the grant committee information you need."

Looking around, she spotted an ink pen and wrote the names and numbers Carolyn gave her on a napkin.

"That was fast," she said. "I appreciate it."

"I figured the sooner the better. Besides, I can't concentrate on anything except Dr. Gilsdorf's murder. Any sign of Dr. Wilheim?"

"No, not that I'm in any hurry to see him."

"I don't blame you. Have you decided whether you're going to go after the grant?"

Yakanon.

Startled by the word Talio had thrown at her yesterday, she looked around, half-expecting to see the older Hoh. The walls closed in around her.

"Stay?" she muttered.

"Are you there?" Carolyn asked. "I can't hear you."

Instead of answering, she stepped outside. No matter how intently she stared all around, she saw nothing.

Yakanon.

Her mouth dried.

"Winter, are you all right?"

She opened her mouth, but before she could say anything, a whispery sound reached her. Maybe it was Wolf, maybe not.

"Winter?"

The whisper again, a little stronger this time. Unmistakable. *Wolf.*

"I'm here," she said around the lump in her throat. "And, yes, I'm staying."

Some five minutes later, she was in her cabin. Even though she was certain it wouldn't do any good, she tried to get a Wi-Fi connection for her laptop so she could run a search for Yakanon. After giving up, she scanned through the graduate course notes in her files, copies of Doc's lectures he'd given her, even outlines of Dr. Wilheim's classes, but didn't come up with anything. Maybe the explanation was on Doc's laptop or in his backup. Maybe she'd have to ask Talio.

By now, it was late afternoon, and when she stepped outside, she realized she'd soon have to put on a jacket. If she were still in San Diego, she'd be looking forward to the cool of evening, but it was different here.

Everything was different in Olympic.

Everything had changed for her.

Determined to rejoin the real world, she headed toward the Potlatch office. The shadows were so long that little sunlight reached her, and she couldn't help but wonder if someone might be watching. No matter how firmly she told herself that Doc's murder was responsible for her paranoia, she couldn't shake off the suspicion. Maybe if she were back in familiar territory—

Maybe if Jay were with her—

No one was outside near the office, and there was no sign of Doc's body bag.

Suddenly afraid for the man who'd done so much for her, she picked up her pace. She should have stayed around to make sure he was properly cared for.

The office door opened, and Jay and Michael stepped out. Michael barely acknowledged her before striking off for a park service vehicle. Jay headed toward her. Next to Michael and Booth, who both carried the strain of their day, Jay looked as if he could keep going indefinitely.

"What happened?" she asked.

Jay came closer than her nerves needed. "They're taking the body to Seattle for an autopsy. Michael is going to the ranger district office in Quinault. I'm not sure what he hopes to accomplish there. Mostly, he probably can't bring himself to just wait for the process to play itself out."

"What about the investigation?"

"A couple of law enforcement rangers stayed where we found Dr. Gilsdorf, and Christian has been in contact with them. Christian wants to turn his attention to the cabin to possibly determine if there's a connection. They might not bother looking for fingerprints, because they'd have to have a testing kit brought in. Besides, anyone focused enough to take what he did would have worn gloves. Christian said he doesn't want to wait too long to interview the two of us."

Thank goodness for food in her stomach. Otherwise, her sudden lightheadedness might've gotten the better of her.

She debated telling Jay that she might have heard Wolf again, but she'd only be giving him a partial story if she didn't mention Yakanon's role, and she wasn't ready to do that. One more thing, she wasn't sure she should tell him about her conversations with Carolyn. Given everything Jay had done for her, she hated keeping anything from him, but she first had a lot to ponder.

She nearly told Jay she wasn't sure she could add anything valuable, but the interview might provide her with the opportunity to ask the investigator if he had any suspects.

Suspects? She was an anthropologist, not a detective.

A woman being *stalked* by a spirit wolf.

"What are you going to do?" she asked.

"Michael asked me to try to convince Christian to rethink his decision to close the trail to Ghost Totem. I agreed to bring it up. That's part of why Michael's going to Quinault. He's hoping the Pacific ranger district will put pressure on Christian." Jay ran calloused fingers through his thick, dark hair. "I'm sure they'll trust Christian to do his job."

"I wonder if he has any idea who did it."

"I don't know."

Jay hadn't closed any more of the distance between them, so why did she feel as if he was trying to draw her toward him? Maybe the sensation came from within her.

"Did he say anything to you?" she pressed.

"I'm not law enforcement, so I'm not the one he'd be discussing suspects with, but I'm sure he's compiling a list of everyone who had recent dealings with Dr. Gilsdorf."

Which included Dr. Wilheim, Michael, Booth and the Native Americans.

Jay's gaze became even more sober. "I didn't tell Michael about you staying in one of the cabins after all."

"Why not?"

"If he can use you to his advantage, he will."

"You sound sure of that."

He nodded. "He tried it with my people."

"What did he do?"

"He's long wanted to put us on display. This spring, he attempted to talk my uncle and other Hoh elders into conducting a potlatch on the border between the park and our reservation to entertain the public."

"Which you didn't want to do."

"It didn't personally involve me, Winter. I'm not part of those discussions."

But he wanted to be. His expression left her with no doubt. "Doc didn't tell me much about his relationships with other people here." She paused. "I wish he had. Dr. Wilheim is on his way here."

Jay frowned. "Why?"

"I'm not positive, but I have my suspicions. Have you said anything to Christian about Doc and Michael's relationship?" *Or what the Natives thought of Doc?*

"Not yet, but I'm going to. A heads-up about Michael—he doesn't handle confrontation well. Most times he backs down, but he has a temper. You saw a taste of it."

"Yes, I did. It seems strange to me that someone with a short fuse has gotten promoted like he has." Feeling chilled, she started rubbing her arms.

"Look, it's going to get cold in a hurry. Maybe you should go to your cabin. I'll tell Christian where you are."

"Jay?" She stepped into his space, once more feeling his heat. "Are you going to say anything to Christian about Wolf?"

His eyes narrowed. "Of course not. Are you?"

"And have him believe I've lost my mind?" Wishing Wolf would step out of the forest, she looked around. Jay was right, it would soon be dark. She was trying to decide what to do when Jay reached out, captured her wrists and drew her arms to his sides.

"There's something I need you to consider," he said. "The spirits are sacred to my people. They'd never forgive you if you say anything."

If he wanted to intimidate her, he was doing a decent job of it—all except for the part of her that wanted more than his fingers around her wrists. As evening took away the distinction between man-made structures and nature, what Jay represented became even more important.

"You indicated you don't believe as some Hoh do. Would you ever tell someone who isn't a member of the tribe about Wolf or other spirits?"

"I'd never say anything to an outsider."

Outsider. Her throat went dry, compelling her to swallow several times.

"That's something to take pride in. To be certain who and what you are..."

"Don't envy me, Winter. Be proud of what you've done with your life."

"I'm a survivor."

"What made you like that?"

His voice stroked her like a night breeze. Nothing existed except the two of them—and the barriers she'd erected around herself. "A lot of things I don't want to talk about." *Can't talk about.*

"Like not knowing whether your parents are alive."

Instead of giving her time to come up with a response, he drew her closer. As her breasts pressed against him, her heart started beating in double time. Her cheeks, throat and points south heated. In her mind's eye, he carried her into his cabin, stripped off her clothes, laid her out on a narrow bed and settled his naked body on top of hers. She spread her legs for him and wrapped herself around him. Made him hers. Became part of him.

"Damn it!" He shoved her away. "I know better. So do you."

He was right, terribly right. As she spun around so she didn't have to look at him, she swore she'd never get close to him again.

Chapter Thirteen

Jay's feet dragged as he made his way to Dr. Gilsdorf's cabin, but it had nothing to do with reluctance to deal with law enforcement or the long day catching up to him. No matter how much he might want to deny it, and he wasn't sure he did, he couldn't get Winter out of his mind.

Or wanting to touch her.

Needing to make love to her.

Where had that last thought come from? Granted, he hadn't had a romantic relationship since his divorce, but sex with Winter wasn't in the realm of possibilities. Was it?

"You can't go in there," Art, a ranger he occasionally worked with, said as he approached the cabin.

"I didn't figure I could. Besides, I've already seen what I need to. Christian's in there?"

"Him and one other person." Art spread his arms. "I'm the only one still standing guard. You and the woman were at the murder site, right?" He stuck out his hand. "Jay Raven, right?"

Jay shook hands with Art. "I don't know much about murder investigations," he admitted. "Do you have any idea how long it'll take?"

"None. Being trained in how to conduct one is a different story from the real thing. I don't need to tell you that murder and Olympic aren't synonymous."

He studied the closed cabin door. "I have no idea what they're going to find in there."

Art nodded. "I feel sorry for the woman who found the body. I heard she thought a lot of the victim."

"She did."

"And she discovered this place" — he pointed at the cabin — "had been ransacked."

"I was with her."

"Heavy. Robberies happen here. And how many car break-ins have we had this summer? Me, I believe it's kids." Art chuckled. "Back when I was a teenager, I did some pretty stupid things. Good thing I didn't get caught. Otherwise, I would have never gotten this job."

If he'd broken any laws, Uncle Talio would have hauled him before the tribal council and compelled him to confess. Unfortunately, a strong father figure and close-knit tribe hadn't kept Floyd sober.

Winter didn't have any kind of family.

He was still drawing comparisons between his support system and her lack of one when the door opened and Christian and a ranger who usually worked around Sol Duc Hot Springs emerged.

"Any chance what happened in here might lead you to Dr. Gilsdorf's killer?" Jay asked Christian.

"It's a possibility, but, right now, I wouldn't give you odds. You were in here both before and after the break-in, right?"

Jay nodded.

"How good is your memory?"

"I didn't pay much attention to the interior," admitted. "Winter might be more help."

Christian pulled a notebook from a back pocket and held it up to the waning light. "Booth Deavers told me Dr. Gilsdorf had borrowed a number of volumes from the park library. I've asked him to give me as complete a list as possible."

Christian was in his early fifties. As with Michael and Booth, the day had taken a lot out of him. Did he intend to spend the night at Potlatch? And if so, where did that leave Winter, since Jay had put her in the only unoccupied cabin? Darn it, he should have thought of that before now.

"You up to answering some questions?" Christian asked.

"I'm dead on my feet, but I want to talk to you while your

memory's fresh. I need to do the same with Ms. Barstow. The two of you came right here when returning to Potlatch, right? How would you assess her emotional state?"

Strong and fragile. "She was pretty upset last night, but she's doing better today." *Maybe no longer being haunted by Wolf.*

Christian nodded. "That'll probably come and go." He glanced at his watch. "I want to go home and get a change of clothes. I'll probably spend the night there then come back in the morning. Do you know where Ms. Barstow is? The sooner I do this the better."

"You want me to get her?"

"If you don't mind."

I'm not sure how I feel about seeing her again so soon. "She informed Dr. Gilsdorf's son of his death."

"Tough job. I'm going to want to talk to the son, as well." Christian withdrew a cell phone from a carrying case on his belt. "I need to make some calls, so if you don't mind bringing her here —"

"Will you want her to go into the cabin? I'd like to prepare her, if that's the case."

"Yeah. She might have a better idea than anyone at Potlatch what the professor had with him of a personal nature."

"About those personal items, do you think she can have a few of them?"

"I don't see why not. I'd better square that with the son."

Jay left Christian and headed toward the cabin where Winter would be staying. Part of him wished she'd go back where she'd come from so she could start to put her life back together. But the rest of him, the man part, wanted her around. Maybe because of her unsettling impact on his senses, he felt more alive than he had since before the cracks in his marriage started. He wanted to ask about her easy acceptance of Wolf. Anyone else would have thought they couldn't have heard or seen what she had. Instead, it was as if she was grateful for the spirit's presence. Accepting.

Why did she have what eluded him?

Maybe equally important, why had she placed a wolf head tattoo over her heart?

He took a step then stopped with one foot off the ground. The back of his neck prickled. Someone was watching him.

Instantly alert, he stopped and studied what little he could see. The longer he stood there, the less certain he was that the watcher was human—or maybe the truth was his need for the spiritual connection Winter took for granted was responsible for his thinking.

"Are you there, Raven?" he whispered. "If you are, I open my heart to you. I'm sorry I—sorry I turned my back on you."

He waited, remembering when he could barely wait to be considered a man so he could begin his spirit search. Then things had changed, and, by the time he reached eighteen, he was in full rebellion mode.

"Raven, forgive me. Don't desert me." About to say more, he stopped. Strained to hear.

Hell. It wasn't Raven. Just his desire to make the impossible happen.

And maybe whoever law enforcement was looking for was still around.

Was that possible? If he'd killed someone, the last thing he'd do was stay anywhere around the scene of the crime. But then he didn't think like a criminal.

It didn't make any sense that someone would be watching him. If there was any danger, it would be aimed at Winter because of her close ties to Dr. Gilsdorf.

Concern for her prompted him to pick up his pace. A few minutes later, he reached her cabin and knocked. When she didn't immediately respond, he knocked again, louder this time.

"Winter," he called. "It's me. Are you all right?"

"Jay? Just a minute."

She'd turned on one of the lamps. As a result, when she opened the door, light from behind seeped into her hair to give it red highlights.

"What is it?" Her eyes were wide.

Let's go inside. "Christian wants to talk to you. I offered to come get you."

"He's at Doc's cabin?"

"Yeah. If it bothers you too much, I'll see if he'd talk to you in the office."

"No." She ran her fingers through recently shampooed hair. "That's all right."

Don't touch her. "He's going to ask you to look it over. He might let you take Dr. Gilsdorf's personal items."

"He said that?"

"I asked."

"Oh. Thank you." Her head drooped, and she stared at her shoes. "Damn," she whispered, "damn."

"What is it?"

"Nothing." When she drew herself upright, he looked for tears but didn't see any. "I'm lying. A lot's wrong tonight."

"I'm sorry."

"It isn't your doing. I really appreciate your asking Christian what you did about Doc's belongings."

"Because Dr. Gilsdorf's that important to you?"

"No." She looked down again, then up. "You are."

Two simple words. Throwaway words. Maybe.

"I care about you, too." *More than I had any idea I would.*

Then they were inside the cabin and together again. Steps taken by each of them. Arms extending. As he clutched her to him, her clean scent filled him, but it was more than that. Arousal.

Hunger.

"We shouldn't—" she started.

"I know," he finished.

He touched his lips to her forehead, between her eyes, the tip of her nose. Her fingers were fisted in his shirt at the waist, wrinkling the fabric. When he kissed her eyelids, her breathing picked up. Something surged to life inside him. He both fought and encouraged the sensation by spreading his fingers over the sides of her neck so he could hold her head steady. That accomplished, he tipped her head upward. Their mouths all but slammed together. Taking. Demanding.

She dragged down on his shirt as if trying to force him to his knees. Even as he countered her surprising strength, he remained keenly aware of the soft woman inside her practical clothes. She might resist both him and herself, but she couldn't get past her sexuality any more than he could stop being a man. He didn't take advantage of her smaller body. Instead, he celebrated it as he worked his fingers under her collar.

Her flesh was so soft! Enticing. A threat to his sanity.

Unable to keep his hands still, he explored her as far as the damnable fabric allowed. Then, frustrated and determined, he attacked the top button. She made no effort to stop him. Instead, she freed not one, not two, but three of his shirt buttons. He wasn't sure whose breathing was loudest, couldn't control his. When he'd dispensed with the last button, he drew her blouse over her shoulders. He could have stripped her if she lowered her arms to her sides. Instead she clung to his shirt.

Breathed as if she were dying.

Another dangerous step had been taken. Their mouths continued to take and bruise. He ran his hands up and down her back, settled his fingers over her spine. The longer he held her against him, the slighter, warmer and more alive she felt. He was beyond being embarrassed by his erection. The message behind her now parted lips and the sweet tongue gliding between his said she'd fallen under the same erotic spell.

A harsh shudder ran through him. Gripping her arms, he struggled to determine what had happened. When she ran her fingers over his waist and burned his flesh, he realized she'd pulled his shirt out of his jeans.

She scratched him over his ribs. Wondering if her intention was to destroy him, he dragged her hands off him and placed them behind her. That done, he stopped kissing her and leaned back. The contrast between lamplight and approaching night complicated his view, but only one thing mattered — how she looked.

The wolf tattoo just above her bra.

"What are we doing?" she whispered.

"I don't know." He couldn't stop looking at the detailed predator head. His erection continued to throb. It would until — until when?

"Jay, we shouldn't be doing this."

No, they shouldn't. Shaking with the effort, he brought her arms back in front, settled her hands against her middle and released her. His sides where she'd scratched him hummed.

"I'm sorry." She pulled her shirt back over her shoulders but didn't hide the tattoo behind the fabric. "If I led you on, I'm sorry."

"You didn't."

She sighed then filled her lungs. Started re-buttoning her buttons. "I can't focus on what just happened. Maybe — it'll have to wait until my emotions are under control."

That was why she'd engaged in a little making out, so she'd have something uncomplicated to focus on. It wasn't as if she saw him as some great stud, more like a diversion.

Even as he tried to sell himself on the explanation, he suspected their brief groping would haunt her as long as it did him. They'd have to find a new way to interact, one that called for keeping their hands off each other.

Somehow.

Chapter Fourteen

Approaching headlights in the distance told Winter that someone had just arrived at Potlatch. Much as she wanted to head for Doc's cabin so hopefully she could put some distance between Jay and herself, she stopped. When she changed direction and headed for the office, Jay kept pace.

"I'm guessing I know who it is," she said. "If I'm right, I need to talk to him."

"You're talking about Dr. Wilheim?"

She nodded and kept moving. By the time they reached the parking area, a well-dressed, six-foot-plus man with long arms and legs was emerging from a vehicle. Her heart sank. "That's him all right."

"It didn't take him long to get here."

Even though she'd known he was on his way, she wasn't prepared. She wondered if he'd used university or private funds to pay for his plane ticket and rental car, not that it was her business.

"We don't have to have that conversation tonight."

She nearly laughed at an image of herself hiding behind Jay. "Don't tempt me. No, the sooner I get this over with the better."

Dr. Wilheim started for the office. Thanks to the still-on car headlights, she could tell he was frowning. She'd never seen Dr. Wilheim in anything except dress shoes. New-looking tennis shoes made for a strange contrast with his dark slacks and collared shirt.

"Dr. Wilheim," she said as he reached for the stair handhold. "I don't believe anyone's in there."

As had always been his way, Dr. Wilheim didn't rush

turning around. When she'd first met him, his overly long limbs had made her think he'd be awkward, but he wasn't because he took care to connect with every part of his body before making a move. He was going bald, but if it bothered him, she'd never seen any sign. Prominent frown lines and creases at the corners of his mouth resulted in a somber, disapproving expression.

"Winter."

Just her name, no other acknowledgment.

"The park budget officer, Michael Simpson, told you what happened to Doc," she said. "If you're looking for him, you'll have to wait until tomorrow. Michael left a while ago." She glanced at Jay to see if he'd add to her comment. He didn't, and if he ever looked at her like he was at Dr. Wilheim, she'd want nothing to do with him. Had he been this hostile toward Doc?

"What are you doing here?" Dr. Wilheim gave no indication he was aware of Jay's scrutiny.

"Where else would I be?"

He looked down his narrow nose at her. "You can't have forgotten the conversation we had right before you took off. I made it clear I couldn't spare you for more than a few days. With Anthony dead, I'd assumed you'd have given your professional responsibilities priority. Not to be insensitive, but he no longer needs you. I do."

"Pompous ass," Jay whispered.

When she'd first been assigned to him, Dr. Wilheim had intimidated her, but Doc had told her she'd better get over it, because, otherwise, Dr. Wilheim would run over her. "I can't leave," she told the professor. "For one, law enforcement needs to interview me."

"So the investigation is underway," he said. "Michael wasn't sure how long that would take." He angled his body to Jay. "And you are?"

"Jay Raven, ranger. I was nearby when Winter found Dr. Gilsdorf's body."

For the first time, Dr. Wilheim looked less than confident.

She couldn't remember ever seeing him like that.

"Do you know Michael?" she asked.

"As a matter of fact, I do. This is far from the first time I've been to Olympic."

She was aware of that. What surprised her was that Dr. Wilheim hadn't said anything earlier. Neither had Doc. "When were you here before?"

He extended his arms. "Don't question me. What matters are the circumstances that brought me here today."

Even though she'd rather be doing just about anything other than listening to his sharp tone, she nodded. "It's a long day for you." *Me too.*

"It certainly is. I'll be staying at a motel in Olympia, but I wanted to come to Potlatch before I settled in. So Michael isn't around. I don't suppose you can tell me where Booth Deavers is."

"He spends much of the summer at the Lake Quinault Lodge so I suggest you start there. That's where the library is located," Jay said.

She wondered how many people Dr. Wilheim had interacted with during his visits and why.

Dr. Wilheim waved bony fingers at Jay. "I'm aware of that. He was here today, right?"

"Yes," she said.

"He probably left," Jay said. "Gilsdorf's cabin was broken into and a number of things taken. That's our immediate concern. Why are you asking about Booth?"

"That's personal. What's missing?"

When Jay didn't respond, she explained that some of the items were library property.

"I trust Booth has a list of what's missing," Dr. Wilheim said. "Hopefully, it wasn't the oral histories."

So Dr. Wilheim knew about them. She supposed Doc could have told him, but it didn't seem likely. Perhaps he'd learned about the histories from Booth.

"I'd love to see them," she admitted.

"The contents aren't your concern," Dr. Wilheim said. "I

understand your feelings where Anthony is concerned. The two of you had a unique relationship, one I didn't entirely approve of. But he's dead. You have a job to do. It isn't here."

"Even if she wanted to leave," Jay said, "she can't. I thought she made that clear."

Dr. Wilheim snorted. "Your hostility doesn't surprise me, Mr. Raven. I warned Anthony he'd have his work cut out for him trying to win the Natives over."

She'd never been sure whether Dr. Wilheim was arrogant or simply insensitive. Didn't he realize his attitude would antagonize Jay?

"Winter," Dr. Wilheim said. "You can't possibly comprehend the complexity of this situation. Neither did Anthony. He was so focused on uncovering obscure and unimportant settlements that he didn't get the bigger picture. I attempted to warn him he was in over his head, believing he could get the Natives to cooperate. I learned that lesson years ago while doing fieldwork with the Cheyenne."

She didn't care what Dr. Wilheim had to say. She wasn't sure she ever would again. Right now, it took all her self-control not to scream that her friend had been murdered. Didn't Dr. Wilheim feel the slightest bit of loss?

How would he react if she told him that Doc had gotten his hands on a priceless artifact—and it was in her car trunk?

"I'm sorry we haven't been properly introduced." Dr. Wilheim extended his hand toward Jay. "You're Native American? The lighting could be better."

Jay closed his fingers around Dr. Wilheim's. "Hoh."

Dr. Wilheim pulled free. "So you're both Native and a ranger. Is there a conflict of interest? I want to learn everything I can about those in a position of influence here. I'll admit, my time with the Cheyenne would have been more fruitful if I'd known that then."

Dr. Wilheim had spent not quite three months with the

Cheyenne. Afterward, he'd written articles for academic journals. She'd been struck by how superficial the pieces were. Doc had told her that, in part, was why Dr. Wilheim's grant proposal had been rejected.

"So." Dr. Wilheim drew out the word. "It appears there isn't anyone I can talk to tonight."

What about me? Don't you want to know what happened to Doc?

"Law enforcement is here," Jay said.

"Of course, and I do need to be informed of the status of the investigation. However, I doubt they'll be in a position to tell me anything of importance for a while." He stretched. "Winter, where are you staying?"

"Here."

"Hmm. Tomorrow we *will* talk about your return to the university."

University. The word and world it represented had become foreign to her. In contrast, the forest represented something she needed.

Chapter Fifteen

"How can you stand to work for him?"

Winter watched Dr. Wilheim's departing car until she could no longer see it. "I don't have a choice. The administration assigned me to him."

"Now there's my idea of the perfect suspect," Jay said. "Lock him up and throw away the keys so we don't have to put up with him."

"Are you serious?"

"About thinking he could have killed Dr. Gilsdorf? I can't answer that." He placed his arm on her shoulder. "Does he care about anything except himself?"

She'd put on a jacket after re-buttoning her shirt, but that wasn't what was keeping her warm. Just having Jay with her served as a physical and emotional barrier between herself and the man responsible for her salary. Jay was her connection to Olympic forest, the one person capable of understanding her complex relationship with the world she found herself in.

"I'm not sure he does." Their shoulders touched. When he placed his arm around her, she struggled to focus on anything except him.

"About what he said," Jay said after a silence that had her wondering if he too was reacting to the contact. "Your continued employment depends on you going back as soon as possible?"

"Yes."

"Don't you care?"

"I do and yet... I worked so hard to get that degree, and I definitely like the salary, but... Right now, I feel disconnected from that life. Probably come morning…"

"After you've rested."

"Of course," she said, even though she wasn't sure that was true. For the first time in her life, she had financial and housing security, only, right now, it didn't matter.

The moon was almost directly overhead and surrounded by a riot of stars. Much as she loved a desert night, this moment was precious. Maybe because of the man she shared it with.

Wolf, are you here? I need you and what you represent. "I can't leave. If I do, it's as if I've abandoned Doc and everything he stands for."

"Just Doc?"

"No, not just him. To have Wolf…"

"Have Wolf what?"

"Anchor me," she whispered as she slid her arm around Jay's waist. Regardless of the danger, she needed the closeness.

"In what way?"

Too late, she realized how much she'd said. "I don't know who I am. Not beyond the superficial, anyway."

"You mentioned that, but I don't understand."

"I don't expect you to. I barely do myself. Please don't ask me to say any more than I have. It's—complicated."

"All right." He hugged her. "Winter?"

"What?"

"I don't want to say this, but Christian does need to talk to you."

"Yes, he does." Her life had been turned around. Maybe that was why she was having so much trouble concentrating—and maybe Jay's presence had more to do with it than she was ready to acknowledge. "I've been putting something off. Maybe I should do it before I see Christian."

"Telling Dr. Gilsdorf's son about the theft?"

"Yes."

* * * *

Christian was standing outside by himself when she and Jay reached Doc's cabin. Her conversation with Pearson had been short because she hadn't wanted to delay seeing Christian. Someone had turned on the outside light, and Winter saw that Christian was on his cell phone. He ended with a simple, "Yes, of course."

"Thanks for agreeing to see me," Christian said as they shook hands. "You've been through a lot, but I'd like us to talk while your memory is fresh."

She explained that she'd written down everything she could think of and would turn that file over to him. "Maybe your questions will take my mind in new directions, but before we get started, Doc's son wants to talk to you."

He nodded then rubbed the back of his neck. "And I need to talk to him."

Aware that Jay hadn't left her side, she punched Send. When Pearson answered, she explained why she was getting back to him so soon and handed the agent her phone.

After expressing sympathy, Christian listened for several seconds, nodding as he did. "Of course," he said. "I realize how difficult this is for you."

No, you can't, she wanted to scream. Instead, she looked up at Jay. The lightbulb had given his face a yellow cast, but he was still the most arresting man she'd ever seen. She'd have to find a way to tell him about having possession of the mask without it destroying their relationship.

Christian handed the phone back to her. "I assume you know what he asked."

She nodded.

"He'd like you to send him everything of a personal nature when I'm ready to release the items. He apologized for not talking to you again, but his daughter was crying."

"She's only ten. She loved her grandpa. Do you know when the release might happen? There's a lot I need to do tomorrow."

Jay stared at her.

"There are some things you can take now." Christian yawned. "Not everything, I'm afraid, but I want to be as sensitive as possible."

"I'll help you carry the items to your car," Jay offered.

The car with the wolf mask in the trunk. "I appreciate the offer, but until I know what I'm dealing with — "

"Why don't we go inside," Christian suggested. "Unless it's too unsettling for you."

"I'm all right." She wasn't.

Jay remained close as she followed Christian into Doc's cabin. Later, maybe, she'd tell Jay how grateful she was for his distracting presence. However, if she did that might expose too much about her emotions where he was concerned. The way Christian looked at them made her wonder if the agent had picked up on the energy.

After looking around, she decided nothing had been moved since Jay and she had been in here. She couldn't bring herself to look at the bed where Doc had lain and hated the idea of picking up his toothbrush or comb.

"You look as if you've been kicked in the gut, again," Jay said. "Why don't you point? Christian can tell us whether the item needs to stay or can go."

"Thanks for the suggestion. I might take you up on it."

Jay smiled and, suddenly, things were easier. "Doc hated buying clothes. I doubt if he bought anything new for himself since his wife died. Pearson sent him some things, and I bought a pair of slacks and a shirt so he'd look presentable for a conference. I'm sure he didn't bring that outfit here."

Realizing she was stalling, she walked over to the open closet and pointed at a shirt. Christian nodded.

"Here." Jay held out his hands. "Load me up."

Collecting Doc's clothes didn't take long. While she dealt with Doc's scent on his limited wilderness wardrobe, Jay carried the items outside and came back in empty-handed.

"They're on a log. What else?"

Her gaze had already settled on the brown slippers she'd given Doc at Christmas. Blinking back tears, she picked them up. As she did, something slid from the toe of the right one and landed against the inner part of the heel. Hoping she wasn't giving away what she was doing, she reached into the slipper. She didn't want to take a chance on looking at the object, but was pretty sure she was touching a memory stick.

She palmed it and slipped it into her pocket.

This was *hers*. Only she had a right to it.

* * * *

"I'm sorry you have to do this now," Christian said as the two of them sat in the Potlatch office.

Jay had made coffee, then he had left so the investigator and she could have privacy. She'd sidestepped Jay's offer to put everything in her trunk by asking him to place Doc's belongings in her cabin. She didn't know where Jay was.

"It's all right," she said belatedly. She sipped the coffee. "I'm going to regret having caffeine this late. How much more do you have to do tonight?"

"Just talk to Jay and make sure the cabin's secure." Christian withdrew his notepad from his pocket. "I've never been in charge of a murder investigation. Depending on what I learn from the autopsy, I might call the FBI. The amount of violence—" He leaned toward her. "I'm sorry you have to hear this, but my training tells me that this was what they call a crime of passion. Someone's idea of revenge."

She struggled to keep her head up. "I hate hearing that."

"I'd like to begin by having you tell me everything you can about what brought Dr. Gilsdorf to Olympic. That might give me an idea who'd have it in for him."

Her mind felt fuzzy and her body sleep-deprived as she told him about Doc's premise that ancient Northwest

Natives had established inland communities instead of spending their entire existence along the shoreline. Doc had examined well-known histories from Natives and white trappers and had conducted a detailed study of the earliest maps. Olympic Forest was nearly perfect for on-site work, because it was under federal protection and little had changed there in thousands of years.

"Can you come up with a reason why anyone would object to his project? It seems innocuous to me, but then I'm not an anthropology expert."

With his comment, her exhaustion fled. She sat up straight and leaned forward. He wouldn't call Doc's work innocuous if he'd seen the mask.

What if someone other than her was aware of what Doc had done?

Doc hadn't stumbled upon the mask while hiking. He had to have known where to look or — was it possible someone had given it to him? She couldn't understand how anyone could have hated Doc enough to do what she'd seen. What was it she heard on TV programs and in the news, that the obvious suspects were those closest to the victim?

Northwest Native Americans had been opposed to having him here. It made no sense for one of them to give Doc the mask, but what — what if whoever that person was had changed his mind and tried to get it back?

And now, because she had the mask, was she in danger?

A cold sweat broke out all over her. She couldn't speak.

"Winter, if you suspect someone, I'd like to hear who and why."

Feeling out of her league, she told Christian about Dr. Wilheim's resentment and jealousy. She'd never seen him angry, but he was often impatient. Christian jotted down a few things but didn't ask questions.

Bringing up what she perceived as Michael's irritation with Doc's refusal to cooperate with him felt like a stretch. "He just seems so uptight," she said. "Maybe it wouldn't take much to set him off."

Christian looked up from his notebook. "You've been considering this."

She took a deep breath. "Of course. Doc wasn't just killed. He was—it was overkill."

The investigator studied her. "It looks that way. Can you come up with anyone else Dr. Gilsdorf might have pissed off?"

'Pissed off' was hardly strong enough, considering what Doc's last minutes of life had been like.

"I'm mentioning Booth because I can't help but wonder if he's responsible for the theft. He went to a great deal of effort to prepare the oral histories. Maybe—I don't—maybe he thought Doc had taken advantage of his work."

"Hmm. Anyone else?"

"He wasn't happy with the reception he received from the local Natives."

"Wouldn't they just leave him alone?"

Instead of kill him? Probably, unless Doc and one or more Natives had started to trust each other only to have that fragile connection shatter.

"You're right," she said. "I shouldn't have said anything."

Christian looked at his watch. "Don't apologize. I need to consider all possibilities. Before I talk to Jay, I'll walk you back to your cabin."

"I don't like hearing you say that."

Christian put down his notepad. "Whoever killed Dr. Gilsdorf might not be done. You were closer to him than anyone else here."

Her body sagged. "I've thought about that."

"You need to. When will you be leaving?"

I can't. "I need to make some calls tomorrow. Hopefully, I'll have a better idea then."

"Keep me informed. No agenda is worth your life."

She clenched her teeth in an attempt not to shiver. "No," she managed. "It isn't." *But I can't walk away.*

* * * *

148

"Damn it, Floyd said he'd be there," Jay said in response to what his uncle had just told him. He stared at the outline of his cabin but didn't really see it. He lifted his cell off his ear. "I should have guessed he'd keep drinking."

"It isn't that late," Uncle Talio said. "He might still show up."

"Maybe." Jay didn't believe that and suspected his uncle didn't, either. "How do we get through to him that he's throwing his life away?"

"We can't. It hurts every time I remember how proud he was when he was old enough to participate in the chalAt'I'lo t'sikAti ceremony."

"I remember how excited he was. I'd taken part in it the year before and didn't think he understood that the ceremony was to honor our land and not just a reason for dancing and eating. But about that time he started really paying attention to the stories you'd been telling us."

Uncle Talio chuckled. "Three days of being immersed in his culture made an impact with him, same as it had with you. He was so little his first year of watching the ceremonies, I gave him a beaver hat to wear because the masks were too heavy and he couldn't see out."

Neither of them spoke, and Jay suspected his uncle was remembering when he'd played a major role in the rituals that were part of chalAt'I'lo t'sikAti. Hoping to keep Uncle Talio from focusing on what he'd lost, Jay brought him up to date on the investigation into Dr. Gilsdorf's murder.

Uncle Talio didn't ask many questions, but he was used to that. To the older man's way of thinking, a person learned from their own experiences and not lectures. Much as he appreciated being raised that way, he couldn't help wondering if he and Floyd would have turned out how Uncle Talio had hoped if they'd been given more direction.

But that wasn't entirely true. The man who'd raised them had gifted both boys with a rich legacy.

"I don't know what's going to happen regarding the work Dr. Gilsdorf was involved in," Jay said. "The other professor — Dr. Wilheim — you met with him, didn't you?"

"Unfortunately."

Despite his worn-down brain, Jay smiled. His uncle was a good judge of character. If someone wanted his opinion of another person, he gave it.

"What were your conversations about?"

"I wouldn't call it an exchange. Dr. Wilheim was even more adamant than Dr. Gilsdorf that we Hoh *had* to cooperate with higher education. According to him, we owed civilization something. Fortunately, he wasn't here that much."

"Just enough to rub our people the wrong way. Now he's determined to make it clear to Winter that she has to get out of his way."

"How do you feel about that?"

Wasn't the logical question whether Winter agreed with Dr. Wilheim or intended to oppose him? That would matter to most people, but his uncle wanted something deeper.

"I'm not sure. I just got through talking to the lead investigator. He has concerns for her safety, and I tend to agree." He glanced out of his cabin window. Christian hadn't come out and said he believed Winter was in danger. He'd said it was a possibility, which was why he'd asked Kasey Rasmussen to spend the night at the Potlatch office and periodically walk around the settlement. "But this is more than an academic agenda for her."

"Yes."

Yes, as in continue. "You were right. It's personal for her."

"And now for you."

As Jay hung up, he once more acknowledged how well his uncle knew him. What was it? Maybe his tone when mentioning Winter's name had sent out vibes that sprang from when they'd torn at each other's clothes. He needed to keep his distance from her — act like a forest ranger and not some sex-hungry male.

Not see her anymore?

He couldn't do that.

Chapter Sixteen

Winter pulled the memory stick out of her pocket and sat at the table where she'd placed her laptop when she'd moved into the cabin. She trembled, not from exhaustion any longer but in anticipation. Doc had meant for her to find the storage device. He'd placed it somewhere that had no meaning for anyone else. While she waited for her laptop to boot up, she took off her shoes and stretched her spine.

She'd done what she could to lock the door—not that it would keep anyone out if they were determined enough. Even with the security Christian was providing, the logical thing would have been for her to get in her car and head for the nearest town. She'd check into a secure-looking motel and engage the deadbolts. Come morning, she'd contact Christian and ask him what else she should do to ensure her safety.

But Christian might remind her that she was no longer needed here. Ask her why she wasn't returning to San Diego.

She couldn't, because Wolf might not be anywhere except here.

Eyes partly closed, she cupped her hand over the symbol of what had anchored her childhood. Without the wolf of her dreams, she wouldn't have had anything to hold onto. Wolf had disappeared when she became a teenager but fortunately had returned. The mask that had been Wolf's conduit was her responsibility. She had to find a safe place for it until she decided what to do with it—and until she could give it up.

She tried to picture herself handing it over to Jay, only

to surrender to thoughts that had nothing to do with an ancient artifact. Being around Jay was like standing over a flaming campfire. She'd get burned if she got too close, but the flashing reds mesmerized her. He made her hot, turned her reckless, challenged her to see what would happen if she stripped off her clothes before him.

Like you don't know.

When the cursor started blinking, she fought her way back to the present. She pushed the memory device in and accessed the drive. A long list of files popped onto the screen. The one with her name caught her eye, and she opened it.

This isn't the time for pleasantries, she read. *As I see it, you'll only be looking at this if I'm dead.*

Her hand went to her throat. She glanced around, reluctantly lingering on the dark window beyond the small table. Still battling fear, she forced herself to start reading again.

My guess is you're in shock. I would be, too, except I'm dead. For the record, I deleted all files from my laptop. Maybe you already know that. However, it's possible that whoever did me in — sorry for the euphemism — got his hands on my computer. I've been using it in part because I want whoever is watching me to believe he knows where he'll find everything.

How long had he been in fear for his life, and why? Determined to learn more, she went back to reading.

The joke's on that bastard. You believe I'm a benign and boring university professor, but being here is bringing out a side of my nature I wasn't aware of. Survival instinct, for lack of a better term.

"You didn't survive," she muttered.

I wish I could see you right now. Please, damn it, don't let what I'm writing be for nothing. Who found my body?

"I did. Damn it, I did."

Sorry, I'm rambling, but it never occurred to me that my life would be in danger. Someone doesn't approve of what I'm doing. Unfortunately, I'm not certain who, even though I have suspicions. Winter, I'm not perfect, as you're about to discover, but you're one of the best things that happened to me. I wasn't the perfect husband or father, but I believe I had the capacity to be a first rate grandfather.

The words blurred. She wasn't sure she'd show this to Pearson.

I hope I made a positive impact in your life.

"You did."

You're so self-contained. I've told you that enough times, but now I have a larger point to make. I have no doubt your first reaction to my death will be to work to take over the project. You'll believe you owe it to me, but you don't. I helped guide you toward you a way to support yourself, but you taught me a great deal about what it means to pick oneself up by her bootstraps. Independence. We're even.

Much as what he'd written enriched her, she suspected he was putting off telling her something. Maybe she shouldn't continue until she'd emailed the file to Pearson. They'd read it at the same time. Make a joint decision.

No, not Doc's son. Instead, she'd go to the person who'd made the most impact on her since she'd come here.

She'd stood up before what she'd just done sunk in. Much as she needed Jay around, she didn't dare let him see this tonight. Maybe she never would.

It's time to tell you about the mask.

She'd been leaning against the chair while reading but couldn't continue until she was again sitting. She felt hot and cold, scared and excited.

I was committed to finding proof of Natives' presence inland. I'm convinced Natives kept a number of their sacred objects somewhere safe from the elements. I consider that statement the ultimate carrot I dangled before the grant committee. I wasn't sure they'd buy my argument that Northwest Natives had gone to extraordinary lengths to protect their valuables. I may have overstated my conviction. Hell, between you and me, I deliberately did.

Her mouth sagged as she reread the last few sentences.

Doc had never said anything about attempting to con the grant committee.

Are you shocked? Maybe you no longer respect me. Of course, the ultimate success would be if I uncovered a treasure trove the likes of which the world has never seen, but the sad truth is, I fabricated some of the so-called hypothesis. No one, not even Dr. Wilheim, tried to verify my statements. To put it crudely, my BS worked.

Her head pounded.

Call me self-absorbed. Call me crazy for wanting to be remembered for something other than teaching classes and writing articles. When I was putting the grant request together, I did so much fantasizing about what I hoped to accomplish that I now wonder if I lost the line between hypothesis and reality. A part of me realized my mindset had become skewed, but the rest — that glorious and childish rest believed that ancient Native treasures were out there waiting for me to uncover.

"I wish you'd told me."

Here's the rub, Winter. I was right. Stop and digest that, let it sink in. Ancient Northwest Native Americans indeed had a location where they safeguarded what was sacred to them.

"How did you discover..." She felt drunk. "Did you just stumble...?"

This is the really difficult part, the great confession. I'm tempted to go to my grave not telling anyone, especially you. But if I do, what I started will end with my death. All you'll have is the ceremonial wolf mask. I want you to go forward with this. Hell, I need you to. At the same time, am I asking you to risk your life? At night, when I'm in the cabin, I sometimes sense a presence. Sometimes, when I'm in the field, the feeling of eyes on my back comes over me. There have been sounds —

"Wolf? Oh Doc, has Wolf..."

Being stalked is unnerving. That in part is why I decided to write this.

"Why didn't you tell me or law enforcement?"

I'd like to insist I bear no responsibility for my death, but that's not true. Winter, I did something no one in my position ever should. Searching the forest for signs of an ancient Northwest Native American settlement armed with old maps and a few writings of the area's early explorers was a fool's mission.

How that must have hurt.

I asked the local tribes to work with me, but they refused to. The Hoh denial was particularly disappointing, because I saw Hoh River as my jumping off place.

Michael Simpson – have you met him? – is a man with his head in a financial noose. He'd love for me to put the forest on the map. Keeping him off your back isn't going to be easy. Simpson isn't the only person here I'm having issues with. As the park historian, Booth Deavers wears a number of hats. Where Simpson is desperate, Deavers is ruled by ambition that's almost laughable, considering how few people care about what he does. I am impressed by his efforts to get Native oral histories into a permanent form and have borrowed them. I didn't give him the due he believes he deserves, and our relationship has eroded.

Wilheim has become a real irritant. He's concerned as I am that our department will experience cutbacks. Maybe the bean counters will decide that anthropology doesn't need two senior professors. He believes he'll be safe if I fail here and he rides in to save the project. What concerns me is if you and he lock horns over who takes over. He's the one with clout.

"But Dr. Wilheim isn't aware of Wolf." She pulled back her top so she could see the tattoo.

Here comes the hardest part. The thing I wish I didn't have to tell you. I bribed someone. Waved money and, more importantly, liquor in front of him. He works part-time at a sporting goods store in Forks, so meeting and talking to him about what kind of hiking gear I'd need looked innocent. In truth, I'd been looking for a Native with weaknesses I might be able to use to my advantage. His brother unwittingly led me to him.

She'd already been sick to her stomach, but this made it much worse.

I asked the brother, a totally physically competent man if there ever was one, how the local Natives earned a living. Only a handful work for the Forest Service like he does, and I –

Moaning, she began rocking.

I'm sure he thought I was a fool, because many Natives are involved with local fishing. He probably explained as much as he did so I'd leave him alone.

"I don't want to do this. Damn it, Doc, do you have any idea how wrenching this is?"

Long story short. The ranger was worried about his brother's drinking, but at least he had a job. He said enough about that job that I was able to narrow my search. Winter, I found a Hoh who was willing to talk to me in exchange for alcohol.

"I hate this! Damn it, Doc, I hate you!"

Her ears were still ringing from her outburst when she thought she heard a howl. Galvanized by the sound, she hurried to the door and started to open it only to slam it shut. She listened intently for several minutes, then, awash with emotion, returned to the laptop and forced herself to continue.

I befriended the young Hoh. He wants to do right by his heritage, but the devil has a powerful hold on him. When he's drunk, he talks. Floyd's parents are dead. He and his brother were raised by their uncle, who is a tribal elder. His addiction embarrasses him. He has disappointed his relatives. He feels isolated from other Hoh. I was there when he needed to talk, someone who listened without judging.

"Do you mean it or were you exploiting him?"

I'm tempted to give you the details of what we talked about, but that's because I'm still attempting to justify my actions. To cut to the chase, after several weeks, I took him out for drinks and dinner. It wasn't the first time I'd supplied him with what loosens his tongue. I didn't want to pull information out of him he wasn't ready to give, because he might see through it. We had a wonderful meal, steaks. And drinks. More drinks on his part than mine. I told him I was getting discouraged. He wasn't the only one who felt as if he'd failed.

Doc had always been able to use words. As a result, she had no trouble imagining how he'd pulled Floyd into his lies.

I confided in him when no one had done that with him for a long time. My guess is one of the last things he remembered before he got too drunk that night was his new and much older friend admitting he felt like a failure because there weren't any Native artifacts for that drinking buddy to bring into the light of today.

A blank page briefly made her fear Doc hadn't written anything else. Maybe he'd unconsciously left his finger on the enter key.

Two days later, Floyd brought the wolf mask to me. He didn't say anything, just walked into my cabin and handed it to me. I watched him leave. I couldn't speak. The mask was – I don't have to tell you what it meant to me.

"No, you don't."

I attempted to call him, but he didn't answer. As soon as I could get away – Michael wanted to hook me up with Seattle media – I went to see him. Floyd wanted nothing to do with me. He said he'd done something he couldn't forgive himself for. I tried to convince him that the world deserved to see what his ancestors had created, but he ordered me to leave. I couldn't tell whether he'd been drinking. Finally, I begged him to at least tell me whether the mask represented what I hoped it did, which was part of a greater whole. He nodded. That's all he did, just nod.

A whispery sound touched her nerve ends. Wolf. No doubt. Was the spirit aware of what she was reading? Once, she would have laughed at the thought. Now, she closed her eyes so she could concentrate on the quiet howl.

"What am I supposed to do, to think?" she whispered. "To believe?"

The howl rose and fell. She followed it in her mind until she half-believed she was drifting through the night with it. Much as she wanted to step outside and join the predator, she remained behind the closed door. Wolf was her past and present, maybe her future, but tonight belonged to Doc and what he'd left for her to read.

Whimpering, she opened her eyes and waited for the words on the monitor to become clear.

I saw Floyd the day I mailed the mask to you. I wanted to let him realize I'd help him make a decision he could live with so we could work together. He was drunk. Wasted. Winter, that, in part, is why I wanted you up here. You're Native. If anyone can gain Floyd's trust, it's you.

"You were willing to exploit me? Use me?"

So here we are. Floyd is too young for his life to be over. If he gets help, if we can bring his brother on board — what am I saying? My dream remains the same. I don't want my career and life to end without giving the world some reason to remember me.

Faced with another blank screen, she scrolled down, but Doc hadn't written anything else.

After closing the file, she staggered to her feet and walked over to the window closest to the door. The moon wasn't doing enough to lessen the night forest's impact. Everything Doc had written tumbled inside her.

Doc had warned her of danger, but he'd told her to come anyway.

He'd exploited Jay's brother's weakness. As a consequence, he could prove the theory that had been his driving force for years. More than just prove a theory.

Now, the risk and potential rewards were in her hands.

She pulled out her cell phone and started to dial Doc's son to tell him about the memory stick, only to put the phone away. Jay would hate Doc for what he'd done. Maybe he'd blame Floyd.

She couldn't turn the mask over to him or Talio without implicating Doc and Floyd. Better to protect them.

Until what or when?

"Too many questions," she moaned. "Not enough answers."

After unsuccessfully listening for Wolf for a few minutes, she debated going to bed, but she wouldn't be able to sleep. It was better to do something. A perusal of several files revealed no useful information, but then she came across one containing material from Native oral histories that had been recorded more than a hundred years ago. Booth had fleshed out some of the transcripts based on, he said, what explorers had observed. Doc's accompanying notes made it clear he viewed Booth's work with skepticism. She found nothing she didn't already know about Pacific Northwest Natives lifestyles, but their legends and beliefs served as a refresher course.

Passages about Raven reminded her that a person's spirit was more than a guide. Like many other Native American tribes, those of the Northwest saw Raven as the Trickster. No other supernatural being was as skilled when it came to outwitting whoever Raven wanted to outwit. According to the Tlingits of Alaska, Raven's uncle Nascakiyel had created the world, but it took Raven sneaking into his uncle's house and stealing the sun from the box where Nascakiyel kept it to light the world.

How did Jay feel about such ancient legends? Maybe he wanted Raven as his spirit.

The screen blurred, and she rubbed her eyes. Then the word 'Thunderbird' jumped out at her. Many tribes had believed in a version of Thunderbird. If she wasn't so tired, she'd probably be able to recall the Northwest Native American version. Tonight, however, she was glad Booth had recorded what he had.

Thunderbird had lived on top of the highest mountain peak and had a lake on its back. Thunderbird kept lightning as its pet. All Thunderbird had to do to cause a storm was to flap its wings.

Yakanon.

Shivering, she squeezed her eyes shut and then opened them. That was the word Jay's uncle had used the first time he'd seen her. There wasn't much about Yakanon in either Booth's or Doc's notes, just that the being or spirit or whatever it was had been able to speak with Thunderbird.

"Not enough. Damn it, not enough," she muttered after running a document search.

Leaning back, she laced her fingers together under her breasts and looked around. The room had no answers, prompting her to once more close her eyes. She started to

159

drift.

A sound. Faint. Beyond the walls.

Determined to capture what she could, she let darkness continue to surround her. The quiet, soft vibration seemed to be coming from all directions. Thinking it might get louder, she steeled herself, but the chant—yes, a chant— remained as much imagination as reality. She couldn't call it a song or even a rhythm. Rather, it was as if a number of people were whispering in several languages.

Were the Natives out there? Conducting some kind of nighttime ceremony? Maybe asking the spirits to—to what?

Stop it! There weren't such things as Ravens that stole the sun or Thunderbirds capable of creating storms.

And yet there was Wolf.

How could she explain Wolf?

Chapter Seventeen

Thunderbird was in a benevolent mood this morning, Jay concluded as he stepped into the forest behind his cabin. According to the Old Peoples, Thunderbird's eyes gave off lightning, and his wings were responsible for creating thunder. The spirit might change his mind before noon and fill the sky with clouds, but, right now, only bright blue showed above the treetops.

To say he'd slept would be an exaggeration. He'd dozed off a few times but had been unable to turn off his mind, which had bounced between images of what he and Winter had seen at Ghost Totem and questions his sleep-deprived brain couldn't process. He'd be late for work, but there was no way he could concentrate on what he needed to do until he'd gone for a solitary walk.

More than a walk, he unnecessarily reminded himself. He waited until he reached an elk trail before facing what he needed to. Uncle Talio and other tribal members, mostly the senior ones, accepted their spirits without question. As a child, he'd assumed that in time he'd find his own spirit, which would guide him through life, but that belief hadn't survived his teen years. All the time he'd been away from there, he'd managed to shove the question of what he did or didn't believe into the back of his mind.

Shortly after his return, he'd started taking a mature look at the fiber of Hoh principles. He'd done so in an analytical way while keeping what he thought was an open mind. He might have given the subject more attention if he hadn't been so busy with work, helping his uncle get back on his feet, and doing everything he could to keep his brother from self-destructing.

Then Winter had driven into his world.

Winter, who said she'd seen and heard Wolf and had had a wolf's head image imprinted onto her flesh.

He stopped and looked up. "Raven? Are you waiting for me to ask you for help? Maybe you want me down on my knees begging for you to — to accept me."

The wildlife was out in force this morning, but for too long he tried to convince himself that that wasn't what he was hearing. He needed to believe his spirit was reaching out to him. Then a chickaree clinging to a limb high over his head started chattering, and he had no choice but to stop deluding himself. When he whistled at the rodent, it responded by shaking its bushy tail and climbing higher.

When he could no longer see the chickaree, he started walking again, but so many bracken ferns were on the elk trail that he turned around so he wouldn't destroy the fragile fronds.

And because he needed to see Winter.

Five minutes later, he approached her cabin and knocked. When she didn't respond, he tried turning the knob. It was locked, but a shoulder to the door would probably pop it. He nearly called her cell number, but wouldn't she have contacted him if she'd wanted to get in touch?

Maybe she couldn't? Maybe something bad had happened to her? The question knotted his belly, and he looked in the windows. She'd straightened her sleeping bag and the open bathroom door told him she wasn't in there. He didn't see a reason for her to return to Ghost Totem. What made the most sense was that she'd decided to go somewhere that called for getting in her car.

He leaned against the cabin wall and stared at his cell phone, willing it to ring. Equal amounts of irritation and concern overtook him. Still, he talked himself out of attempting to get in touch with her. The better part of a minute later, he punched Floyd's number. The cell rang four times then went to voicemail.

"Where were you last night? Did you forget about our uncle? Look, I'm not going to say more, because I'll regret it. I want you to get in touch with me. Now."

Still holding the phone, he stared at his world. Floyd was too easily swayed. Combine that with too many beers, and he might believe what a number of Hoh had said about Dr. Gilsdorf having no right to be in Olympic.

Had his drunken kid brother picked up a fish-flaying knife and —

No!

When the possibility returned to haunt him, he highlighted his uncle's number and hit send. Uncle Talio answered after the third ring.

"I might be out of range today," he said in response to the older man's hello. "I wanted to get in touch with you before that happens. Have you heard from my brother?"

"No, I haven't. Jay, I don't mean to cut this short, but several tribal elders are on their way."

He stared at the ants around his boots. "A meeting?"

"An informal one. There's considerable concern about what's going to happen now that Dr. Gilsdorf is dead. Dr. Wilheim wanted to talk to me last night again, but I put him off. I'm sorry I gave him this number."

Damn. "Do you have any idea what he wants?"

"Cooperation, which he isn't going to get. I don't like his ways."

Uncle Talio didn't make judgments about people, so hearing him say that pulled Jay's attention off the ants.

"He and Winter want the same thing," he said.

"No." Uncle Talio spoke slowly. "They don't."

* * * *

Winter was pulling out of the office parking lot when Jay reached it. She slowed but didn't stop, and he wondered if she was debating punching the gas. Then the wheels stopped turning, and she rolled down the window. Despite

163

his inner battle with what she represented, he wanted to cup his hand around her jaw so he could steady her head while he touched his mouth to hers.

"Where are you going?" he asked.

She squeezed her hand around the steering wheel. "Probably to Forks. If I'm going to be here for a while, I need to get some groceries."

"Are you coming back after that?"

She blinked and looked out of the front windshield. "Yes."

To hell with giving her the space she obviously wanted, he thought as he rested his hand on her shoulder. "The way you said that, it sounds as if you don't want to."

"I do. Believe me, I do."

Intrigued by the passion behind her words, he rubbed her shoulder. She continued to avoid his gaze. "But not under these circumstances."

"No, not under these circumstances. Jay?"

His name coming from her increased his awareness of the fundamental difference between them. She was a woman, he a man. Right now, everything else came after that.

"What?" he finally thought to ask.

Sighing, she faced him. "You and I aren't law enforcement. It isn't our job to figure out who murdered Doc."

"But you can't help wondering."

"Of course. Doc didn't have enemies. Even Dr. Wilheim— their conflicts were professional, not personal." Tears filled her eyes, and she all but slapped them away. "Who killed him?"

Just like that, her pain became his, compelling him to run his knuckles over the side of her neck. She leaned into the touch. "I can't answer that. I'm not sure when I'll get off work, but, when I do, I'll come to your cabin. You'll be there, won't you?"

"I believe so."

Alone. Maybe vulnerable. No, damn it, he wasn't going to make things any worse for her by bringing up that hopefully remote possibility. Just the same, he needed to call Christian and ask whether an officer would remain around Potlatch.

"In any number of ways," he said, "this is my land. What we saw at Ghost Totem shouldn't happen to anyone. What if you and I work on a list of suspects, come up with reasons for why each of them could or couldn't have murdered your friend."

She shuddered. "You think it'll do any good?"

"It's better than doing nothing."

"I *am* doing something." She stopped looking at him. "Making decisions."

"What decisions?"

When she didn't answer, he was forced to acknowledge that her lack of openness hurt. "Maybe it'd help if you had someone to run your options past."

"I'm not sure."

"We're far from strangers. We've already shared a great deal."

"Yes, we have."

"You might want to pick up something to drink," he said. *I might need the same thing if my brother winds up on that list.*

* * * *

Jay. Jay of the firm knuckles, dark eyes and deep voice. Jay, who'd only seen her for a few minutes this morning but had touched her and left his imprint on her.

It was all his fault, she told herself as she exited the long, narrow storage unit she'd placed the package with the wolf mask in. Thanks to him, she felt as if she was abandoning the mask she didn't dare keep with her.

She slipped the newly bought lock through the door slider and locked it. There. Now she didn't have to worry about Jay finding it and her having to explain.

She'd think about the mask's impact on their relationship later.

Weary of her thoughts, she left the small storage facility

and headed back toward the town of Forks. Except for the mountains in the distance and the smell of sea air, downtown Forks reminded Winter of countless small towns. There was a chain grocery store, but she opted for a mom-and-pop off the main street. Relieved to be doing something normal, she stocked up on meats and cheeses from the deli and talked to the young woman running the only cash register. The cashier had heard about Doc's murder, but that wasn't about to stop her from spending the weekend camping in the park with her boyfriend.

"We're taking Ryan's mutt with us," she explained. "Pee-Wee weighs over a hundred pounds and sleeps right outside our tent. Besides, those who say they won't go anywhere near Olympic until the killer's caught are letting their imaginations get away with them. That anthropologist was targeted specifically. Whoever did it couldn't care less about the rest of us."

Winter envied the clerk's self-confidence. At least she no longer felt as unsettled as she had before she'd come to Forks. A few hours of sleep had helped, as had getting away from the forest. But she was already missing Olympic. Before she returned, however, she had several calls to make.

She'd placed her groceries in her trunk and was debating starting the car and heading west so she could enjoy the Pacific Ocean when her cell phone rang. She looked at the display. No, Jay hadn't called.

The moment she heard his voice, she recognized Christian. "I want to get in touch with Dr. Wilheim," the law enforcement officer said. "He's here and staying in one of the towns. Would you happen to have a number for him?"

She told Christian she did, in her phone's address book. "You don't think he had anything to do with Doc's murder, do you?" Do I?

"What made you ask?"

"He and Doc were rivals."

"I'm aware of that. Is that your only reason for bringing

up the possibility?"

"I briefly saw him last night. He's determined to take over control of the project."

"Determined enough to kill his rival?"

"That's a stretch."

"Someone did."

And Dr. Wilheim, maybe, had a motive.

An older pickup pulled in next to her and a heavy-set Native American got out. They nodded at each other, then the man headed for the grocery. Floyd! She should tell Christian about Floyd.

Before talking to Jay?

"Let me ask you something," Christian said. "How do you and Dr. Wilheim get along?"

"Until this happened, I was barely on his radar. Now, he wants me out of his way. Back in Southern California."

"Are you going to leave?"

Not if my being here leads me to the mask's origin. "I'm not sure."

"I strongly suggest you think about it."

"I have a lot of decisions to make."

"Just don't forget what I said last night about your safety."

"I won't."

"Keep me informed of where you are. I'm not sure I can justify requesting manpower to keep an eye on you, since you don't have to remain in Potlatch. If anything makes you nervous, call me."

"I will."

They hung up so she could look up Dr. Wilheim's number. After calling Christian back and giving him that information, she leaned against the steering wheel and stared at the pitted parking lot. She didn't want to go to the ocean after all, not with the forest calling to her, waiting for her to return. Christian would never understand why leaving Olympic wasn't an option.

Hoping Wolf would be there waiting for her when she arrived, she straightened and reached into her pocket for the numbers Carolyn had given her yesterday. It was time to present her argument for continuing the work Doc had begun.

To her surprise, the head of the grant committee answered. After introducing herself as Dr. Gilsdorf's colleague to the older-sounding woman, she asked if the committee members had heard that he'd died. She deliberately didn't say he'd been murdered.

"Robert, he's on the committee, called me about an hour ago. We're in shock."

"It's a shock to everyone, me in particular because I'd helped him pull his presentation to you together." She took a deep breath. "I'm in Washington and in possession of his files."

"You are? How did that happen?"

"Like I said, we worked together. He'd taken the precaution of setting up a system to safeguard his work. In honor of his memory, I want to do right by what he entrusted me with."

"It's personal then?"

She filled her lungs. "Yes."

Hoping she was saying the right things, she pointed out that she was in a position to go forward with the study and hoped to do so as soon as possible, starting with getting the grant monies transferred to her. She only mentioned Dr. Wilheim in passing.

"Dr. Gilsdorf was my mentor," she finished. "I want nothing more than to finish what he started."

"Email me the specifics of your intentions. Be sure to detail everything you have."

Even as she agreed to do so, memories of what the wolf mask had looked like sitting in the corner of an otherwise empty storage unit distracted her. Despite what Doc had done, she still loved and owed him, but that debt might jeopardize not just that one mask but everything it represented.

Turn Jay against her.

She'd weathered the horror of Doc's murder in part by focusing on her determination to continue his work, but that was before she'd learned about his methods. Maybe more to the point, she wasn't sure how she could move forward without implicating Floyd.

Floyd, who perhaps had justified killing Dock. Floyd, who perhaps had hoped the Hoh never learned he'd given Doc the wolf mask.

Earlier, she'd pondered how she might find Floyd without letting Jay know. She hated going behind Jay's back, but if she didn't, she'd have to tell him about Doc and Floyd's relationship. Sick at heart over the possibility that her actions would spell the end of their fragile relationship, she drove to the public library, where she was able to get a Wi-Fi connection. A Google search to locate Floyd revealed the name of the only sporting goods store in Forks plus three bars. She first went to the store where the disgruntled manager told her that Floyd hadn't shown up for work today. A twenty-dollar bill earned her Floyd's last-known address, but when she went there, a woman with a baby told her she'd been living in the apartment for a month.

Fighting discouragement and her instinctive need to return to the forest, she drove to the bars. At the first, a fairly new place next to a motel, Floyd's name elicited blank looks. Except for a couple of elderly men hunched over beers, the bartender was the only other person in the second place. He knew Floyd but hadn't seen him for several months and didn't expect to because Floyd owed too much there. He suggested she might have better luck at Seger's.

The rain and humidity hadn't been kind to the cheaply built Seger's Bar. It smelled of beer and sweat, and the interior was so dark she couldn't see into the corners. A big man with a large belly covered by a stained apron sat on one of the stools, watching TV. The look he gave her left her with no doubt that she didn't belong.

"Sure," he said in response to her question. "He's in here more often than he's probably home. Does he owe you money?"

"No. We have a friend in common. The friend told me to look Floyd up when I came to Washington. He said Floyd might be willing to show me where his people fish."

The man she assumed was Seger stared at her. "His people. You aren't from around here?"

Maybe. Instead of answering, she explained about her unsuccessful attempt to find where he lived.

"He's renting some trailer. At least, that's what he told me. There's a trailer park near the north end of town. He might be there." Seger frowned. "Hmm. He wasn't here last night. Judging by how he's been acting lately, I shouldn't be surprised."

"Why not?"

"He said he wants to stop drinking because it gets him into trouble. I told him, if he wants to get sober, he needs to stay away from here. But he said he didn't have anywhere else to go."

"Did he mention what kind of trouble he was in?"

Seger frowned again. "Floyd's an easygoing kind of guy, but, lately, I could tell he had some heavy shit on his mind. I told him to confide in his brother—he's always looked up to him—but Floyd said that was the last thing he could do." Massive shoulders lifted as Seger shrugged. "My guess is Floyd owes his big brother money."

It might be worse than that.

* * * *

Winter had just finished carrying groceries into her cabin when her cell phone rang. Spotting Jay's number, she stared at it then answered.

"Where are you?" he asked.

She sat at the kitchen table before telling him. Hearing his voice heated her body but didn't kill her fear that what little they had could shatter. All too soon, she'd have to tell him why she'd been looking for his brother.

"Michael just contacted me," he said. "He wants to talk to you."

"What about?"

"I asked, but he danced around it. I'd be surprised if it isn't a repeat of what he tried to talk Dr. Gilsdorf into."

Thank goodness for Jay. He'd just reminded her that Floyd wasn't the only person who'd had dealings with Doc during the last days of his life. "Did you give him my number?"

"No. I told him I'd relay the message. If you're willing to sit down with him, I want to be there."

I want you there. After she thanked him for the offer, they agreed that the meeting should take place on neutral territory. Jay suggested the Potlatch office in two hours.

"I know something about him he probably doesn't believe anyone here is aware of," Jay said. "How he reacts could be revealing."

"Are you going to tell me what it is?"

"I'd rather not. That way, he won't feel as if we've set him up."

Jay had her back. She just wished she was worthy of it. "Maybe you should tell Christian."

"Let me see how Michael reacts first."

"All right. I just—do you really think he's capable of—"

"I can't believe any human being is capable of what we saw, but it happened."

She reluctantly hung up then stood and walked over to the door. She stepped outside. Thunderbird must be in a peaceful mood today. The spirit had painted the sky in bold blue, tempered with a handful of clouds, and the endless green seemed even more vibrant than it had this morning. Always before, she'd given Mother Nature credit for the weather, but coming here had opened her to another option. Maybe she should tell Jay that she was moving closer to his people's beliefs.

Just his people?

Chapter Eighteen

Two hours later, Winter watched as first a Forest Service truck then a private sedan pulled into the Potlatch office parking lot. She should study Michael in an attempt to get a handle on his potential for violence, but only seeing Jay again mattered. How long ago had she told herself she needed to keep as much distance as possible from him? What a lie that had been. Watching how easily Jay exited the high cab of the truck made her ache to see him naked. He acknowledged her with a casual nod that hurt until she realized he was probably putting on an act for Michael.

Besides, given her emotional turmoil, she was in no condition to judge what kind of relationship they were or weren't building.

"We don't need you here," Michael said to Jay as the three entered the cool office.

Jay chose the chair behind the desk. "Let me be the judge of that."

Looking less than pleased, Michael planted his hands on the back of one of the two chairs on the other side of the desk. Winter positioned the remaining chair so she could see both men and sat down.

"I asked him to join us," she told Michael, less than truthfully. "I'm having trouble concentrating and am hoping he'll keep me on track." She risked a glance at Jay, but nothing in his expression gave away his thoughts.

Naked? Yes, she'd love that.

"What did you want to see me about?" she asked Michael in an attempt to get her mind back where it belonged.

Michael pulled three yellow sticky notes out of a front

pocket. "Two TV stations and a newspaper are working on pieces about Dr. Gilsdorf's murder. Because I've dealt as extensively as possible with the media, they naturally contacted me. I was expecting this and am committed to doing everything possible to minimize the negative impact to the park."

"You can't downplay a murder," Jay said.

"Of course not. The point we need to make is that this is an isolated incident."

Jay leaned forward. "Is it?"

Chilled, she divided her attention between the men.

"There's no madman running around looking for more — sorry, Ms. Barstow, I didn't mean to cause you any more distress. My problem..." He looked down at the sticky notes he still held. "My problem is that there have been a number of cancellations. People are afraid to come here."

She shook her head. "Not everyone. I talked with a woman from Forks who said her boyfriend and she plan to camp here this weekend. They're bringing along their dog."

Jay frowned. "We have rules about where dogs are allowed within the park. If she lives locally, I'm surprised she doesn't know. Of course, maybe she doesn't care."

Whoever had killed Doc hadn't cared about human life.

Michael repeatedly turned the notes over. "It's possible you won't have to worry about the mutt, because that couple could have a change of mind. I attempted to impress upon the reporters how much they're going to hurt the park if they sensationalize their stories, but that isn't their focus. It's news, they told me. They have a responsibility to warn the public." He stared at Jay and her by turn. "Warn? That's not what those articles and TV segments will be about. Ratings. Well, their damn ratings are going to financially kill Olympic."

You should have thought about that before attacking Doc, if you did.

"The park is larger than a single crime," Jay said.

Michael snorted. "I realize the forest's economic health

doesn't concern you, but it's vital to me."

"As you keep mentioning." Jay rested his spine against the chair back. Despite his relaxed position, she tried to imagine him as her protector and guardian, something she'd had little of in her life.

Michael studied Jay before turning toward her. "I'm a methodical man, not impulsive. Rash decisions backfire and cause untold problems, which is why I spent so much time today coming up with the most logical plan of action. It involves you."

"How?" she asked.

Michael waved the notes at her. "These are the names and numbers for the members of the press. Your Dr. Gilsdorf was so obsessed with the history here that he ignored my suggestions about how to expand his agenda into something that would benefit the park. I'm asking you to consider what Olympic meant to him when you contact these people."

She made no move to reach for the papers. "Why me?"

"You have to ask? Because they'll listen to you. You, a lovely young woman committed to carrying on your colleague and friend's work. For now, all you have to do is tell them you're staying and see no reason why anyone should avoid Olympic. You're convinced the forest is safe."

"I can't tell them that. There hasn't been an arrest."

"And as far as I know," Jay added, "a suspect hasn't been identified."

Michael's fingers dug into the notes. "If, as I believe, Dr. Gilsdorf's murder was a random act, the responsible person is hundreds of miles away from here. They're never going to find him." He shook his head. "It was unfortunate, of course, a real tragedy, but Dr. Gilsdorf wouldn't want the park to suffer for it."

"Have you talked to Dr. Wilheim?" Jay asked Michael. "You must be aware that the question of who, if anyone, is going to take over for Dr. Gilsdorf hasn't been decided."

I want to make that happen, Jay. And if I'm successful, maybe you and I —

"Dr. Wilheim called me this morning," Michael said. "At first, I was surprised, but then I realized he's wasting no time trying to get various park staff members to back his appointment to the project."

Pressure built up in her forehead, and she pictured herself locked in a staredown with her supervisor. Maybe it would turn into a physical fight.

With knives?

"What did you tell him?" Jay asked.

"That I'm in no position to say whether he or Ms. Barstow is more qualified." Michael smoothed the crumpled squares of paper. "He doesn't need to know we're having this conversation."

"What if I tell him?" Jay asked.

"What?" Michael spluttered. "Why would you do that?"

Jay stood and placed his hands on the desk top. "Why not?"

"Dr. Wilheim doesn't grasp how special Olympic is. You do. So does Ms. Barstow."

Watching Michael attempt to keep an eye on Jay and her at the same time would have been funny if she hadn't picked up on the tension between the two men. The tendons stood out on the sides of Michael's neck while his fingers kept closing and opening. Fortunately, the papers were now on the table, because otherwise he'd probably tear them.

"Neither of you understand how desperate the situation is." Michael's stare made the hairs on the back of her head stand up. "You *have* to get the press to listen. Go in front of the camera and give the reporters plenty to quote about your conviction that Olympic is safe. You can become the park's voice. You must."

"Stop it," Jay warned.

"I can't. The park's financial situation—"

"You don't care about that," Jay interrupted. "The only thing that matters to you is holding onto what's left of your career."

Michael shoved the chair he'd been gripping so it banged into the desk. "I've given everything I have to keeping the park's finances in the black. You've seen the results of cutbacks. Surely, you don't want it to get any worse, to have to look for a job yourself."

"I can always find a job," Jay said, "but you're afraid you can't, which is why you're groveling."

"How dare you say —"

"I used to live in Seattle," Jay broke in. "I was there when you came within an inch of being charged with fraud."

Her mouth opened, prompting her to cover it. What had Jay just said?

"That's right." Jay nodded at her. "My former father-in-law was one of nearly two dozen trusting men and women you deceived."

"You can't prove anything," Michael said. "Shut up. Just shut up."

"What?" Jay challenged. "You can't take the truth?"

Much as she needed to concentrate on the words the men were saying, their animosity kept distracting her. By the time she'd accepted it, Michael had stopped telling Jay to shut up and was leaning across the table at him.

As she understood it, Michael had handled events at a Seattle convention center owned by a group of investors. They'd hired Michael, trusting he'd bring in revenue via a series of venues.

Michael had inked a contract with Jay's father-in-law and others who wanted to put on an antiques show and had taken a sizeable deposit.

"My father-in-law was one of the first to arrive so he could set up his antiques," Jay explained to her. "Not only hadn't the heat been turned on, but the floor was dirty, there was no sign of the promised booths and tables, the bathrooms were locked and the health department had closed down the kitchen. Even more important, the security guards they'd been promised were no-shows."

"I was in charge of booking and promotion," Michael

insisted. "You can't hold me responsible for what the janitors did or didn't do."

"I'm not the one pointing fingers. My father-in-law's group went to the investors, demanding their deposit back. They also contacted several other groups and learned their experience wasn't unique. You lost your job when cancellations started piling up."

"I wasn't fired. I resigned."

"Because you had no choice." Jay gave her his full attention. "I don't know how or why the Forest Service hired him. It certainly wasn't because anyone in Seattle recommended him."

"Why *did* you come here?" she asked Michael.

"I believe I can answer that," Jay said. "He went from a private position to a public one. He presented the Forest Service with a résumé I'm sure omitted the jobs he failed at. How many were there, Michael? You're afraid that this is your last chance?" He paused. "You were hired to increase revenue at Olympic National Park, but that isn't going to happen because of something you might have done."

The back of Michael's knuckles whitened. "What are you talking about?"

"You're angry," she said, because it was time for her to carry her weight in the conversation. "My guess is it's all you can do not to attack Jay. Did Doc make you even angrier? He refused to let you exploit what he was doing for your gain and—"

"You repeatedly knifed him," Jay finished for her.

Michael slammed his palms against the table. "You're crazy! I'd never—my god, this is a nightmare."

"Yes," she whispered, "it is."

* * * *

"What do you think?" Jay asked as, from the porch, they watched Michael speed away from Potlatch.

Winter sighed. For a second, he thought she was going to

lean against him, but she straightened and focused on the wilderness. Was that longing in her eyes?

"He certainly wasn't going to confess," she said. "You were right. Bringing up what happened in Seattle caught him off guard. He revealed more than I'm sure he intended to. I'm sorry for your father-in-law."

He almost reminded her that George was a former in-law, but why make a point of his marital status? "George isn't one to hold grudges, but he has strong opinions of what's right or wrong. That's why I haven't told him about running into Michael. Suing Michael will never get his money back."

"It sounds as if you admire George."

"I do. He's a good man. Not having him and my former mother-in-law in my life anymore was one of the worst things about failing at marriage. Relationships come in many forms."

"Yes, they do."

Being around Winter was even more difficult than he'd thought it would be. He had no intention of leaving her to obsess over who'd killed her friend, but neither were they in a position to play amateur detectives. What mattered to him was that he'd held her, kissed her, touched her tattoo, envied her relationship with Wolf. Worried for her safety.

"What now?" He framed the question in an attempt to take his thoughts off her impact on him. "We need to bring Christian up to speed."

For the first time since Michael had driven away, she gave him her full attention. Her eyes were asking something he didn't grasp and maybe she didn't want to voice. "You're right." She sounded distracted. "I, ah, need to talk to him about several things."

"Like what?"

When she lifted her hand and covered her throat, he saw it as a self-protective move. But was she afraid, or determined to keep something from him? "I don't..."

On the brink of asking her to continue, he keyed into her body language. She was listening to something. If it was

Wolf, he —

No, not her spirit, but an approaching motor. He positioned himself so he'd be between her and the vehicle. Then he recognized the car Dr. Wilheim had been driving last night.

Winter cursed. "I'm not ready for this."

"What does he want? I thought he'd made his position with you perfectly clear yesterday."

"I did something behind his back."

Was it behind my back, as well? Instead of asking, he studied her, willing her to continue.

"I got in touch with one of the people responsible for the grant," she said. "My guess is Dr. Wilheim found out."

"You — What did you say?"

She lifted her head. "I asked what their procedure was for making a formal request to have the grant transferred to me."

"Already?"

"Yes, already."

If they'd had more time, he might have asked when she'd intended to tell him, but what if she told him it was none of his business? Damn, things with Winter Barstow were becoming more and more complicated.

"You again," Dr. Wilheim said after he'd climbed the stairs. "What are you, her bodyguard?"

Does she need one around you?

"You could have called me," Winter said. "What if I hadn't been at Potlatch? You would have made this trip for nothing."

"But face-to-face confrontations are more effective."

She shrugged. "Is a confrontation necessary?"

Jay had no desire to immediately jump into the conversation. Maybe he'd learn more by observing. Winter had seemed vulnerable yesterday, which, considering what she'd gone through, was understandable. He liked seeing her stand up to Dr. Wilheim.

Dr. Wilheim squared his shoulders. "You certainly didn't

waste any time going behind my back."

"That wasn't my purpose. I needed to learn what I had to do to get started."

Dr. Wilheim shot a glance at Jay. "Did she tell you what she did?"

I'm learning just now. "Yes."

That seemed to surprise the man. "What's going on between the two of you?"

I don't know. I wish I did.

"He helped me get through one of the worst nights of my life," she said. "That's all."

No, it wasn't, Jay wanted to protest.

"Excuse me if I don't take that at face value," Dr. Wilheim retorted. "You've demonstrated that you can't be trusted."

"Can't be trusted to what?" he asked when he'd just told himself to let her handle the conversation. His stereotyped impression of what university professors were like was being shot all to hell. "Let you walk all over her?"

"Hardly. What I'm doing is reminding her of our relative positions." Dr. Wilheim stared at Winter. "I was dumbfounded when I heard you'd already contacted the grant committee. *I'm* determined to salvage the work Gilsdorf began. As for you, you aren't presenting yourself as the grieving *friend.*"

No tears formed in Winter's eyes, but Jay felt her battle to keep control over them. Yes, she was one strong woman. One he could grow to care about even more than he already did.

"I have no intention of bowing out," she said. "And I'm not going to waste my breath explaining my reasons." She looked around, her expression becoming less tense as she did. "I can't leave," she whispered.

"Can't?" Dr. Wilheim parroted. "Damn it, Winter, if you expect to keep your job, you *will* return to San Diego as soon as you can get packed."

"I told you, I can't."

Dr. Wilheim jabbed a finger at her. "I'm not interested in

your nonsense. In case it didn't occur to you, the reason you beat me to the punch is because I was putting other things into play. First thing this morning, I contacted one of the university's attorneys. He needs to do some research, but he believes we have a case for demanding the historian turn everything in his possession over to me as a representative of the university. That material belongs to the federal government, not him."

"What material are you talking about?" Jay asked. "Wasn't that taken from Dr. Gilsdorf's cabin?"

Dr. Wilheim snorted. "I've made connections here and know things neither Winter nor you are aware of. One thing I learned is that Booth wasn't totally forthcoming with Gilsdorf about the extent of the records he's collected."

"And you believe they're valuable," Winter said.

"Indeed I do. I'd be surprised if they don't play a key role in my success here, which is why I'm involving the university's legal team."

As Jay saw it, Dr. Wilheim was taunting Winter. Instead of responding, she studied her surroundings. Uncle Talio did that sometimes, his expression gentling as he did. Jay couldn't wrap his mind around why Winter should feel at peace right now. At the same time, he envied her.

"You've outstayed your visit, Winter." Dr. Wilheim again thrust a finger in her direction. "There's no way the grant committee will choose you over me, especially once I have possession of what Deavers has been holding back. Let me say this as clearly as possible. Within an hour, you *will* be on your way back to the university."

If she left, he might never see her again.

But even as his stomach tightened, he read her decision in her body language.

"I'm staying here," she said simply. "As for my reasons — that's personal."

"Then you're fired."

"On what grounds?" Jay demanded when she didn't react.

181

"Isn't that obvious? She's defying me. Believe me, I can make it happen."

"That sounds like a bluff." He wasn't sure it was. Damn it, how could Dr. Wilheim slam a door on the career she'd put so much into? "Considering what she's been through, the university will—"

"Jay," she interrupted, "I don't care." She spread her fingers over the hidden tattoo, and he nodded.

"I don't believe you," Dr. Wilheim spluttered. "How will you support yourself?"

"That isn't your concern."

When Dr. Wilheim started to speak, she shook her head. Then she left the porch and headed into the forest. Jay tried to determine what she'd been looking at but saw nothing out of the ordinary. Leaving the professor to maybe make sense of what had just happened, he took off after her.

"Winter, wait," he called out once they were out of Dr. Wilheim's earshot and before he lost her in the tangle of vegetation.

She stopped but didn't turn to him. The shadows were so deep she seemed part of her surroundings. He'd immediately fallen in lust with the woman he'd married, but experience had soon taught him that physical attraction wasn't enough. By the end of their marriage, he could no longer remember what he'd once thought they had in common. In contrast, Winter Barstow was breathing the air that had given him life. She'd told him very little about her past, just enough for him to conclude she was searching for a place to belong to.

How would she respond if he told her he believed she'd found that place? If he went that far, he'd also have to tell her he was afraid she might jeopardize her sense of belonging because of her debt to Dr. Gilsdorf.

"Damn him." Even though he wasn't sure she wanted him around, he closed the distance between them. "Dr. Wilheim shouldn't have handled things the way he did. In addition to backing you into a corner, he deliberately kept things from you."

She whirled around, surprising him with how effortlessly she moved. "Isn't that what you accused me of? You thought I should have cleared everything with you before going to the grant committee."

He had believed that, but his reasoning no longer mattered. Keeping his hands off her earlier hadn't been easy. Now, it became impossible. Trusting his body to do the right thing, he took hold of her arms and drew her close.

"I don't want us to fight." He bent over so their mouths were only inches apart.

She started shaking. "I don't want to, either."

She was still keeping things from him, details that had to wait because he stopped from wrapping his arms around her and hauled her against his chest and erection.

"Jay," she mouthed as she arched her pelvis at him. "Oh, Jay."

Jay what?

Then she lifted her head, her heated breath slid over his face, she held tight to his waist, and there was nothing else. He wanted to hand her butterfly kisses. Instead, his mouth attacked hers. Her strength met his. Crashed over him. Feeling powerful and out of control, he backed her against a tree, ran his knee between her legs and slipped a hand under the hem of her top so he could feel her soft flesh.

Wherever insanity was taking him, she was on the same journey, cupping his buttocks and grinding against his pelvis while low sounds rumbled in her throat.

Just when he was certain he was going to take her, she let go of his buttocks and pushed against his chest. He started to swat her hands away.

"Wolf," she whispered. "I hear Wolf."

"No." *Damn it, no!*

"I have to..."

"What do you have to do, Winter?"

She started shaking. "I don't know."

183

Chapter Nineteen

Dark leather chairs flanked the oversized fireplace in the Lake Quinault Lodge, but only a few people were in the large rustic structure where the park's combination of library and museum was located when Winter walked in. Instead of asking what she intended to accomplish by coming here, Jay had simply said he'd accompany her. He'd already told his supervisor he wouldn't be going back to work today. She hadn't discouraged him, and not just because she wanted him around. Jay's roots were here. If Booth was in possession of something that would enrich his comprehension of those roots, he had a right to them.

Maybe she did, too.

Maybe whatever she could uncover of her origin was more important than anything else.

The drive had frayed her nerves, and, judging by Jay's silence, he was experiencing the same thing.

They shouldn't have held onto each other or kissed.

But they had. Again. Fierce and hungry.

She hated keeping the mask from him almost as much as she hated not telling him what Doc had revealed about Floyd. Why couldn't things be simple and clean between them? Maybe attraction would deepen and become that vague *something* she'd long been looking for in a romantic relationship.

Don't, she ordered herself as Jay's shoulder brushed hers. She wouldn't think about what might be. The man who'd meant the most to her had been murdered. Only justice and fulfilling his dream mattered.

Her intention had been for Jay and her to go directly to

the library, but when she spotted the fireplace and nearly floor-to-ceiling windows on either side of it, she stopped and took it all in. The setting was so peaceful, set aside from life and responsibilities, perfect for lovers.

No! Silence those thoughts!

Stifling a moan, she removed her attention from the logs burning in the fireplace. Because of the dim lighting, it took her a moment to locate the door labeled 'library.'

"You're sure you're up to this?" Jay asked.

She forced a laugh. "Why not? It isn't as if I have a job."

"Dr. Wilheim might have been calling your bluff."

"Even if he was, I don't care."

He studied her. "Because Olympic and Wolf have too tight a hold on you."

You're part of that hold. "Maybe it was being confronted by Michael and then Dr. Wilheim, but suddenly all I could think about was plunging into the forest. Never returning."

"Everyone wants to escape sometimes."

She nodded but didn't risk looking at him. "Not escape. Finding myself." Unnerved by how much she'd revealed, she gave herself a mental shake. "All right, let's do this."

As he led the way across the room, a couple of women stopped their conversation and stared at Jay. *You can't have him. He's —*

No, he wasn't hers. Would never be, because, eventually, she'd have to tell him the truth.

When Jay opened the library door so she could enter ahead of him, she didn't see anyone. Then she heard Booth's voice. It sounded as if he was in a room beyond the library. Jay and she exchanged a multilayered look. That done, she took in her surroundings.

Several glass cases held Native American tools and weapons, as well as printed notations explaining how the items had been used and what they'd been constructed from. Front and center was some well-preserved traditional rainwear made from cedar bark. The notation explained that the garments had once belonged to the Nootka, whose potlatch ceremonies often celebrated the child or young man designated to take over the honor and rank of chief.

A timetable stretching from ancient times to the present filled most of one wall. On the left of the timetable, someone — Booth, she surmised — had documented what was known of life in the Pacific Northwest over thousands of years. The right detailed what had been going on in the world during the same timeframe. Obviously, Booth wanted visitors to be able to draw comparisons between this isolated setting and the larger historic context.

"Look around," Jay whispered. "I've seen it."

"What's your reaction to what Booth has done?"

He shrugged. "Typical museum stuff."

Spotting a locked glass bookshelf, she walked over to it. There were two shelves. One contained commercially available books about the park and Northwest Native Americans, while the other held a number of cardboard-backed eight-by-ten old photographs. The top photographs were of a collection of fish-drying racks, a small cedar canoe with two Native men wearing rain capes and hats beside it, and an ancient woman in a feathered headdress that had been worn by shamans. The photographs were nothing unique. Like Jay had said, typical museum stuff.

This couldn't be everything. Booth must've kept valuable material away from the public. What the room held disappointed her. The Olympic Forest was a fabulous ancient rain forest. Plants that didn't exist anywhere else on earth flourished there. Even the most jaded traveler couldn't help but be impressed by the giant trees, lush ferns and wealth of plants. In the short amount of time she'd been in the park, she'd seen a number of unique birds. There were flies — the thought made her shiver — but Olympic was also home to countless insects, amphibians, rodents, predators and prey.

Wolf.

In addition to the ocean, there was a multitude of creeks, streams and rivers. Those waterways were as special as the land, and it was a shame visitors couldn't find information about them here. Given more room, commitment and imagination, this could become much more than the name 'library' on the door.

"Winter. I didn't expect to see you here."

Feeling torn, she faced Booth. Next to his immaculate dress shirt and slacks, she felt shabby.

"Why didn't you?"

He opened his mouth to respond, only to frown at Jay. "Your bodyguard?"

"Does she need one?" Jay asked.

"Not here she doesn't. Did law enforcement assign you to keep an eye on her?"

When Jay didn't answer, she decided to let the question slide. "When I told Jay I wanted to see the museum, he offered to drive. I took him up on it. I needed..."

"Something other than what happened to Dr. Gilsdorf to focus on? So, what's your impression?"

I'm disappointed. She pointed at one of the enclosed cases. "That caught my eye. I've never seen an authentic woven bark rain hat or cape anywhere except in a museum."

"I thought Dr. Gilsdorf might make the same observation, but he barely looked at them. The rainwear belonged to the family of one of the first white settlers to the area. They weren't forthcoming about how their great, great grandfather had gotten his hands on the items, and I didn't ask."

"What are they doing here?" Jay asked.

Booth all but puffed out his chest. "I heard about the estate sale the family was having. Apparently, they'd come upon hard times. I approached the county historic society and convinced them to let me use some of their funds to bid on certain items."

Something about his explanation didn't sound completely ethical to her — until she compared it to what Doc had done.

"How long have you been working here?" she asked.

"Going on two years. Unfortunately, it's been an uphill

battle to convince the feds to adequately fund the library. There's some potential from such sources as estate items, and I'm committed to adding to the collection despite the budget constraints."

Having seen the university deal with the same thing and hearing Michael talk about his budget issues, she understood Booth's frustration. "Speaking of the collection..." Her attention went to the two shelves of books and photographs.

Booth walked over to the shelving and patted the glass. "Not much to this, is there?"

"No, there isn't."

"That's because I belatedly learned to safeguard what's of value. My predecessor here wore a number of hats. As a result, he didn't devote much time to this space." He paused. "I discovered a closet filled with items that hadn't seen the light of day for a long time, including dozens of audio tapes."

"The oral histories?"

"Exactly. Their existence isn't well-known. They were made thirty, forty years ago. Once they were in my possession, I made a number of efforts to record the memories of elderly Natives. Those turned out to be both successful and rewarding in terms of prestige, however limited, and interested Dr. Gilsdorf. The old tapes are another story, because they were done in the Quinault language."

"My uncle said he remembered his father talking into a recorder," Jay said.

Booth shrugged. "I hired an old Chinook woman to handle the translation. She got through two before she died a couple of months ago. I attempted to do some of the work myself, but that was a fool's mission. Finding another translator has been difficult in large part because tribal elders now refuse to cooperate with me."

Jay gave Booth a sideways look. "I'm aware of the lack of cooperation."

Not giving herself time to question what she was doing,

she asked Booth how many people were aware of the Quinault tapes.

"More than I'd prefer. The woman who did the translating was quite the talker. There were legends in there even she didn't know about, plus stories about conflicts with other tribes, wolves and grizzlies. Exciting stuff."

"What about where people were living at various times?" she asked.

Booth lifted his eyebrows, telling Winter that he'd picked up on the layers behind her question. "Some. The problem is there's no modern reference for the names the Natives gave for settlements. I'm hoping location placement will become easier once all of the tapes have been translated."

If they ever are. Just the same, she understood why Dr. Wilheim was determined to get his hands on them. Did Talio speak Quinault? Would he agree to work with her if the tapes were in her possession?

"As for why I've put so much energy into this project," Booth continued, "at my core, I'm a historian. A literary geek, you might say. Winter, you're an educator, so you understand. I have the utmost respect for the past and am excited about what the present generation can learn from it. Maybe my obsession comes from losing my parents at an early age."

She'd been trying to get a reading on Jay, but Booth now had her full attention. "I'm sorry."

"After they died—my father when I was five, my mother three years later—I went to live with my aunt. She had four children and was quite the disciplinarian. The only way I was going to earn her respect and attention was by excelling at academics."

Listening to Booth, she realized Jay knew less about her past than they did about the historian. She'd always kept those years close to her heart, but Jay deserved more.

About a lot of things.

"It looks as if you've taken your childhood and fashioned it into a career you love," she finally thought to say.

He shook his head. "Love is a pretty strong word. When I applied for the position—I'd been working for a county library system where there was no hope of advancement—Michael assured me that funding for this" he indicated their surroundings—"was going to become a Forest Service priority. Obviously, that didn't happen."

"Do you feel you were lied to?" Jay asked.

Booth ran his fingers through his spare hair. "Not at all. In its attempts to balance the budget, Congress needs to know whether projects are self-supporting. If you've listened to Michael, and I don't see how you can't have, you realize the parks are under pressure to carry their own weight. I can't expect any increase in my operating budget until and unless it pays for itself."

"Any ideas how you might make that happen?" Jay sounded as if he cared.

"Several." For the first time, Booth smiled. "Jay, Olympic is unique. Even with selective logging, it stands as a testament to the past. I want to build on that so when people come here they're able to step back in time. All they need is a reason to take that first step." He pointed at the wall with the timeline on it. "I'm working on a brochure that includes this so when a visitor steps on one of our many trails, they can connect where they are right now to what took place from the beginning of time."

Connected spelled out how she'd felt from the moment she'd come to Olympic, except, for her, the richness went beyond looking at thousand-year-old trees.

"Have you discussed your project with park leadership?" Jay asked.

"Just in a broad way. I'm hoping to include specifics about the Native American impact, complete with a map highlighting where historic settlements were located."

"Which settlements?"

Alerted by Jay's clipped words, she waited for Booth's response.

"Surely you don't need to ask," Booth replied. "A number

along the Hoh River have been identified, but there are more, their location buried within the oldest tapes."

"The settlements are sacred to the various tribes." Jay's mouth thinned. "They'll oppose having them become amusement parks."

"I would never do that," Booth snapped. After a moment, his features relaxed. "I'm sorry if I sound defensive. The last thing I'd do is exploit historically significant sites, but there's no reason why the present generation can't look at them and imagine what life there was like when they were vibrant communities."

Jay's fingers fisted. "Those sites are sacred."

Torn, she tried to split her attention between the two men. She'd love nothing more than to hike to where her maybe ancestors had lived and stand where her great, great grandparents might have smoked fish and raised their children. At the same time, she didn't want outsiders crowding around, taking pictures and keeping the spirits away.

"Doc wanted to identify as many sites as possible," she said. "Is that what he was looking for when he borrowed what he did?"

Booth walked over to the door to the rest of the lodge and looked out. "He didn't spell out his intentions, not that I blame him. I've been closed-mouthed about my plans for increasing revenue because—I'll be honest—I'm committed to making and keeping that *my* project. We all want to shine."

"And yet you were willing to share some of the oral histories with Dr. Gilsdorf," Jay said. "I'm assuming those are the ones you conducted."

"I had no choice but to comply with a request coming from a representative of a public institution. However, in light of the cabin break-in, I regret my decision." He stared at Jay. "I have the utmost respect for you, but I suspect that at least one of your people is responsible for the theft. The tribes want the histories returned to them. I believe they're seeking legal means in an attempt to have that happen."

Jay walked over to the case holding the cardboard-backed photographs, then looked over his shoulder at Booth. "Where are the oldest tapes?"

"I'm not going to tell you. Rest assured, they're in a safe place."

Just like the wolf mask.

Chapter Twenty

The closer Jay and she came to the Hoh reservation, the more aware Winter became of the ocean smells and sounds. Thick woods crowded the edges of Highway 101, and the deep gray clouds that had been building for several hours further isolated her from the outside world. They hadn't passed any buildings for miles and miles. They hadn't spoken during that time.

Once they'd left the library, Jay had unsuccessfully tried to get in touch with his brother. From what little Jay had told her, she realized he was upset with Floyd for not spending last night with their uncle. With a second night approaching, he needed to check on the older man. Jay wasn't content to simply talk to Talio, because his uncle tended to downplay his limitations. Jay had offered to take her back to her cabin, but she wanted to see Talio. Maybe even ask him to explain what Yakanon meant.

Jay pulled off the highway and onto a thread of road snaking through ancient forest. She felt both trapped and embraced by the vegetation, wished she could reach out and touch the man sitting to her left.

"How many people live on the reservation?" she asked.

"A couple hundred, tops. Some moved away because erosion got so bad, but a few are coming back now that we've been given more land."

"If it wasn't for your uncle, would you live in the area?"

"I don't know. Maybe."

As they reached the clear spot that constituted the residential district, she understood his hesitation. From what she could tell, there was just this single street. A few of the weather-beaten houses had low cyclone fencing around them. Otherwise, it was impossible to tell where one property line ended and another began. None of the houses looked as if they'd been painted recently. A tall, slim dog without a collar stared at them from the side of the road. How would the dog react if a wolf approached it?

Jay had already explained some of the houses that had been built near the seashore or the Hoh River had been flooded and consequently abandoned. Those were the people most interested in relocating to the newly acquired land. Fortunately, his uncle's father had chosen a homesite above the flood plain. Jay had given up trying to get his uncle to leave the house and was in the process of updating it.

He turned onto a single lane dirt road. They immediately started climbing. Some three or four minutes later she caught sight of where Jay and Floyd had grown up. Judging by the location, the view of the ocean from the house should be spectacular, but she couldn't take her attention off the structure ahead of her. She guessed it to be around fifteen hundred square feet. The new metal roof was steeply pitched, and she hoped Jay hadn't done it without help. It looked as if he wasn't quite finished installing the gutters. She noted a heavily patched stone chimney. Most impressive was the sturdy redwood front porch.

When he pulled in next to a nearly new pickup, she faced him. "How is he going to feel about me being here?"

"Ask him."

She nodded. Then, because the need to touch Jay was becoming stronger by the second, she opened her door and got out. Talio must have heard them coming, because he'd already stepped onto the porch. She took a second to look behind her. Numerous trees filtered her view of the ocean, but it stretched out below and beyond. Timeless. Filled with whispers. Even more impenetrable than the forest.

Her heart felt as if it was expanding. If she spread her arms, would she be able to fly? "I'd live here," she whispered.

"The view—"

"It's isolating."

She turned into the sea-scented breeze. "I've been isolated all my life."

* * * *

Uncle Talio had never been one for idle talk. As a result, as soon as they went inside, Jay gave his uncle a brief overview of what he and Winter had been doing during the day. Judging by how she studied walls adorned with clam baskets, bone-barb fishing hooks, part of a cedar canoe he and Floyd had found years ago, a bear pelt that had always been there, and a ceremonial rattle representing a raven next to the fireplace, he wasn't sure she was paying attention to what he was saying.

In response to his question, his uncle said this morning's meeting hadn't resulted in any progress in the tribes' efforts to place Native sites under their control. The legal firm they'd hired was still studying the laws to see what their options were.

"Does that bother you?" Winter asked. Jay couldn't tell how she felt about what she'd just learned.

Uncle Talio leaned forward in the hardwood rocking chair his father had made. "The young are more impatient than someone my age. Besides, don't you want things to remain as they are? This way, you can simply step into Dr. Gilsdorf's shoes."

Even with the two Thermopane windows Jay had installed this spring, the lighting in the living room was dim. A few raindrops slid down the glass.

"So much is out of my hands," she said. "I'll give the grant committee what they want. Right now, mostly I have to wait."

"Where will you do your waiting?"

His uncle didn't probe. That he was doing so with Winter told Jay there was nothing casual about the question. She'd

195

been sitting in a blanket-covered chair to his right, but now she stood and walked over to the raven rattle.

"Can I touch it?"

"Yes," Uncle Talio said.

She lightly stroked the over-emphasized beak and large, deep blue eyes. "Cedar," she whispered. "How old?"

"I'm not sure."

Still stroking, she nodded. "Maybe it's better that way. A continuum. Do you use it in ceremonies?"

"Yes."

Nodding again, she angled her body to Uncle Talio while keeping her slender fingers on the rattle. It was the poor lighting, of course, but suddenly she was no longer wearing a blue front-button shirt, but a deerskin dress decorated with abalone shells. Her waist-length black hair with an eagle feather woven into it flowed down her back.

"Then you're a shaman," she said.

Uncle Talio sent Jay a look he wasn't sure he understood. "An honorary one. You know your anthropology."

After studying the image a little longer, she walked over to Uncle Talio and knelt beside him. "It's more than a field of study for me. A lot more."

His uncle touched her head. "I know."

She sank down a little and stared at the rug under her knees. No one spoke for the better part of a minute while Jay's heart both ached and beat double time. When he'd first spotted his uncle on the porch, he'd thought he looked tired, but now the older man appeared animated. On their way here, he'd repeatedly asked himself if he dared tell her about Grandparents Cave. Now the only thing that mattered was that they were together. She was in his world today, absorbing his life. Turning her back on the career that might threaten his people's past.

"I asked Jay to let me accompany him because I hope you'll tell me about Yakanon," she said as she placed her hand over Uncle Talio's. "I attempted to research the word, but all I came up with was that Yakanon and Thunderbird can communicate with each other."

"Who is Thunderbird?" Uncle Talio asked.

She smiled. "Jay said you were a teacher. Thunderbird is a spirit, a powerful one that can control weather."

"Part of an ignorant people's superstition?"

"No!" She pulled back but didn't release her hold on Uncle Talio. "I have a pretty good idea what you're thinking, that anthropologists are academicians determined to be as accurate as possible about ancient lifestyles. They can't crawl inside the hearts and minds of those who believe in spirits and go on spirit quests. It's a field of study for them, not reality."

"You aren't talking about yourself," Jay said. Much as he wanted to stand behind her so she could lean against him, he didn't move.

"No, I'm not."

Heat and cold warred inside him as she let go of Uncle Talio and reached for the top button on her shirt. She flicked a glance in his direction and then gave Uncle Talio her full attention. From where he was sitting, he had a clearer view of Uncle Talio's expression than hers. Someone who hadn't grown up around his uncle probably wouldn't have caught the faint widening of his eyes or nearly imperceptible nod.

"I don't know who my parents are," she said as she undid the second button. "If they were ever part of my life, I don't have a memory of that. About the only thing I'm sure of is that I'm Native American. Just looking in the mirror tells me that."

"Yes," Uncle Talio said, "you are."

She blinked repeatedly. "Thank you. I needed to hear you say that. This" — she ran her fingers over the newly exposed wolf head image — "represents what constitutes roots for me. There wasn't a night of my childhood that I didn't dream of a wolf. Countless times during the day, I'd think about what I came to call my imaginary friend. The experience was never frightening. I didn't once feel as if I were in danger."

197

You weren't completely alone. You had this. "Did you tell anyone?" Jay asked.

Her eyes glittered. "No. Wolf was mine. I didn't want to share him."

Uncle Talio's attention stayed fixed on the tattoo as he straightened and pressed his hand against his thigh. Outside, the wind had picked up while the only sound Jay could hear in here was his heart beating.

"What did Wolf do in your dreams?" Uncle Talio asked.

"He'd walk with me. I dreamed a lot about walking. I saw myself as being on an endless journey. I wasn't lonely or scared, because Wolf was by my side. I'd wrap my arms around him and smell his fur—dreams aren't supposed to include a sense of smell—and he'd lean against me. We'd stay like that until I felt like walking again." She started to cover up the wolf image, only to leave it exposed. "As a teen, I convinced myself that my dreams had been my way of dealing with what was going on in my life. I'd created Wolf to sleep with me, keep me from getting cold."

"From feeling alone." He might have said more if his throat hadn't closed.

"Yes," she whispered.

Uncle Talio lifted his hand from his leg and touched his forefinger to the wolf likeness. Jay waited for her to object, but she remained within easy reach.

"What you have here duplicates what you saw in your dreams?" Uncle Talio asked.

"As close as I could make it. I drew it and told the tattoo artist to follow it exactly. I love what he created."

There was nothing sensual in how Uncle Talio's rough finger traced the image. Either his uncle was committing it to memory or was comparing it to something he believed in.

"When did Wolf come into your life?" Uncle Talio asked.

She closed her eyes. "He's part of my earliest memories, which started when I was approximately five. I've tried and tried but can't remember anything before I was found."

"Found?" Jay parroted.

She focused on him. "I'm not sure whether to call it a campground or roadside rest. I was alone."

"Someone dropped you off?" How could anyone do that to a child?

"There are so many holes in my early years. When I was in my late teens, I went to the social service agency that initially took responsibility for me to fill in the gaps, but they said the records were locked."

I hurt for you. "What about your name?"

Uncle Talio's hand slid to his lap. Winter stood and returned to her chair but didn't seem to realize that he could still see the wolf head along with the swell of her breasts.

"It was January when a truck driver found me. He called me Winter. He contacted the police, and they took me to a hospital where they determined I was around five years old. My clothes must have been indistinguishable. I didn't have any scars or marks that might have helped them narrow down who I was. The press ran my picture, but no one stepped forward to identify or claim me."

Alone. So alone. "What about DNA or blood type?"

"That was before DNA matching became the tool it is. My blood type is common. There was nothing wrong with me, so I couldn't stay in the hospital. The social workers wanted to give me another name, but I insisted I already had one."

"The one the truck driver used."

"Yes. I remember him putting his coat around me and carrying me to his cab. I must have been scared. Confused. I cuddled against him and fought when the police separated us. He came to see me when I was in the hospital. They let him take me outside so I could see his rig in the daylight. The way he called me Winter, I loved it."

"What about your last name?"

"The trucker—Salvador Rambo—told everyone that because we were in Barstow, California, and I might have died if he hadn't found me, he had the right to give me an identity. He asked what I thought of Winter Barstow, and

199

of course I said I loved it."

I'll never forget this moment. "Has he stayed in touch?"

She shook her head. "Salvador was killed in an accident on an icy road about four years after we met. He was the only person I could call family. I kept being sent to different foster homes. I probably wasn't the most lovable little girl. I didn't like being hugged and people getting into my personal space."

Not touching her was killing him, but he was afraid that might spell the end to what was happening that afternoon. "Why do you think you were like that?"

"I was too young to fully comprehend what it meant to be abandoned, but I was scared of going through the sense of loss again, so I held back. I had to live under whatever roof I was sent to, eat the people's food, live by their rules. But either I had no idea how to trust or none of those families knew how to give me what I needed."

"Wolf did," Uncle Talio said.

Eyes wide, she nodded. "Wolf was my rock, my pretend friend." She looked out of the window. "At least, that's what I believed he was until I came here and… Salvador and I were comrades, pals, family. Because of his job, I only saw him a few times a month, but those visits were the highlight of my life. He told me it was the two of us against the world. He said he was trying to get custody of me, but he'd been in prison. Between that, the trucking, and his being Mexican and single, he was afraid it wouldn't happen."

"Do you believe he was telling you the truth?" Jay asked.

She kneaded the chair arm. "Even if he wasn't, he gave me what I needed."

"No one just abandons a child. I mean, yes, it happens, but someone somewhere would notice that a child was missing. And when that child's picture winds up on the news—"

"Salvador said maybe my parents had come a long way from where they were living before they dropped me off."

"Or your parents were dead," Uncle Talio said. "Maybe

you'd been stolen from them."

Jay thought she might recoil, but she simply nodded, and he understood this had occurred to her before. "There are a lot of possibilities. Believe me, I went over and over them, but I couldn't make something out of nothing."

He couldn't stay where he was any longer, not with her looking so alone. He stood, positioned himself behind her, and rested his hands on her shoulders, careful not to touch her flesh. "Then you came here, and Wolf reached out to you."

"And you're asking yourself if this is where you began," Uncle Talio added.

She covered his left hand with hers but kept her attention on Uncle Talio. "Is that possible?"

Jay wasn't surprised when his uncle didn't respond, because only Winter could answer her question, not with a birth certificate but a feeling in her heart. Wolf's howl.

"I wasn't an easy child to be around," she whispered. "I don't remember wanting to be cuddled. No wonder no one stepped forward to adopt me. Sometimes I did things I shouldn't have, just to see what kind of reaction I'd get. My probation officer called me an outlaw."

"Probation?"

"I was a juvenile delinquent. Locked up for stealing when I was homeless."

His hold on her shoulders tightened, and his heart ached. "You were homeless?"

"Self-imposed, because I kept running away. It was—I was always looking for something even though I wasn't certain what it was."

Something to belong to, a place maybe. "You had Wolf."

"Not really, because, like I said, by my teen years I'd convinced myself that Wolf was a figment of my imagination. I wanted to be so damn mature, not rely on an imaginary creature."

I did the same, turned my back on my spirit.

The silence following her comment about how she'd come

to perceive Wolf wasn't uncomfortable. He nearly thanked her for being so honest about her early years before he remembered her question about Yakanon. Wondering if his uncle was thinking the same thing, he looked at him.

Uncle Talio nodded. "Winter, you have proven yourself worthy of understanding why I said what I did when we first met."

Under his hands, her body became wire-tight.

"That day, my spirit guided my words in ways it seldom does. Usually, Eagle rests in my heart, and I'm sure I'm on the path He wants me to be on. Restlessness had brought me to Potlatch. I thought maybe Eagle wanted me to tell my nephew something, to again try—but it wasn't that. Only Jay can decide how he wants to walk through life."

"But it wasn't that," Jay said hoping to bring his uncle back on track.

"No. Winter, you might not believe what I'm telling you, but, because of Wolf, you will. My role the other day was to hand you a message. Not just from my spirit, but others, as well."

Her shaking increased, prompting him to reach over her shoulders and rest his fingertips on her throat. Close to her tattoo.

"Thunderbird does more than control storms. He gives Yakanon a voice."

"Why does Thunderbird have to do that?" she asked.

"Yakanon doesn't have form. He's an essence, a sound, a message."

When she muttered something that might have been a prayer, his heart went out to her.

"What is the message?"

Uncle Talio stared at the window then at her again. "It relieves my heart to realize Wolf resides in your soul. Maybe his presence will make this easier for you." He sighed. "Yakanon's voice is a lament for the death of a soulless one."

"Soulless one?" she whispered.

As Uncle Talio started rubbing his thigh again, Jay wondered if he was aware of what he was doing.

"Eagle tells me that, through most of Hoh history, Yakanon seldom spoke. There was little need, because those who lived here walked a clear and righteous path, but there were a few times when the ancients heard Yakanon. Not even the shaman was certain whether the cry was for the living or dead."

"Is the cry a warning?" she asked, leaning forward.

Uncle Talio's features sagged. "My spirit hasn't told me."

"So." She sighed. "There's no way I can be sure whether Yakanon is saying someone without a soul has died or that death is coming."

Uncle Talio extended a hand toward Winter. "I'm sorry. I wish I could tell you which it is. Jay, I've barely slept the past few nights. My heart is heavy."

"Why didn't you tell me?" he asked.

"Because you've already taken on so much."

* * * *

Before they left Talio's place, Winter helped Jay bring in enough wood for a couple of nights. Much as she'd wanted to hug Talio, she was afraid either the man or his spirit might be able to read her mind. Maybe Talio's heart was heavy because he knew the wolf mask was missing from wherever it had come from. Perhaps he hadn't said anything because he wanted to see if she was capable of being honest. Worthy of Wolf.

"He's an amazing man," she said as Jay and she neared Potlatch. "I can't help but wonder…"

"What?"

She probably wouldn't have responded if Jay hadn't reached over and rested his hand on her thigh. Just like that, she mentally relived how she'd revealed what she understood about her past.

"This is going to sound crazy, but my childhood might

203

have been different if I'd had someone, a grandfather maybe. I would have an anchor. Not need to rely on an imaginary playmate."

"There's nothing imaginary about Wolf for you."

Propelled by the warmth over her knee, she squeezed his hand. "I know that now. If only there'd been someone I could tell about Wolf all those years ago."

He threaded his fingers through hers. "Don't. Live in the present."

A present that revolved in large part around him.

"Thanks for helping with the wood," he said. "My brother should have taken care of that."

Unless Floyd had fled after killing Doc.

Half sick from the thought, she struggled to focus on her surroundings. The drizzle Olympic was well-known for gave the forest a misty quality. Between that and the setting sun, she felt caught in a netherworld where time didn't matter. It was becoming dark, but that state might last for hours.

"What are you going to do next?" he asked as he pulled into the Potlatch parking area.

Out of the corner of her eye, she glimpsed his profile with the wilderness just beyond. The fingers of his left hand clenched the steering wheel.

"I'm not sure. I can't leave."

"How are you going to support yourself?"

She'd barely given that thought. Even with his question, it didn't matter. "I should have worked on getting my information to the grant committee."

"You couldn't because you're being bombarded with the question of who killed your friend."

Except for Floyd, she'd talked to everyone she considered a suspect. As she slid around for a clearer view of Jay, she likened their relationship to glass. It might shatter.

"You can't do anything tonight," he said. "Let it be until morning."

"I want to."

He faced her. "Go to your cabin. Get some sleep."

I don't want to sleep. I want you.

The admission echoed, making her wonder how long it had been waiting to be expressed. "Jay?" Just saying his name made her shiver. She tried to calm herself by concentrating on unfastening her seat belt, but wound up cupping his hand between her palms.

"What?"

"I don't— I've forgotten what I was going to say."

"Have you?"

Jay's black Hoh eyes dug past countless layers. He touched her heart and nerve endings, made her acutely aware that she was a woman.

"Come in with me, please."

"You're sure?"

She nodded. "I've never been more sure of anything."

Chapter Twenty-One

Winter had hunched her shoulders and held her collar against her throat during the short walk to her cabin, but the light rain reached her anyway. Her side next to Jay remained warm while the other became chilled. The *splat-splat* of drops striking the path gave the evening a rhythm but made listening for Wolf difficult. If Jay had asked what was on her mind, she would have told him she was hoping Wolf would approve of what they were about to do. But even if her spirit didn't, she wouldn't have changed her mind.

They had tonight.

As soon as they stepped inside, Jay started crumpling newspaper in preparation for starting a fire. She got a towel from the bathroom and dried her hair. After closing the wood stove door, he took the towel from her. Unsure what to do with herself, she removed her jacket and laced her fingers together.

"I have food if you're—"

"Not now."

Watching him remove his coat tightened her throat. He still had on his Forest Service uniform, not that it mattered, because she was seeing the man and not the federal employee.

"My uncle wants to accept you," he said. "But he isn't sure yet."

Talio wouldn't want to have anything to do with her if he knew what she'd done with the wolf mask. Maybe his admitting he couldn't sleep had been his way of hinting about his knowledge.

No. Talio didn't play games.

"What's wrong?" Jay asked. "Maybe his hesitancy concerns you."

"It's not that. I comprehend his reservations. He's everything the words 'Native American' represent, while I..."

He brushed damp hair back from her face. "Just be you."

For tonight, his touch and expression seemed to say that only the two of them mattered. She could love a man like this. Maybe she already did.

No. Love didn't happen in the space of a few days. Desire, yes, wanting to sleep with him, certainly yes, but love took time.

More than she'd ever taken.

"I shouldn't have said that," he said with his hand against the side of her neck. "I'm telling you to be comfortable in your skin when I'm not in mine."

She continued to lean into his touch. "You're not?"

"I've been lying to myself." He pressed his mouth to her forehead. "All my damn insistence that I'm content living in today's world—it isn't that simple."

Thunder rumbled, sounding so far away it barely made an impact, although maybe the truth was she couldn't concentrate on anything except what Jay was saying and her need for him. Casting aside all doubt and fear, she flattened her hands over his chest.

"We're both on journeys," she said. "Attempting to weave the ordinary world with something that goes far beyond that."

His expression eased a little. "Thanks for keeping it basic."

They kissed, not a simple thing, nothing gentle or questing about the contact. Ruled by want, she wrapped her arms around his neck, rose onto her toes and pressed her body against his. All the while, his lips bruised hers, and she met his message with her own. Thunder grumbled again, adding strength to her desire. She felt drunk. His erection pushed at her. Moist heat flooded her crotch. Her mouth still sealed to his, she whimpered.

His greater strength closed around her. Held her prisoner against his fierce male body.

"Wait." The single word from masculine lips vibrated through her. "Something—" Groaning, he forced distance between them while still holding onto her. "Protection. We need—"

"I'm on the pill. I don't sleep around, but I'm not a nun. I'm also not good mother material right now." *Someday, please.*

"I have condoms. For the record, they've been in my wallet for a while."

"I want you," she managed.

"I've hoped this would happen from the first time I saw you."

She couldn't say the same, because, back then, concern for Doc had consumed her, but this was tonight. After he'd settled her arms by her sides, he reached for her shirt's top button. Suddenly weak, she locked her knees.

"Thanks for showing your tattoo to my uncle," he said.

Speak. Don't miss anything. "I had to. If anyone can explain the connection between Wolf and me, it's him."

"He won't spell things out for you. He believes it's your journey."

Her eyes burned, but for one of the few times in her life, she didn't care whether someone saw her emotions. "At least he knows."

Even with desire filling her veins, she wished Jay would say more about his uncle's reaction to the wolf likeness. Maybe after they'd had sex, he would—what was going to take place between them? Was it simply sex or were they after lovemaking?

Feeling as if she was being tossed between two very different acts, she didn't move as Jay slowly dispensed with her shirt. To her mind, sex was a physical act, bodies seeking and achieving satisfaction. Lovemaking went deeper and was a place she felt a stranger to. She'd wanted to fall in love, had twice believed that was what she felt, but the condition hadn't lasted.

Looking into Jay's dark eyes, she realized it was different this time. No matter what happened tomorrow, she'd never forget him.

And in the world she desperately needed, what had begun between them would never end.

"Lovely," he muttered. "Perfect."

Where had she gone while he was unfastening her bra? Judging by how she was shaking, obviously her body had remained in the moment.

"Will you do something for me?" he asked. "I'd like to watch you get rid of the rest of your clothes."

Her garments consisted of jeans, panties, socks and tennis shoes, none of them seductive, but she wanted to please Jay. She sat on the side of the bed and leaned over to untie the laces. Her newly exposed breasts and firm nipples were now in full view.

"You're making me crazy."

Still bent over, she studied him. He'd gone to the table and leaned his hip against it. His fingers were maybe a foot from her laptop where she'd read Doc's confession. If anything was to come of what was beginning between them, she'd have to tell him what Doc and Floyd had done.

But not now.

She dispensed with her shoes and socks, then stood. She managed to unhook her jeans before Jay's stare got to her. He'd cupped himself, and his head was tilted to the side. Sucking in her stomach, she eased down the zipper and pushed the denim over her hips. Excitement had already drenched her panties, her teeth felt as if they were floating and she kept having to swallow.

Despite her clumsy fingers, she got the denim past her buttocks. An awkward shimmy resulted in a wad of fabric around her ankles. She had to sit down to finish the job. Then, she stood and took hold of her practical white panties. Wishing they were red or black and hugged her navel, she started them on a downward journey.

"Wait." He pushed away from the table. "My turn."

She had no objections. She even managed to stay in place when he pressed his palm against her belly. Shaking, she planted a hand on his shoulder to brace herself and lifted one leg and then the other so he could slip her feet through the panties. The job done, she stood naked and vulnerable before him. He settled his hands over her hips before leaning down and running his lips over her tattoo. Need crackled. Her nipples ached and heat built on heat in her core.

"The bed."

Galvanized by his raw order, she stumbled over to it and collapsed. She covered the wolf head with one hand and cupped her mons with the other. "Your turn. I need you naked."

"Maybe you want to—"

"I can't. Please do it."

Jay Raven dispensed with his clothes, keeping her riveted on every move. She didn't care that he had a matter-of-fact way about him. He was doing this for her. His body wasn't perfect. A surgical scar on his right elbow and a wide, pale-healed gash over his left calf spoke of a physical life. Fine, dark hairs dusted his chest and ran down his flat belly. When he revealed it to her, his fierce, jutting cock stopped her breathing. He hadn't been circumcised.

Wonderful, she wanted to tell him. *You're wonderful.* Instead, she pressed her legs together.

"You're all right?" he asked.

"What? Yes."

"You look, I'm not sure, scared."

If she was afraid of anything, it was herself. She'd never wanted something as much as she wanted Jay inside her. Sex might destroy her, emotionally rip her apart, but it was worth it. "Come here."

He nodded then picked his jeans up off the floor, extracted his wallet and pulled out a foil-wrapped package. Seeing the condom in his hand made what they were going to do even more real.

When he sat on the bed next to her, his greater weight pulled her toward him. She'd never ripped herself open to anyone like she'd done with Jay Raven.

"I think," she said, "we shouldn't talk about certain things."

He rested his hand on her thigh. "I'm not interested in talking."

Of course he wasn't. When he turned toward her, she placed her fingers on either side of his face and touched her lips to his chin. "I haven't had much success with relationships."

"I failed a pretty big one myself."

She took a deep breath. "Tonight's all that matters."

"What about tomorrow?"

"I want it to be good for us, but I can't promise—"

"One step at a time." His breath dampened her face. "That's how we have to do this."

"You're right." *No insane thoughts about walking hand in hand into the future.*

His fingers began a slow, seductive march up her thighs toward that already heated place. "I'd like to have tomorrow off and spend it with you."

Yes! "Maybe you could take me to some of your favorite places. No agenda, just..."

"The two of us?"

Speechless, she again pressed her lips to his chin. He looked down at his hands as if reminding her of what he was doing

She spread her legs and fell back on the bed. He propped himself on one elbow, then brushed her sex with a work-roughened finger. Gasping, she dug her nails into the cheap spread.

"You're hot," he muttered. "I wasn't sure—so soon."

"I didn't know it would happen like this," she told him as she lifted her buttocks off the mattress in invitation. "It feels..."

His face went out of focus as he leaned down. Then he licked the breast closest to him while cradling her mons, and she understood this was what it felt like to die. Much as she wanted to hold still, she couldn't. A nail snagged, but that didn't stop her from clutching the spread.

He repeatedly deposited moisture on her breast, chuckling low in his throat when she whimpered. Her nipples became so hard they hurt while juices trickled from her. Even with her labored breathing, she heard rain hammering the roof. No one would be out tonight. Whatever happened between them would remain their secret. Their world.

When he drew her breast into his mouth and pressed his tongue against her aching nipple, she scratched his chest. His breathing became deeper, faster. She sounded the same. The hand covering her mons began a downward journey, touching the hot, soft flesh there.

"Yes," she gasped and arched upward again. "Oh, yes."

To her great disappointment, he straightened. The moisture on her breast started to cool, distracting her a little from the teasing touches to her sex.

"Sorry," he muttered. "My back wasn't made for that position. Besides, there's something I need to do while I can still function."

Watching him open the condom package and roll it over his beautiful penis seemed unreal. This was happening to someone else, a woman in control of her life.

Desperate to have him over her, she started to scoot higher on the bed. He helped her turn so she was lengthwise on it and stretched out on his side next to her. She faced him, then lifted her leg over his hip. When his erection stroked her lower belly, she arched her pelvis toward him.

He slid a hand between them and from there to her core. "You're ready for me?" he whispered.

"Yes. Oh yes."

A single move on his part and he was inside her, the connection made. The penetration wasn't deep, and their ability to move was restricted, but she loved being one with him. When he splayed his hand over her back to hold her in place, she silently thanked him by lightly rubbing his arm. She wasn't relaxed, hardly that, but neither did she want to hurry. Judging by his long, slow thrusts, he felt the same way. Sighing, she pressed her thigh against his buttocks. Her breasts brushed his chest.

It was happening.

Time passed. Her mind sank into a secret place. She experienced arousal and peace, expectation and relaxation. Connection. A deeply imbedded heat kept growing. At first, she was barely aware of where the journey was taking her, but then her awakened body surrendered to necessity. With every breath she took, with each masculine invasion, she became hungrier.

Bordering on desperate, she scratched his shoulder.

"What?" he muttered.

Tonight, you're my world. "Just getting your attention."

He pushed into her. "You already have it."

The exchange distracted her from ever-building desire. When she reconnected with her body, she realized her desire had doubled. She again scratched his arm, harder this time. He pressed his fingertips against the small of her back. Lightning seared her channel.

An animal-like moan escaped her. Feeding off it, she kissed the man who'd become the most important person in her life. He answered with a bruising kiss of his own, then clutched her to him and rolled her under him. He slipped out. Staring up at him, she opened her legs.

Instead of stretching out over her as she expected, he straddled her hips, his knees pressing into the mattress. Grabbing her around the middle, he lifted her waist off the bed. She bent her knees, and he settled into the space she'd created. Using her heels for leverage, she rose up and offered her sex to him.

He again filled her, the penetration deeper this time, wild. She flung her head to the side and closed her eyes, slipped into sensation. He continued to hold her up and in perfect alignment. Eager to let him know this time meant everything, she ran her hands over his thighs. She didn't care whether he was looking at her or had closed himself into his own world. Their bodies had become one.

More than just their bodies. Jay Raven was no longer the stranger he'd been a few short days ago. He'd become her lover as fully as she'd become his.

He repeatedly pushed into her, prompting her to set a pace designed to create as much inner friction as possible. Her body started to melt, a delicious sensation she wanted to continue for the rest of her life.

Her life.

Joined with his.

Calling what tore through her 'heat' didn't come close. She loved to climax and had taught herself the art of self-pleasure. But those solitary hours always left her slightly unfulfilled, more alone at the end than when she began. That was in the past, because she and Jay had connected.

Become one.

Moving toward the same goal.

Flame bled into flame. No longer content to let him direct the pace of their lovemaking, she clutched what she could of his thighs and pulled him toward her, trying to deepen the union. As she did, she repeatedly clenched and released her sex muscles. She was riding something without form or direction, still floating, panting.

Her breasts jiggled, her nipples pulsed, her juices bathed his erection, and she breathed.

Sex.

Giving this man her all.

Climaxing.

Crying unshed tears.

* * * *

Long seconds later, she came back to earth to realize Jay had climbed off her and was on his side. His attention was on the window behind her.

"What is it?" she asked.

"Listen."

The rain hadn't let up, but there was more to the night. Interspersed with the drumming, she heard a welcome sound. The low vibration touched her everywhere.

"Wolf," she whispered. "He doesn't mind the rain."

"He's communicating with you?" Jay asked.

"Yes."

He nodded and continued to stare at the window. After a few seconds, his eyes widened. "There," he whispered.

Shock briefly stole her voice. "You heard?"

"Yes."

They stared at each other as the long, otherworldly moan continued. When it ended, she waited, hoping Wolf would start again. Jay slid off the bed and walked over to the window. She couldn't stop looking at his naked silhouette or feeling his emotion.

"So that's what you've been hearing?" he asked.

"Yes."

He faced her. "It's so clear, so easy to identify, but I couldn't until tonight. Until us."

Thank you, Wolf.

Chapter Twenty-Two

Last night had been more than Jay had believed a night with a woman could be. They'd made love a total of three times while it rained and Wolf's cry echoed what was happening inside. He'd hoped there'd be time for one more round before they addressed what today needed to be about, but when he'd cupped his hand around her breast and started to kiss Winter, she'd slipped out of bed and gone into the bathroom.

As the shower ran, he called his uncle. His veiled attempt to see how Talio was doing didn't fool the older man, who'd told him he hadn't slept well.

"I'm not sure what it is," Uncle Talio said. "Something isn't right in the land of my ancestors. I need to stop focusing on myself and open my soul to Eagle."

Uncle Talio had never been self-absorbed. Besides, Eagle wouldn't blame him for concentrating on recovery. After telling his uncle he'd try to see him later, he again punched in Floyd's number.

"This isn't funny," he said to voicemail. "Man up, bro. Call me back. Or at least call Uncle Talio."

"I take it you didn't have any luck reaching your brother," Winter said. She'd come out of the shower and was reaching for a flannel shirt.

Noting that she was avoiding his eyes, he didn't bother shaking his head. He wasn't his brother's keeper. Maybe Floyd was in jail, which might be the best thing for him. "I'd like to show you some of my favorite places today, if that's what you want to do."

She closed the fabric over her front. "Why wouldn't I?"

"Something's on your mind," he made himself say. "If you're regretting—"

"No." She started buttoning buttons. "I'll never regret what happened between us, but Jay..."

Here it comes, he thought. She was going to tell him that what she felt for him didn't go deep enough for a relationship, but how could that be when Wolf— "But what? I want honesty between us."

"Honesty," she repeated on the tail of a long sigh. "You're right. I have to— Jay, would you take me to see your brother?"

He hadn't seen that coming. After pushing his naked body off the bed and grabbing his clothes, he started for the bathroom, only to stop because he didn't like anything about what was happening.

"I should have said something before." She clutched at fabric. "But it was so damn hard. Your brother and Doc— they were working together."

He felt as if he'd been punched. Images of Floyd as a hero-worshipping kid brother filled his mind's eye. "I didn't. You're sure?"

"Yes, unfortunately I am."

Where was Wolf? Why the hell couldn't he and Winter go back to last night? "Give me a minute to—never mind. Tell me now. Whatever happened between them wasn't simply work, was it?" He had to force the question. Had to accept what his brother had kept from him. "You wouldn't be this upset if it was. And Floyd would have told me."

Leaving her shirt half-buttoned, she collapsed in one of the two kitchen chairs. "Do you believe I want this conversation? Suspecting Floyd of— It's the last thing I want to do."

His head roared and, for an instant, he wondered if he was having a heart attack, but it was only shock.

The worst kind of shock. "Wait, what? Are you saying my brother might have killed Dr. Gilsdorf?"

Her silence and lack of eye contact told him more than he

wanted to know. Being naked added to his vulnerability. He needed to ask himself why Wolf had revealed his existence just before his world twisted.

"I'm taking a shower. Don't go anywhere," he said. "It can't remain like this."

"I know." The way she was looking around, he suspected she wanted to escape as much as he did.

He spent more time than necessary in the shower, because he couldn't get his mind to stop spinning. He found nothing. Refused to believe his brother could be capable of murder. Wondered whether he understood Floyd at all.

Unlike Winter, he didn't exit the bathroom until he was dressed. She was at the stove, cooking something but, although his stomach grumbled, he didn't give a damn about eating. He poured coffee for both of them, not bothering to ask how she took hers. As she placed scrambled eggs on two plates, he buttered the toast she'd started. They sat across from each other.

She picked up a forkful of eggs then set it down. She nodded at her laptop, which she'd moved to the recliner.

"Doc left me a letter. A file, really."

Be part of this conversation. No matter how difficult it is, face it. "When?"

"I'm not sure when he wrote it, not long before his death. It was in a storage key I found in his cabin."

Anger fought for a toehold in his mind. "And you're just now telling me about it."

"Jay, please hear me out. I need to say this before it becomes even harder."

For the first time since daylight, she truly looked at him. Her expression put him in mind of a trapped animal. He didn't hate her but couldn't say how he felt. She stumbled over the telling, but he got the gist. A worried-for-himself Dr. Gilsdorf had come up with a way to pass some key information on to Winter. She didn't go into the specifics of Dr. Gilsdorf's relationship with Floyd, and he had no doubt she was keeping things from him, but apparently the professor had paid Floyd to help him with his project. Things had gone well for a while, but then they'd had a falling out and Floyd had refused to have anything more to do with Dr. Gilsdorf.

"Doc can—could—be incredibly persistent when he wanted something," she said as their eggs cooled. "I wouldn't be surprised if he kept pressure on Floyd. Maybe—damn it, I have to be honest." She looked beyond him to the mist-filled morning. "I want to avoid saying certain things because…"

"Because it'll change how you think about Dr. Gilsdorf."

It had been a guess on his part, but, judging by her flared nostrils, he was right at least in part. "He was my hero. He still is. Knowing someone killed him tears me apart."

It can't be my brother, damn it. He wouldn't — "You aren't going to let me see what he wrote, are you?"

She shook her head. "Not now. I can't."

How in the hell had she been able to dismiss her suspicions of his brother while they fucked?

He tore his toast in half, then held the pieces up and studied the ragged edges. "If they'd disagreed about working conditions that would be the end of it. Dr. Gilsdorf would look for someone to take his place." He dropped the toast on top of his eggs. "My brother was a hell of a lot more than a guide, wasn't he? What couldn't Dr. Gilsdorf let go of? What was enough to—oh, hell, I can't believe I'm saying this—what would make my brother desperate enough to kill?"

She stabbed her eggs. "What makes you suspect he was desperate?"

Or drunk. "I shouldn't have said that. Floyd isn't a violent person."

Her hand jerked up and down as she poked more holes in her breakfast. "I don't want to think anyone is capable of that kind of violence, but someone is. Someone with a lot at stake."

He grabbed her wrist, stopping her action. "Like Dr.

Wilheim. Maybe Michael or Booth." He wouldn't be surprised if Michael had been furious at Dr. Gilsdorf for giving him the brush-off, but Booth wasn't out of the realm of possibilities — unless whoever had knifed Dr. Gilsdorf hadn't known his victim.

Yeah, right. Mad Slasher running though Olympic. Happens all the time.

"Jay?"

There was the vulnerable tone he'd heard before. "What?"

She got up and walked over to the window. After wiping condensation off it with her sleeve, she peered out. The weather forecast was for a return to sunlight. He wondered if it would make a difference to Wolf.

"What if Floyd had shown Doc something he shouldn't have?"

His heart pounded. No way would Floyd reveal the existence of Grandparents Cave to an outsider — unless he'd been too drunk for caution.

"Is that what he did?" He didn't trust himself to touch Winter. "You're convinced my brother revealed something, and Dr. Gilsdorf wouldn't let it go."

"*Couldn't* let it go," she corrected. "Jay, Doc's whole career had led up to what he hoped to accomplish here. The stakes were so high."

They couldn't have been any higher than what a sober-again Floyd might have been forced to face. If he'd told Dr. Gilsdorf about Grandparents Cave, he could have believed only the professor's death would ensure the safety of what was in it.

He imagined turning Winter around. They'd wrap their arms around each other. Their mouths would meet. Maybe they'd return to the narrow bed and silence thoughts with sex. He'd listen for Wolf, thank Wolf.

Instead, he said, "I'll take you to him."

* * * *

Jay had had to clench his teeth to keep from commenting on his brother's housing. Floyd wasn't making much money, but he could have afforded something better than the single-wide trailer at the rear of a wrecking yard. Apparently, the previous renter had gotten free rent in exchange for guarding the rusting vehicles, and Floyd had agreed to do the same. Considering how many evenings Floyd spent at Seger's Bar, Jay didn't see how his brother could guard anything.

Winter looked around as he eased past the cars and trucks, but she didn't say anything. They'd barely spoken during the ride into Forks, and he'd spent it mentally trying to flesh out what she'd told him. No matter how much he needed the truth from Winter, she hadn't given him enough. He refused to beg, vowed to get Floyd to tell him everything.

Seeing the yard from her perspective embarrassed him. Accepting Floyd was one thing, but showing someone he cared about what his brother's life consisted of was something else. He wanted to explain that beneath the drunk was a good and sensitive man.

A man capable of murder?

So many weeds and bushes were between the trailer and business that most people weren't aware it was back there. Probably the owner's intention. He was so intent on dodging potholes, he nearly reached the trailer before he spotted Floyd's pickup. Seeing it here on a weekday surprised him.

"What is it?" Winter asked.

The concern in her voice ended his vow to say as little as possible. "He should be at work."

"Why didn't we go there?"

"I have a key to this place. I wanted to see if there was anything in there that might tie him to Dr. Gilsdorf."

"You think—"

He pinched the bridge of his nose until it hurt. "I don't know what to think."

"I'm sorry I asked you to come here. To involve you."

221

"Too late."

She stared at the trailer. "I don't want to do this."

Not as much as I don't. "Let's get this over with. He might be drunk. Maybe he lost his job. It's possible he hasn't been answering his phone or seeing Uncle Talio because he's ashamed. Hell. Oh, hell."

Her big, black eyes nearly undid him. "I wish it were last night," she whispered.

Me too.

The narrow wooden steps leading to the trailer tilted under Jay's weight. There wasn't room for both of them, and he'd deliberately taken the lead so — what? So he could confront his brother?

Although he knocked repeatedly on the flimsy metal door, Floyd didn't open it. The tension that had wrapped itself around him from the moment he'd spotted his brother's truck was getting worse. He couldn't deny the sick suspicion he didn't want to see what was inside. Finding the knob unlocked only added to his impulse to run.

"What is it?" she asked.

"I don't know." Had his brother drunk himself to death?

Too many seconds passed before he pushed the door in. It was so dark he could barely make out the secondhand couch and small TV on a box. Then he spotted his brother on the floor near a tipped-over chair in the space between the living room and kitchen.

"No." The word came out a whimper, a moan.

He couldn't say what reservoir of courage got him into the claustrophobic space. His brother was dead, lying on his side with his legs out straight and his arms curled in toward his chest. Blood stained the yellowed linoleum and thin carpet. Too damn much blood.

"Maybe he committed suicide," Jay heard himself say. "He killed Dr. Gilsdorf and then — "

Winter grabbed his arms and jerked him around to face her. Her face had whitened, but there was a fierceness in her eyes. "We have to get out of here. You aren't thinking straight right now. Don't jump to conclusions."

He dimly comprehended that she was trying to provide logic that would carry him through the nightmare, but it didn't matter.

His brother was dead.

Chapter Twenty-Three

Jay had barely moved since the Forks police arrived. Winter was glad he had his truck to lean against, because she wasn't sure he could support himself. Every time she looked up into his haunted eyes, she was taken back to when she'd found Doc. She'd had Wolf, even if she hadn't fully understood at the time. In contrast, Jay only had her, and she represented so much he didn't want to face.

Floyd was too young to die. Jay would spend the rest of his life asking himself if he could have done something to change the course of his younger brother's life. Right now, she didn't care if Floyd was responsible for Doc's death. She just didn't want anything to do with today – wanted to be in the forest with Jay while he showed her its secret places and told her what they meant to him.

The police chief, a well-built man in his late forties who'd introduced himself as Miles Klein, exited the trailer and headed toward her and Jay. After hauling Jay out of the trailer, she'd called nine-one-one. Would she have to remind him to contact his uncle? Would Jay want her to go with him, and would Talio want to have anything to do with her?

When the officers first arrived, Chief Klein had asked what they were doing here and whether they'd touched anything. The questions had been routine enough, but she'd noted that the chief's gaze had locked on each of them, longer on Jay than her. Maybe he'd seen that Jay was in shock.

"Did you get a close look at your brother?" the chief asked.

"No." Jay started to shake his head but stopped, making

her wonder if he was dizzy.

"Then you didn't see what was done to him."

"Done *to* him?" she parroted. "He— There's no doubt he didn't commit suicide?"

The chief had acknowledged her as she asked her question. Now he went back to studying Jay. "Someone killed your brother."

As nausea washed over her, she struggled to stay on top of it. No matter what the words' impact on her, it was worse for Jay. Hoping to give him strength, she grabbed the hand closest to her and brought it up to her chest.

"Who?" Jay slumped a little. "Who did it?"

"At this point, I'm not going to hazard a guess. I'm sorry, Mr. Raven, but I'm going to need you to work with me so we can identify a suspect." Chief Klein shot a look at the trailer. "We're going to be here for a while. I'm asking you to wait until we're done with the crime scene investigation."

She asked how long that might take, only to be told to be patient. Jay didn't say anything after agreeing to do whatever he could to help law enforcement. When the chief said he needed to go back inside, she opened the passenger door to Jay's truck and steered him into it. Once he was sitting, she went around the vehicle and got behind the steering wheel.

"Someone killed my brother," he muttered. "Did— I don't get how it happened, whether he suffered."

"I hope not."

Jay continued to stare at the trailer. "I have to tell my uncle."

Much as she longed to hug him, she didn't want to hamper his ability to concentrate. "It should be done in person. We owe him that much."

"We?"

Jay had been with her during the worst night of her life. The least she could do was return the gesture.

"After the police are done with me," Jay muttered, "that's when I'll go to Uncle Talio's place."

Don't shut me out. "You don't have to do this alone."

If her words made an impact, he gave no indication as he continued to stare out the window. She was still attempting to accept the reality of how Floyd had met his end, but it was far worse for Jay. She'd be strong for him, accept his moods no matter whether she understood them or not.

After what seemed like forever, he swiveled toward her. "Do you still believe my brother killed your friend?"

"We don't... This isn't the time to talk about that."

"What else are we going to do? This is the last thing I expected to... I didn't want to open the trailer door."

Her need to touch him became even stronger, but she continued to hold back. "You thought he might be — that you might find him dead?"

Jay closed his eyes. When he opened them, he looked as if he'd aged twenty years. "He's always been dependent on Uncle Talio and me. Even when he was sure I'd chew him out, he never told me to mind my own business. I should have — damn it, when I couldn't reach him, I should have come here."

"It was probably already too late."

He flinched. "We don't know how long he's been dead, what was used."

A knife maybe. Like Doc.

The possibility that the same person could have killed both men was more than she could wrap her mind around.

"How long does it take to determine a cause of death?" She was instantly sorry she'd asked.

"I'm not the one to ask." He rested his head against the seat back and again closed his eyes. "Floyd spent a lot of time at a bar. It's a place that's a pain in the ass for police."

I know. I've been in it.

"Cheap booze, customers without a lot going for them, sometimes short tempers. All the owner really cares about is keeping the doors open so he can pay his bills. There was a shooting there last year. A man was shot — in his leg. I think just about everyone there that night got arrested."

"I imagine you tried to convince Floyd to stay away from it."

"I'm not his father. He isn't—wasn't some kid I could ground."

Was this conversation helping Jay accept the reality of his brother's murder? She knew all too well that it would take time, because, in some respects, she still believed Doc was alive.

"Rumors were," Jay continued, "that the regulars at Seger's came armed. Floyd stopped carrying a pistol because Uncle Talio said he was asking for trouble, but he almost always had a knife on him."

And a knife had been used to kill Doc.

"What was it?" Jay's voice dropped "He pissed someone off at Seger's, and that person followed him back here?"

"Do you think that's possible?"

"My brother doesn't have enemies. What he does—did—is drink too much, and when he did he became impulsive. He says whatever pops into his mind, isn't always diplomatic."

That drunken impulsiveness might explain why Floyd had given Doc the wolf mask. "Maybe you can help the police by giving them the names of people he might have pissed off."

"I didn't know everyone Floyd hung out with. I wish to hell I'd made the effort, because maybe he'd still be alive."

No matter what she said, Jay would blame himself. She'd done the same thing by telling herself Doc might not be dead if she'd been with him.

Jay started rubbing his thighs much as she'd seen Talio do yesterday. "This is going to be so hard on my uncle. How am I going to tell him?"

She squeezed Jay's arm but stopped when he didn't respond. His eyes were still closed. She wished he had. Seeing him mourn made her feel as if she was intruding on a private experience, and yet she didn't want him to be alone.

The air inside the truck was getting stuffy, so she opened

her door. Jay didn't seem aware of what she'd done. As the minutes ticked along, she made a mental list of what Jay would have to do. Answering the policemen's questions would come first. Then he'd have to get in touch with his supervisor and tell him he needed some time off. He had to drive to his uncle's place and deliver the devastating news in person. Some kind of funeral would need to be planned, Floyd's belongings dealt with.

Did he want her with him while he was doing those things? Should she offer her body for escape, and would he take the gift?

When she spotted Chief Klein coming their way, her first impulse was to speed away with Jay. Instead, she shook his shoulder. When he opened his eyes, she pointed. Groaning, Jay got out of the truck. She joined him.

"There's going to be an autopsy," Chief Klein said. "Once that's over, we'll release the body to you. I've run into your brother at Seger's. Never had to arrest him or so much as threaten to."

"Could someone at the bar have done it?" Jay asked.

"It's possible. If it wasn't for some of those who hang out at Seger's, the town wouldn't need a police force. My officers are going to be in the trailer a while longer collecting evidence, but I'd like to talk to the two of you in my office. That way, I can record the conversation."

"Yes," Jay muttered. He pushed his fingers into his thick hair. "Did he suffer?"

The chief looked down at the mud oozing around his boots then met Jay's gaze. "He didn't die fast."

She squeezed Jay's fingers. Except for a faint nod, Jay didn't react to what he'd just learned. When he didn't say anything, she knew she had to.

"Was his throat cut? Is that what killed him?"

The chief stared down at her. "What made you— Wait, were you involved with that killing in Olympic?"

She swallowed around a too-familiar lump. "I found the body."

"And you believe there might be a connection between the two?"

Next to her, Jay tensed, adding to the warning bells already going off inside her. "They knew each other," she said. "I'm not sure how well."

"We need to talk about this," the chief said. "The media's going to show up, and I want to get the two of you away before that happens. I suggest we go to the station."

Jay pushed out a long breath. "All right."

* * * *

Jay had appreciated Winter asking him if he wanted her to drive, but maneuvering a vehicle might be the only thing he could control today. Every few seconds, the reality of his brother's murder slammed into him as if fresh. The rest of the time, he felt numb.

They'd only gone a few blocks when she touched his thigh. It took everything he had not to slap her hand away. Didn't she realize he couldn't take anything more?

"Jay, I didn't want to tell the chief about the relationship between Doc and your brother."

"You think their murders might be related?"

"Maybe."

His head cleared one layer at a time until he was staring at the void that had become his life. "I don't want there to be a connection. To wonder if what went on between them was enough for my brother to lose his life over — what the hell brought them together, Winter?"

She flinched. "You don't want to know."

The police station was just ahead. Instead of deciding where to park, he glared at her. "Are you trying to protect my feelings? If that's your intention, it's too late. Nothing can be worse than what I'm going through right now."

"I'm so sorry." She stroked his thigh, gave him too much to concentrate on.

Sorry wasn't enough. He needed his brother alive. "What

are you going to tell the chief?"

Her eyes looked larger than he remembered, full of emotions he didn't have the energy for. "Whoever killed Doc and Floyd needs to be brought to justice. I'll do what I can to help."

The millions of things he had to do today loomed over him, but he struggled to focus on the present. And on what he owed his little brother. "Make me one promise. Whatever it is you're keeping from me, tell me first."

"You want me to hold back from saying anything to the police?"

"When our parents died, Floyd crawled into my bed. We slept together for more than a year. I helped him with his homework, stood up for him when he was being bullied at school. He was my best man when I got married. So, yes, I deserve the truth. The whole damn truth."

She pressed her hand against his thigh. "All right," she whispered and opened the door. His leg where her hand had rested instantly cooled. As he watched her get out, he struggled to mentally return to last night but couldn't.

He didn't know how the hell he felt about Winter Barstow.

Chapter Twenty-Four

Chief Klein talked to Jay first while Winter waited in another room. In answer to her question, the city officer receptionist explained that a reporter from the area newspaper centered in Port Angeles was on his way here. Because the major news media had already reported on Doc's murder, it was possible they'd be interested in Floyd's death to see if there was a connection, but the receptionist hadn't heard from them yet. It felt unreal to Winter to realize Doc's death had resulted in coverage she was unaware of. Wouldn't someone have wanted to talk to her?

Then it dawned on her that the media didn't know where she was or how to get in touch with her. She'd be surprised if Dr. Wilheim hadn't made himself available for interviews. Maybe that was what she should have done if she wanted the grant committee to sit up and take notice of her.

This wasn't about her career or Doc's legacy. It was about two killings that might or might not be connected and about Jay's right to know about the wolf mask.

When Jay came out of where the chief had been talking to him, he looked at her but didn't say anything. His eyes were still haunted, but he seemed to be standing straighter than the last time she'd seen him. If he was getting over shock, grief had begun.

"My conversation with Jay revolved around his brother's comings and goings," the chief said once it was just the two of them. "Floyd wasn't a troublemaker, but he hung around with those we deal with on a regular basis. Jay is taking his brother's death hard."

"Yes he is." Even though she was sure Jay had already

done so, she explained how losing their parents at an early age had bonded the brothers. When she was done, she sat back in the metal chair and waited for the chief to start questioning her. Jay had asked her to hold back everything he deserved to hear first. She wasn't sure if she could do that, but she'd try. She could always get back in touch with Chief Klein.

After telling the officer about her professional connection with Doc and what had brought Doc to Olympic, she explained that, after his death, she'd learned that he'd been working with Floyd. "It wasn't as if Dr. Gilsdorf had formally hired Floyd. He needed someone who was more familiar with the forest. I'm not aware of the specifics of what they did. I'm guessing that in part Floyd acted as a guide."

"You said you learned about their arrangement after Dr. Gilsdorf's murder. How did that come about?"

She'd prepared herself for the question but was afraid her tension showed as she told the chief that Dr. Gilsdorf had left her a letter. "He had concerns about his safety. I believe he wanted to make sure I had the details of what he'd been doing, in case something happened to him."

Chief Klein looked up from his notes. "So you can't speak to whether Dr. Gilsdorf and Floyd's relationship was an amicable one?"

"I wish I could."

"Did you mention this relationship to those investigating Dr. Gilsdorf's murder?"

She frowned. "I don't believe I did. I didn't learn about their relationship until after I'd talked to the park's law enforcement."

"You need to."

Her mind kept spinning. She wanted to yell at Miles to slow down so she could put the puzzle pieces together. "You think—"

"Winter, a knife was used on Dr. Gilsdorf. Floyd almost always had a knife on him. He probably avoided a few fights by pulling it out."

"Jay just told me about it."

"Do you suspect Floyd might have had a reason to kill Dr. Gilsdorf?"

Be careful. Don't say something you aren't ready to. "I did, but Floyd wasn't the only one."

The chief rested his elbows on the table between them. "Who else?"

As she spelled out the competition between Doc and Dr. Wilheim, Michael's frustration and Booth's resentment, she realized she might be looking for motives when there weren't any.

"I should have said more about this to Christian Turney," she finished.

"Why didn't you?"

Because I was determined to defend Doc's reputation. Because having Wolf in my life meant so much. Because I wanted to be with Jay. "I guess I thought—Jay helped me work through my hunches, but that's all they are. I didn't want Christian to think I was trying to do his job."

When the chief didn't respond, she stumbled on. "You see how it is for Jay right now. He's an emotional mess. I was—still am the same way."

The police chief leaned back only to rock forward again. "We don't get many killings in this part of the country. Now, in the space of a few days, there have been two. You're connected to both of them. Closely to the first victim, peripherally to the second."

Guessing what he was about to say, she clenched her hands together under the table.

"Do you think you could be in danger?" he asked.

"It's a possibility."

"Hmm. Then why are you still here?"

Because of Wolf.

Because I want to learn where the wolf mask came from.

Because of Jay...

* * * *

After noticing that his hands were shaking as he opened the pickup door, Winter asked Jay if he wanted her to drive.

"I'm all right," he said and climbed behind the wheel. "I'm going to take you to Potlatch before I tell my uncle."

She hadn't expected that response. "What about what you want me to tell you?" she asked once they were on the road. "We have to talk about that. And I didn't give Chief Klein many details about what had been going on between Doc and Floyd."

He gave her a blank look followed by a closing down that made her feel as if they were thousands of miles apart. "That'll have to wait. I don't want Uncle Talio or the rest of the tribe to hear this from anyone except me."

Chief Klein's comment about her safety concerned her, but her cabin surrounded by large, mature trees represented serenity. Once she returned to it, she'd stand outside and tell Wolf how much it meant to her that he'd howled while Jay and she were having sex. Maybe Wolf would repeat his heartwarming cry. If she remained still and respectful, if she prayed to the forces she might never fathom, Wolf might step out of the shadows. Let her touch him.

Tell her whether Yakanon saw Doc or Floyd as the soulless one, or if —

Stark fear exploded inside her, compelling her to grab Jay's arm. He pulled over to the side of the street and stared at her. Silently demanded an explanation.

"Please take me with you." She didn't care that she sounded desperate. "Talio needs to hear what I have to say."

"Losing his nephew is enough for one day."

"Are you afraid of the truth?" Desperate determination forced out the words. At the same time, she hated every one. "You've been hiding from aspects of your heritage for years, and now you want to believe your brother was someone he wasn't."

Jay lifted his arm as if warding off what she'd just said. She could barely believe what she'd blurted. Surely, what she knew about Floyd could wait.

But Jay would hate her for keeping so much from him.

He probably already did.

* * * *

Uncle Talio seemed to have shrunk since Jay told him that Floyd had been murdered. Despite the cool wind coming from the ocean, his uncle had been outside when Winter and he arrived. Uncle Talio must have read something in Jay's expression, because he hadn't said anything, only looked out at his world. Winter had stood back while Jay knelt, took hold of his uncle's hands, and said the most difficult words he'd ever spoken.

"I won't let the media get to you," Jay said when he finally stood and sat in the chair near his still-silent uncle. Winter had propped herself against the railing and was looking at them. "I told the Forks police chief how reporters could get in touch with me. I'm not sure when we'll be able to bury him."

Watching his uncle slowly lift his head, Jay wondered if the task was almost too much for him. Neither of them had cried, yet.

"Are you here because you want to be?" Uncle Talio asked Winter.

She rubbed her throat. "Because I need to be."

Uncle Talio's hands on his knees twitched, and his chin trembled. "The first time I saw you, I felt compelled to tell you about Yakanon."

She slumped a little. "Yes."

After a long sigh, Uncle Talio went on. "Did I also tell you I didn't understand where the need came from? I've felt like that for days, uneasy in my skin, not wanting to face tomorrow."

A white-throated marbled murrelet was scratching the

ground around Jay's pickup. It reminded him of how he and Floyd had challenged each other to see who could identify the most birds. They hadn't done that in years.

"I thought Yakanon's lament might be for Dr. Gilsdorf," Uncle Talio continued. "I wanted to believe that my disquiet came because a soulless one had died in an area sacred to my people."

"Ghost Totem is sacred?" she asked while Jay wondered whether grief was getting between his uncle and his lifelong refusal to share what Olympic Forest meant to those whose roots weren't in it.

"Maybe I was wrong. Maybe Yakanon is crying for my nephew."

"No!" Jay blurted. "Floyd isn't—"

Uncle Talio held up his hand. "Your brother had turned his back on his upbringing the same as you did. He drowned his soul in liquor."

This wasn't the uncle he thought he knew, the man who didn't judge. Much as he wanted to insist this wasn't the time to bring up Floyd's shortcomings, Uncle Talio needed to say what was in his heart. Maybe once he was done finding fault with Floyd, he could start to simply mourn him.

"Is that what happened to Floyd?" Winter asked. "He killed too many brain cells?"

"He didn't deserve to be murdered," Jay retorted.

"I didn't say that." She pushed herself away from the railing and walked to the far end of the porch. She stood staring out at the forest for so long Jay wondered if she was communicating with Wolf.

Wolf, who'd spoken to him last night.

Looking as exhausted as he felt, she returned. "Talio, you asked why I came with Jay. It's because I need to tell both of you something." She knelt where he had. "This is the last thing I want to say, and I'd put it off if I could, but I can't."

She was so close he could touch her hair but didn't dare. He hadn't felt this sick the day his ex and he'd decided to end their marriage.

"I can't say if Floyd's actions were wrong." She angled her body toward him. "That's for you to decide, just as I've been wrestling with how I feel about Doc. Jay? I told you about a connection between Doc and Floyd."

"Yes."

"Doc left me a message detailing what he'd been able to accomplish here. He had concerns about his safety." She nodded at Uncle Talio. "Maybe you picked up on some of that. Maybe Yakanon did. Doc needed someone to help him locate the remote hunting camps and villages he was convinced existed. He asked the area Natives to work with him."

"We discussed that request," Uncle Talio said, "during a meeting held at Hoh River."

Her head bobbed. "And you decided not to."

"Can you blame us?" Jay demanded. Didn't she realize how unimportant this conversation was? "Relationships between Native Americans and government have always been complex, sometimes hostile."

He thought she might point out that Dr. Gilsdorf hadn't been a government agent, but she let it slide.

"For a while," she said, "Doc worked on his own, but he became more and more frustrated."

"So he approached my brother."

She pursed her lips. "Yes. I can tell you how that came about, but I'd rather not."

Because she wasn't willing to be completely honest after all? The longer he studied her, the more difficult it became to remember that he'd spent much of last night inside her. Or why he'd wanted to have sex with her.

Today, he just wanted her gone.

He wanted his brother back.

"Doc won your brother's trust," she was saying when he pulled himself back. "Floyd had alienated himself from his family. He needed someone to talk to."

He could have talked to me.

237

"Maybe Doc's dream of success became Floyd's. Maybe he couldn't say no. Whatever the reason—this is so hard—Floyd brought an artifact to Doc."

Jay had stood and yanked Winter to her feet before he realized what he'd done. "What kind of artifact?" he demanded.

If it had been him, he would have tried to break free, but she just stood there, looking sad. "A ceremonial mask representing a wolf." She stared at him until he had no choice but to bring her into focus. "Hundreds of years old but in perfect condition. Wherever it had been, it was safe from the elements."

Grandparents Cave!

"Have you seen it?" his uncle asked without emotion.

She trembled. "Yes."

"And because you're an anthropologist, you, what, decided it's authentic?" Why was he challenging her?

Eyes blazing, she leaned into him, challenged him with her presence. "I have absolutely no doubt that it is, but it has nothing to do with my damn degree."

All at once, he didn't want anything to do with her, so he shoved her. She stumbled backward. Watching her regain her balance, he cursed himself. He'd never used his physical strength against a woman.

"How can you be sure?" he asked instead of apologizing.

She stared at him until he wondered if she was looking for his soul. He should tell her he didn't have one. "Doc sent it to me. I was drawn to it. And I put it on. When placed it over my head, I heard Wolf for the first time in years."

We're not having this conversation. Damn it, I can't handle anything more.

"Where is the mask?" Uncle Talio sounded resigned.

Her chest rose and fell. She stopped shaking. "Where it's safe."

"Why didn't you tell me before?" Jay demanded.

He thought she was going to turn and run. If she did, he wouldn't stop her. "Too many reasons, Jay. Doc had no right doing what he did, but even though he was dead, I tried to cover for him. Having the mask made me feel complete. I finally had a connection to something."

He didn't want to care about her, not today with everything else he had to deal with. Wolf embraced her. In contrast, his spirit had abandoned him.

"You had no right to it."

"Didn't I?" She looked as if he'd struck her. Wounded but surviving. "I wanted to know where it came from, but I didn't dare ask anyone."

By 'anyone,' she meant him. "What would you do with the information?" he demanded. He wanted her the hell out of his life so he could mourn his brother. "Become famous?"

She backed away from him. "Damn you, Jay."

"Yes, damn me."

* * * *

The silent trip to Potlatch seemed to take forever. Before she and Jay had covered half of the distance, Winter had shoved aside her internal argument with him. She didn't hate him, she never would. Having sex had been a mistake, a matter of overloaded hormones and not enough considering the consequences.

She'd said things she shouldn't have, but so had he. His comment about her having no right to the mask, coupled with his assumption that she'd exploit it, hurt. She kept reminding herself of his fragile emotional state, but it wasn't enough. Surely he realized how wrong he was to think she'd put career ambition first.

"What are you going to do?" he asked as he pulled in near her vehicle. "You can't stay here much longer."

She would if the grant was awarded to her. More importantly, if what Jay and she'd begun had lasted, she would find a way to rent the cabin.

"That isn't your concern. I've been responsible for myself for a long time."

When he didn't reply, she regretted her words. Everything was such a mess between them, much of it her fault. She had to do something to make things better.

"There's something you deserve to know," she said. "The mask is in a storage unit in Forks."

His breathing hissed. "It belongs here."

Where was *here?* Someplace she had no right to?

"I'm going back," he said. "I don't want to leave my uncle alone."

Don't cry. "I'm glad you have each other."

More silence. More looking at the chasm between them.

"I don't want you staying in the cabin," he said as she got out. "It might not be safe."

The Forks police chief had said the same thing. She wished she could discuss the situation with Jay, but that, like everything else between them, had blown up around her. So much boiled down to whether the same person had killed both men, or whether Floyd had taken a knife to her mentor before getting killed himself.

"I'm not sure where to go," she admitted with her hand on the truck door and her body angled away from him.

"A motel."

What about the next day and the one after that? "I guess."

"Winter, the mask belongs to my people. I want it back."

"*Your* people? What does that make me?"

"I can't answer that."

Don't look at him. It's easier that way. "If you're trying to hurt me, you're succeeding."

"Ask yourself what you want."

How could she have believed she had feelings for this man, that they might have connected? "I will. And while I'm doing that, there's something you need to consider. Maybe Yakanon's lament wasn't for Doc or your brother. Maybe he's mourning an emotional death instead of a physical one."

"You're saying—"

"Where's your soul, Jay?"

Chapter Twenty-Five

By the time she reached the cabin, Winter wondered if maybe she shouldn't have told Jay about the mask. He was a good man, dedicated to his uncle, brother and the forest. Yes, his insistence that she had no right to the mask had hurt, but his brother had just been murdered. His emotions were even more of a mess than hers. Given the state he was in, he might not fully comprehend her connection to the mask.

She placed the key in the lock then stopped. Two warnings about her safety coming only a few hours apart had made their impact. What if Doc's killer was inside?

But why would anyone want her dead? Granted, she had the memory stick, but she didn't see how anyone knew. Just the same, when she pushed open the door, she stood back and waited for her eyes to adjust before entering. The bed where she and Jay had sex caught her in memories. For too long, she couldn't turn her attention to the half-open door leading to the bathroom. Finally, desperate to escape images of two naked bodies coming together, she stepped inside and entered the bathroom. Jay had left the shower curtain open. No boogeyman lurked in the tiny space.

She started to relax, only to realize she was past hungry and on her way to starving. Glad to have something to put her mind on, she started rummaging through the small refrigerator. She'd pulled out cold cuts for a sandwich when her cell phone buzzed.

Jay?

It wasn't his number, and, even though she didn't recognize it, she said, "Hello."

"Where are you?" a semi-familiar male voice asked.

"Who is this?"

"Michael Simpson. You gave me your number, remember? Where are you?"

"In Olympic." That was as close as she wanted to get to identifying her location.

"Are you near a TV? Did you read this morning's paper?"

TV or a newspaper had been the last things on her mind for days, and she told Michael so, followed by questioning why he'd asked.

"Dr. Wilheim is all over the news. He's so damn arrogant saying *I, I, I* until it makes me sick."

"What is he saying?"

"To hear him talk, you'd assume he'd already been awarded the grant and is at work. He didn't get the grant, did he?"

"Not as far as I—no, I'm certain he didn't. It's much too soon for any decision to have been made." *And I haven't formally thrown my hat into the ring.*

"That's what I thought. Why is he doing this? Could he be trying to convince the grant committee?"

"That's possible. He's never been at a loss for confidence."

"That's the impression I got. I met with him yesterday. Or, rather, I should say he insisted on seeing me. He pressed for information about my relationship with Dr. Gilsdorf."

She picked up a slice of ham, put it down. "What did you tell him?"

"I did my best to make it clear that it's essential for whoever does conduct the study to work closely with me so we can develop a coordinated plan designed to financially benefit the park."

She'd heard that from Michael before but didn't say anything.

"He blew me off," he added.

"I'm sorry."

"Are you? Dr. Gilsdorf was the same way, just a little more diplomatic than Wilheim is. I don't get you people.

242

You're—"

"*You* people? You're lumping me in with Doc and Dr. Wilheim?"

"I'm talking about academia in general. You might be easier to work with. Maybe we could develop a mutually beneficial relationship. In fact, that's why I called. I want to talk to you about how you propose to respond to what Dr. Wilheim is doing. I might suggest you use the same media blitz. With your youth, looks and nationality, the public will side with you. I want to give you the names and contact information for the reporters Dr. Wilheim talked to."

Now? Her refrigerator door was still open, not that it mattered. "It's a rough day," she said. "Jay Raven's brother has been murdered."

The second silence lasted even longer than the first one had. "Do you suspect the killings are connected?"

"I don't know." To hell with weighing every word. If Michael had killed Doc, he needed to comprehend he wouldn't get away with it. Eventually, law enforcement would catch up to him. "Maybe."

"Maybe?"

"It isn't as if Doc and Floyd weren't acquainted."

"You're sure about that?"

"Positive."

Michael didn't stay on the phone long. He immediately changed the subject from the relationship between Doc and Floyd to insisting she write down the numbers he'd called to give her. She deliberately kept her mind blank until she'd finished making her sandwich. Then she started replaying what the park's budget officer had said. He hadn't sounded shocked by the news of Floyd's murder.

After setting down the food she no longer wanted, she stared at her cell phone. She needed to talk to Jay, to hear his voice, to ask his help in sorting things out. But Jay Raven was dealing with his brother's violent death. Facing the reality that she had the mask—and had kept that from him.

As if that wasn't enough, she'd asked Jay to consider

whether Yakanon might be mourning his spiritual death.

Considering the stakes, she didn't regret asking Jay what she had, but her timing and how she'd done it had been terrible. She wanted him to connect with his spirit so he could experience the peace and unity she did when Wolf reached out to her. Last night, Wolf had allowed Jay to hear him. Did that mean Wolf believed Jay was getting closer to his spirit?

Jay wanted her to go to a motel, but the thought of closing herself in an impersonal room with nothing except the TV to distract her made her want to scream. Just going to Forks had made her feel as if she were leaving home.

Home. A place to belong.

To thank for accepting her.

Her forefinger shook a little as she punched the first number Michael had given her. As she waited for whoever was on the other end to answer, she pondered what the reporter at the Seattle TV station might be like. What she didn't expect was to hear a feminine "hello." Off balance, she introduced herself as an anthropologist who'd been working with Dr. Gilsdorf. When Lisa Salterson didn't immediately respond, Winter explained that Dr. Gilsdorf had been at Olympic before Dr. Wilheim arrived and that Dr. Gilsdorf's murder hadn't been solved.

"Thanks for the reminder," Lisa said. "I was off yesterday when we ran the piece about Dr. Gilsdorf. Most of it was based on interviews with law enforcement."

"I'm staying in Olympic," she said. *At least I am right now.* "I haven't seen the news lately, but I believe Dr. Wilheim told you he has already taken over Dr. Gilsdorf's project. That isn't true. In fact, I'm going to do everything I can to honor Dr. Gilsdorf's memory by stepping into that role."

"Oh. Okay. I'm not sure why you're calling me."

It dawned on her that her disputing Dr. Wilheim wasn't particularly newsworthy. She'd stepped outside. Last night's downpour had given way to mist in the morning. The afternoon was partly sunny, the ground damp, and drops still slipped off pine needles and leaves. Everything felt right.

Part of her.

"Dr. Wilheim hasn't been cleared as a possible suspect in his fellow professor's murder." For all she knew, Christian and the other law enforcement rangers hadn't tagged Dr. Wilheim as a suspect, but she did, and today that was all that mattered.

"Is that so?" Judging by Lisa's tone, she had the reporter's attention. "Of course, I'll have to verify —"

"While you're doing that, you might look into a possible connection between Dr. Gilsdorf's death and a killing that took place in Forks."

"Wait a minute. I want to check a few things."

Lisa put her on hold, leaving Winter to listen to elevator music. Moving the phone away from her ear, she stepped into the woods toward where she thought she'd heard Wolf last night.

She might not have a job, which meant she'd have to give up her place in San Diego. If the grant was awarded to her, she'd hopefully rent something in Forks, although she'd prefer to stay here.

Just her and Wolf, unless Jay —

How was Jay doing? Should she have found a way to keep things going between them so he'd have her to lean on? Should she have refrained from telling him she had the wolf mask? Much as she wanted to be his rock, there was too much between them, too many cutting words on both sides.

Maybe he just wanted her out of his life. The kindest thing she could do for him was to leave him alone.

But she didn't want to be anywhere else. She needed this place.

"Are you still there?" Lisa said, coming back on the line. "You were talking about Floyd Raven, weren't you? I talked to our crime reporter. He says preliminary impressions are Raven had been dead at least a day when he was found."

A day during which Jay had believed his brother to be alive.

"I also learned a little more about what happened to Dr. Gilsdorf. The same kind of weapon was used on both men."

"Yes."

Lisa muttered something under her breath. "You said you're in the forest. Coming to Seattle will take several hours, but would you be willing to meet me in Port Angeles?"

"So soon?"

"The story won't be ready in time for the evening news, but we can hint about it. Hopefully, I'll have it put together for eleven o'clock. Have you talked to any newspapers yet?"

"No. I was going to—"

"I'd love to talk you into holding off until I've had a chance to interview you. And if you can add anything to punch up your contention that Dr. Wilheim's motives are suspect—viewers love a mystery."

She wasn't interested in the station's viewership. What mattered to her in ways that went deeper than being able to pay her bills, deeper even than learning who had killed Doc, was forging a future for herself in this incredible place.

In showing Jay that she had as much right to claim the mask as he did.

Even though she didn't want to be late for her meeting with Lisa, she had to do something first. As she dug through her belongings for the card Booth Deavers had given her, she considered taking all her belongings with her, but realized that would call for several trips between the cabin and her car. Jay had made an important point. She might not be safe at Potlatch.

Hopefully, she could find a motel in Port Angeles after the interview, come back here, load up and check into the motel before she collapsed.

Before the need to remain in the forest became stronger than concerns for her personal safety.

When Booth answered, she berated herself for not deciding what she was going to say. However, he didn't give her time to stumble through a request that he advocate for her over Dr. Wilheim—unless Dr. Wilheim wound up being arrested.

"Are you calling because you don't agree with Dr. Wilheim's techniques?" he asked.

"I take it you've seen his interview."

"And I read the article in this morning's paper. What do you think of — ?"

"I haven't read it," she said then explained that Michael had told her.

"What does Michael want from you? Never mind. I can answer that. Of course, if my employment was dependent on the bottom line like his is—what am I saying? I, too, am under pressure to produce. Everyone is. So, Winter, to rephrase my earlier question, what do *you* want of *me*?"

Maybe she'd been wrong to believe Booth would support her goal of taking over for Doc, but she had to find out. Wishing she could see him so she could study his expressions, she explained about her upcoming TV interview.

"I'd like to be able to say you and I will work together if I get the grant. That—you might not agree with me—you'd prefer to be in partnership with me over Dr. Wilheim."

He chuckled. "You want me to say I've chosen a young and intelligent woman over an insufferable windbag?"

"I wasn't going to put it like that."

"Let me ask you something. How much credit do you intend to give me *if* we locate the remnants of a Native settlement or settlements? Maybe find one or more valuable artifacts?"

Like the wolf mask. "Is that possible?"

"Maybe."

Tired as she was, she couldn't decipher his mood. What if he'd come across something in the old records and was intending to combine that with Doc's material? Maybe Doc had let something about the mask's existence slip around Booth.

She couldn't quite come up with a smile. Deception didn't come easy. "The chance to make my mark — of course I can't do that without your help. You've been here longer than I have and have so much at your disposal."

"If, and it's simply *if* at this point, we found something, would your budget increase?"

"Are you talking about an essentially intact site?"

He chuckled. "Let's dream big. What would happen then?"

"I'm not sure. It might become a land grab."

"But you and I would get credit for discovering it."

"Of course." She had no idea whether any credit would come their way, but obviously that was what Booth needed to hear.

"Our relationship needs to be formalized," he said. "No more relying on a man's word."

Had Doc promised Booth something? "Certainly. Can I tell the reporter we're in agreement about how we want to proceed?"

"I don't have a problem with that. Is Jay Raven going with you?"

Her heart felt as if it were being squeezed. "Jay? No. Why do you ask?"

"I thought I picked up on something between the two of you. I'm sorry he won't be accompanying you."

"He can't. His brother..."

"What about his brother?"

"He's dead. Murdered."

"Really?"

Yes, really. And it's tearing Jay apart, but maybe you don't care. Maybe you already knew.

Chapter Twenty-Six

Uncle Talio's place was filled with Hoh. Jay wanted to be alone with his thoughts, but his uncle clearly appreciated the support. Several women had brought food, and a half-dozen children were clambering around the front porch. The adults had come inside as late afternoon shadows cooled the air. The talk ranged from funeral planning once Floyd's body had been released, to Floyd's generosity in helping with the fishing that was a vital part of the tribe's economy. No one asked Jay what he'd seen when he opened the trailer door, and he didn't mention that he hadn't been alone.

Would Winter fit in here? Even though he didn't want to think about her and what she'd said about his lack of a soul, he couldn't stop wondering how she would react to the loving support his uncle and he were receiving.

The TV was on, but he didn't pay attention until suddenly all conversation stopped. Everyone stared at the evening news. A camera zoomed in on Floyd's trailer.

"The body of a young Hoh was discovered here earlier today," a disembodied voice said. "Preliminary indications are he was stabbed multiple times and had been dead for a while. Law enforcement declined to speak about a possible suspect except to state that the victim appears to have been targeted specifically, and there's no danger to the public."

That was all his brother was worth—less than a minute, highlighted by the unspoken message that Floyd's lifestyle had led to his death?

"—a twist on a piece we brought you earlier," a tall, slim female reporter was saying when he broke free of his thoughts. "Intrigue and conflict surround the violent death of an anthropologist whose body was found in Olympic. Today, I interviewed anthropologist Winter Barstow, who disputes the statements made by Dr. Wilheim, the anthropologist who stated here that he'll be continuing Dr. Gilsdorf's work. Ms. Barstow contends Dr. Wilheim is a suspect in his colleague's murder. We hope to bring you the full story on the eleven o'clock news."

The teaser ended with a shot of Winter looking into the camera. Seeing her, even with her grim expression, made his heart pound.

What the hell was she doing?

Feeling old, he pushed himself to his feet and walked outside. The children were making so much noise he didn't reach for his phone until he was in the trees. Winter answered after the third ring.

"I just saw the news," he said. "You can't do the police's work for them."

"I can't simply wait."

He shouldn't have called. Her voice was like fire to his nerve endings. Maybe tomorrow he could deal with her, but not on one of the worst days of his life.

"You don't understand?" she asked. "I hoped you would."

His surroundings blurred, and he grabbed hold of a branch to keep from swaying. "Have you told anyone about the mask?"

"I—no."

"I'd like to believe you."

She gasped. "Is your intention to hurt me?"

Maybe. "Stay out of what doesn't concern you."

For a moment, he thought she'd hung up. "The only thing I can do for Doc is attempt to protect his memory. I have to prevent Dr. Wilheim from learning—"

"I get that you don't like Dr. Wilheim, but don't convict him."

"Is that why you called? To tell me I'm crazy?"

"No." He wasn't sure what he felt about anything. "You

need to consider all possible ramifications of your actions before you say anything."

"It's too late. The interview...Jay, Olympic completes me. The mask is part of it."

"Damn it, you shouldn't have waited so long to tell me about it. It belongs to my ancestors, not you."

She hung up.

He tried to call her back, but she didn't pick up, and he didn't leave a message. What would he say?

From where he stood, he couldn't see the house where his brother and he had grown up. Everyone was waiting for him to return. His uncle would shake off his sorrow to again ask if he was all right, and he needed to ask Uncle Talio the same thing. Instead, as the day ended, a mental image of Winter Barstow standing naked and wanting formed in his mind. At first, her dark eyes held him prisoner. Then, his attention moved to the swell of her left breast and the wolf head likeness there.

"Raven," he whispered. "You came to me that day during my spirit quest. For years, I told myself it was my imagination, but it wasn't. I'll never comprehend the way of spirits. Maybe if I hadn't been so determined to focus on my future that I let go of the past...what happened before now doesn't matter, does it?"

He didn't expect a response, but that didn't stop him from listening intently.

When only the forest spoke, he reminded himself that he had an extended family while all Winter had was a howl.

* * * *

Port Angeles was maybe three times the size of Forks and had a number of motels. After narrowing her search down to three possibilities, Winter headed back to Potlatch. She should have nailed down a reservation, but, on the heels of her devastating conversation with Jay, she hadn't been able to force herself to talk to anyone. Besides, it would soon be

251

dark, and she needed to load up her car.

Instead of pulling her belongings together, she turned off her cell phone so she'd be less likely to call Jay, woke up her laptop and put the flash drive in the USB port. She was attempting to distance herself from what had gone wrong between Jay and her by checking files for clues about where the mask had come from. Much as she wanted to dismiss the possibility that Booth had more knowledge about ancient Native settlements than he'd let on, he had pored over the oral histories. It was possible he'd come across a piece of a puzzle she barely grasped. Another puzzle piece might be in Doc's notes. Sadly, she couldn't ask Floyd where the precious wolf likeness had come from.

And she couldn't ask Jay, because he'd say she had no right to that information.

He was wrong! Her being an anthropologist meant nothing next to her Native American heritage.

An anthropologist who'd told Jay she was determined to shed any and all possible light on what had once existed deep in the forest.

She rubbed her forehead, but her attempt to massage away her conflicting thoughts failed. For the first time in her life she felt as if she had a purpose. Maybe discovering where the mask had come from wasn't enough, but with night enveloping the small cabin, Wolf silent and Jay locked in his own turmoil, that was all she had.

Swiping back tears, she stopped looking at the dark window and concentrated on the words on the screen.

* * * *

Most of their visitors had left, and Jay had talked his uncle into taking a painkiller for his aching leg, when his cell phone sounded. His heart thudded, only to resume its normal beat when he realized it wasn't Winter.

"Jay," a male voice said. "It's Chief Klein."

The man in charge of investigating his brother's murder

was the last person Jay wanted to talk to tonight, but he didn't have a choice.

"I was hoping you could help me with something," Chief Klein said, "but, before I get into that, I need to tell you what I learned from the coroner."

"Tonight?" Fortunately, Uncle Talio had gone outside to say goodbye to a cousin.

"I'm sorry. Maybe I should wait until tomorrow, but my guess is you've been contacted by a number of people who were acquainted with your brother. I'd like you to think about this while those conversations are fresh in your mind."

None of the visitors had been Floyd's drinking buddies, but several of the younger Hoh had told stories about hanging out with the fun-loving Floyd.

"First," Chief Miles said after Jay agreed, "we found rope burns and fiber on your brother's wrists and ankles."

"Oh." His mind wouldn't, couldn't compute.

"More fibers were on a chair."

He remembered a tipped-over chair in his brother's trailer.

"Jay, your brother had been tied up."

Horror slammed into Jay. He staggered toward his recliner but couldn't sit down.

"Someone made sure he wasn't going anywhere," the chief went on. "The ropes that had held him to the chair were severed. It's possible your brother struggled, so he and the chair landed on the floor. The killer cut him free so it was easier for him to get to Floyd. I hate telling you this, but a knife was repeatedly used on him before whoever did this buried it in his belly."

He was going to be sick! Only, if he threw up, he wouldn't be able to concentrate. "That's what killed him?"

"The autopsy isn't complete, but my guess is yes."

The room spun and went out of focus. At the same time, his thoughts crystallized. "My brother was tortured."

"I'm afraid so."

253

"Why! Damn it, why?"

"That's what I hope you can help me with. The timing for this conversation sucks, but I have to do my job. Can you think of anyone who hated Floyd enough to do that to him?"

Barely aware of what he was saying, Jay admitted he couldn't. He needed time to process what he'd just learned but would call back. After offering another apology and sympathy, the chief said goodbye.

Uncle Talio and he seldom used the back door, but he went there because he didn't want anyone to see him walking into the woods. He still didn't trust his stomach to hold onto its contents. He could see a few stars but not the moon, because it was behind the treetops.

Neither Floyd nor he had ever been afraid of the dark. Even when he'd snuck up on his kid brother, Floyd had laughed. Floyd, a sober Floyd, would enjoy being out here.

He didn't deserve what had been done to him.

Nightmare!

Jay stopped and pressed his back against a tree trunk, taking strength from the solid growth. His eyes had adjusted to being outside, and he could now make out the faint shapes of his childhood world. Instead of trying to come up with the names the police chief had asked for, he mentally replayed his three-day-and-night solitary trek while searching for his spirit. He'd focused on the stories his uncle and other elders had told him about fishermen whose boats capsized or hunters who fell through frozen lakes. Instead of dying, those people entered the land of the salmon or seals. His favorite had been the story of how K'wati, the shape-shifting Changer, had killed the chief of the wolves and escaped the rest of the pack by striking the ground with his carved comb and creating a cliff the wolves had to run around. Later, K'wati had poured oil on the rocks. The oil had morphed into a river, again slowing the wolves.

Wolf?

Wolf mask.

Jay's mouth dried. He suddenly wanted nothing more than to return to the house, but his mind kept whirling. Processing.

He had no doubt where the ceremonial mask had come from. For reasons he might never understand, Floyd had taken it from Grandparents Cave and given it to Dr. Gilsdorf. The anthropologist had then sent it to Winter. That, more than what she felt for the man she called Doc, was what had brought her here.

Floyd and Dr. Gilsdorf were dead. Murdered in essentially the same way. The only other person to have recently handled the mask was still alive.

A primitive growl slipped past his lips as he hauled out his phone and punched in her number. It went straight to voicemail.

"Call me," he ground out. "Now. You're in danger."

* * * *

Winter's head ached, and her vision kept blurring. She hadn't been at the computer for long, but the day had caught up to her. Exercise in the form of packing up and leaving the cabin made more sense than looking for something when she wasn't sure what that something was. One good thing about being brain dead, the idea of driving away from Olympic wasn't as painful as earlier. She'd take this one day at a time, one step followed by another.

As for being alone, she knew how to do that. Besides, her solitude wasn't total, because she had Wolf.

Not Jay but Wolf. She'd make that enough.

After repacking her groceries, she stepped outside. Because her hands were full, she kicked the door closed instead of putting things down and locking it. Leaving the laptop in there made her uneasy, but she'd be back in about fifteen minutes. She wished she'd thought to put on her headlamp, but the moon helped some. As she made her way down the dirt patch, she thought back to when a foster father had locked her in a closet because she hadn't done her homework to his standards. She'd spent that night and too many others curled up in the dark, but not once had she cried or begged.

That child was a woman now, resourceful and unemployed, independent and confused. Embracing what Wolf and the mask represented while struggling to strip Jay from her mind and heart. She started to shake her head at the contrasts when an unexpected sound to her right caught her attention.

The sound again. Something brushing against vegetation. "Wolf?"

The figure wasn't four-legged. She had a good second in which to comprehend she was being attacked before intense light blinded her. Someone slammed into her, knocking her backward onto the ground. Her head slammed against something. Woozy, she let go of her groceries and attempted to roll over so she could get onto her hands and knees. Masculine strength forced her onto her back again. The heavier body straddled her at the waist. Powerful hands circled her throat. Thumbs pressed against her windpipe. Robbed of oxygen, she thrashed, scratched, kicked.

Pain filled her. And terror. She couldn't breathe! Someone was killing her! Taking her into darkness. Turning off the light.

Chapter Twenty-Seven

Rope circled Winter's wrists, keeping her arms behind her. A gag had been shoved into her mouth and tied around her head. Her ankles were lashed together. Despite her restraints, the realization that she wasn't dead and could again breathe kept panic from winning. As she became more clearheaded, she concentrated on making sense of what had happened. Cool dampness from the ground was seeping through her clothes and making her shiver. Swallowing brought tears of pain. In contrast to the disbelief she'd felt when she found Doc's body, tonight became crystal clear. She'd been captured.

"I did it," a male voice muttered, making identifying him impossible.

She had to be patient, because her survival might depend on it. One thing, the intense light she'd seen earlier had come from the headlamp her attacker wore.

He clamped gloved hands over her shoulders and pulled her into a sitting position. Hard as it was, she kept from fighting him. She had to lean forward to keep from falling back.

"You're going to stay right here while I put those groceries back and get what I need." He slapped her shoulder. "You aren't going anywhere. I've made damn sure of that."

Booth!

He scooped up her groceries and walked away, heading back toward the cabin. She started pulling on the ropes. No matter how much she twisted and strained, however, all she accomplished was to tighten her bonds. Helplessness settled around her, threatening her sanity when she needed to say in control if she stood a chance of living.

All too soon, Booth returned, carrying her backpack and the laptop. He was still wearing gloves, which meant he hadn't left fingerprints. "These are going in my vehicle." He held up the pack and computer. "By the time anyone realizes you're gone, I'll have moved them to where they'll never be found."

But her car would still be in the parking lot.

Booth left her again. Knowing he was taking the laptop with the flash drive in it to the parking lot where, undoubtedly, his vehicle was made her sick. Eventually, unless she stopped him, he'd find Doc's letter.

Did it matter anymore? Did anything matter except staying alive?

When he rejoined her, he didn't say anything as he untied her legs. Judging by his grunts as he hauled her to her feet, she wasn't making it easy for him, but fighting fear taxed her. Hating what she had to do, she didn't resist when he grabbed her elbow and steered her deeper into the wilderness. The headlamp made it easy for him to guide them around one obstacle after another. His breathing was as ragged as hers.

Alone. In ways she'd never fathomed or experienced.

No, she wasn't alone, because her captor was with her. Booth hadn't explained why he was doing this, but there could be only one reason—he'd killed Doc and probably Floyd and intended to do the same to her.

But not right away. Maybe not before explaining what had led him to this point.

Attempting to comprehend Booth's motivation made it nearly impossible for her to concentrate on where she was going. She tripped on a tree root and started to fall. He jerked her upright.

"Don't play stupid games with me, Winter. You don't want to make me mad."

Wasn't he already? Didn't anger drive his actions?

Maybe not. He must want something from her. Until he'd

gotten whatever it was, he'd keep her alive.

Then —

Wolf? Are you out there? Do you see what's happening? Can you stop him? Angry at herself for capitulating with Booth, she dug in her heels. Booth punched the back of her head. She lurched forward.

"You want another lesson? Believe me, I'll do it." He paused. "I've had practice. Be patient. We'll get there."

She couldn't fathom what he meant by *there* any more than she could make sense of anything else tonight. Some twenty-four hours ago, she'd been taking off her clothes for Jay, and now this.

Jay. Dealing with his brother's murder. Nowhere near Potlatch. Unaware of what had happened to her. Wanting her out of his life.

Hating her for keeping part of his legacy from him.

* * * *

Night lurked behind Jay as he opened the door to Winter's cabin. When he'd seen her car in the parking lot, he'd been torn between anger and concern. It didn't matter whether she returned his call, as long as she understood she was in danger and did something about it. Her fascination with Olympic could wait until the area was safe. He'd parked near her vehicle and jogged to her cabin as different scenarios played out in his mind. She might have fallen asleep without hearing his message or been too upset to listen to it. He could handle either of those possibilities. What he couldn't handle was finding her dead.

He switched on the light and stared at the lifeless space. This wasn't right. She should be in here.

Holding on to his nerves as best he could, he took inventory of what was inside. It looked as if she'd been in the process of moving out, so where was she?

Even though it was the last thing he wanted to do, he made a mental journey back to Ghost Totem and the sight of Dr. Gilsdorf's body. If Winter hadn't been looking for her friend, he might have never been found.

"Winter." His voice echoed in the claustrophobic space, and he stepped outside. "Winter! Where are you?"

No matter how much he strained to hear, his pounding heart was making too much noise. There was only one explanation—someone had her.

The same person who'd killed Dr. Gilsdorf and maybe his brother.

"Winter! Answer me." *Please.*

Even with the familiar night sounds, silence pressed around him. She could be anywhere. Unable to respond. Maybe so far away she couldn't hear him.

Maybe dead.

"No." The sound of his voice surprised him. He couldn't remember ever feeling this desperate. Fighting a fear that made breathing difficult, he called her name once more. He knew this part of Olympic as well as anyone, not that it made any difference, because the forest was a tangled maze of primal growth.

"Raven," he whispered. "Please, I can't do this on my own."

His body felt as if it might snap as he waited and then waited some more. Until the last few days, he'd relegated his spirit to an untouched corner of his mind. Like someone who never prayed until hit with a crisis, he had no right to expect Raven to acknowledge him.

But he had nothing else. He needed Raven.

"Please." He worked to make his voice sound stronger. "I'm sorry. So sorry. I shouldn't have given up on you. Raven? Are you out there?"

A gentle wind rattled the treetops to his left.

Chapter Twenty-Eight

Winter and Booth had walked for what felt like at least a mile when light from his headlamp revealed a grove of big-leafed maples. The thick trunks were partly covered in moss. More moss clung to exposed roots while lacy leaves served as a stark contrast to the aged trees. He shoved her toward one of the huge maples with a hollow at the base. Only a few hours ago, she would have loved the site. Now the thought that she might die here chilled her veins. She didn't want to die!

"On your knees." He didn't give her time to decide whether to obey but again hit the back of her head. She barely had time to turn her face to the side before she slammed into the tree. Booth kicked her feet out from under her, and she landed chest-down half inside the opening. The smell of damp age filled her senses.

Booth snaked a rope around her ankles, and, despite her struggles, jerked it tight. That done, he rolled her over so she looked up at him with her arms bowing her back. No locked or barred door had been this confining.

"There. I can't believe— Damn, I really did it."

Desperate for an explanation, she chewed on her gag. Another wave of fear threatened to overwhelm her, but she fought it as she'd fought parts of her childhood, by separating herself from her body.

She wasn't Booth's prisoner after all. Instead, she'd gone hiking with Jay. When they were sure no one was around, they'd stop where the ground was soft and no insects lived. Hungry for each other, they'd sink to their knees and reach out. First one of them and then the other would whisper of need and commitment. He'd forgiven her. Doc and Floyd were alive. Olympic embraced her.

"Where is it?" Booth demanded.

Confused, she shook her head. The headlamp half-blinded her, preventing her from seeing his expression.

"You have it. I have no doubt you do."

Despite her turmoil, she put one and one together. It was Booth who'd broken into Doc's cabin, but he hadn't found what he was looking for.

Again, she shook her head.

He loomed over her. "Let me explain something. I'm good at planning what I need to do. It's vital. No one will be coming in or out of Potlatch until morning, so I have plenty of time. More than you do." He grunted. "I found your car keys in your pocket while you were unconscious. My vehicle's at the Sol Duc campground. It was a hell of a walk to Potlatch, but I don't want anyone knowing I'm here. That way, I won't get caught. I cover all my bases. When I'm done with you, I'll take your car. Make it disappear."

Like I will.

She had no idea how long it would take him to reach Sol Duc after, she assumed, hiding her car somewhere in the forest, but it didn't matter, because, by then, she'd be dead.

Dead. Her life over.

He positioned himself near her head and stared at her. If only she knew what he intended to do with her.

"I'm going to remove the gag, but you'd better not yell." He held up a knife so the light glinted off it.

Had this weapon killed Doc—and Floyd?

Jay!

"There's no one back here, and the forest swallows sound." He placed the knife on the ground and reached behind her head. The gag loosened. "You and I are going to talk. We have to."

And then you'll treat me like you did Doc and Floyd.

"All right," he said as he pulled the cloth out of her mouth. When he picked up the knife, she noted that his hand was shaking. "I ask questions. You answer."

She moved her mouth about and licked her lips. "I hear you."

"But you're telling yourself there's no way you'll give me what I want or that I'm really going to kill you. Go on, lie to yourself."

Keeping her head off the ground took effort, but otherwise she'd look defeated. "Why did you kill them?"

"Them?" He wiped his mouth with his free hand. "So you figured out at least some of it. I gave Floyd every chance to tell me what was going on between him and Gilsdorf, spell out what had gotten Gilsdorf so damn excited. He kept praying to—hell, I don't know what he was praying to."

His spirit.

"I told him he didn't have to die, that one secret wasn't worth his life." Booth sighed. "Maybe I meant it. I shouldn't have tried to get him to work with me, but I had no idea he was such a damn mess." He grabbed her hair and forced her head up. "You aren't a mess. You want to live. You'll do whatever it takes to stay alive. The thing is, I can break down your defenses. Unfortunately, I've gotten good at it." He touched the knife tip to her throat. "I need some information from you. I couldn't get it from Gilsdorf or Floyd, but it'll be different this time. It has to be."

Much as she hated the idea of doing anything Booth wanted, in the end, she might not have a choice. Maybe, if she kept him from losing his temper, he'd let her live.

No, he won't.

Mentally recoiling at the thought, she kept her attention on his nearly indiscernible form.

"You didn't come to Olympic because you had nothing better to do." Booth sounded tired. "Gilsdorf confided in you about something. I have no doubt he did. What was it?"

"I don't know what you're talking about."

"Liar." He struck her cheek, knocking her flat. "Judging by the methods I used on Gilsdorf and Floyd, you're thinking I can't control myself, but I know what I'm doing."

"How can you say that? There's no excuse for —"

He slapped her again. "You have no idea what I've gone through, what I've had to put up with. I believe in being rewarded for my efforts. Not being taken for granted."

"Why would someone do that?"

"What a stupid question. Because they're selfish. When I asked Gilsdorf what he thought of the material I generously gave him access to, he said it was useful. Damn it, it..." He sobbed. "My turn! Finally my turn."

* * * *

Night had become his enemy. So had his surroundings.

Nothing was right, everything he needed gone.

Abandoned by Raven.

Jay caught his toe on something and went sprawling. Cursing, he threw out his hands in an attempt to cushion his fall, but his forehead hit the ground. He heard a cracking sound followed by sudden, intense darkness.

Abandoned.

As he got to his knees, he realized the fall had broken his headlamp. He pulled it off and fiddled with it but couldn't get it to turn back on.

Where was he? Did he belong here? More important, where was Winter?

"Raven," he whispered. "Please. I need you as I've never needed anything in my life."

The forest swallowed his words, leaving him alone. Still on his knees, he bowed his head.

"Raven. Please."

Silence.

* * * *

Booth had let go of Winter's hair. Despite that, his tension swirled around her. Judging by his gulping breaths, he was trying to regain self-control. She wouldn't last if he couldn't, but she knew not to say anything.

"Useful! What a demeaning thing for him to say. Ropes and knives are useful. What I loaned him... When he kept putting off returning the files, I got suspicious. When I asked him what he was up to, he said I'd know when the rest of the world did."

She hated the idea of Doc taunting Booth, but maybe that was how Booth had interpreted things.

"What does this have to do with me?"

Booth pulled the lamp off his head and placed it on the ground. The intense light illuminated the forest in all directions for some ten feet. His eyes were half-closed, and yet she recognized savage determination.

"Nothing. Tonight is all about me."

Booth was self-absorbed. What he wanted or believed he was entitled to came before everything else, even human lives.

"Gilsdorf went from acting like we were colleagues to closing up. He stopped talking about what he was doing. Shut me out." Booth again touched the knife to her throat. "Something had excited him. I saw it in his eyes. I deserved to know what it was."

She guessed he felt that way because he believed that what was in the histories had been the key to Doc's discovery. The explanation for what Booth had done to Doc was so simple, at least from his perspective. Except he was wrong. Floyd and the wolf mask had been the key.

"What brought you here? If it hadn't been for you poking around Ghost Totem, there wouldn't have been anything left of Gilsdorf's body."

"Someone would have found—"

"You have no idea how quickly cougars, coyotes and bears can break down a body." He patted her leg. "That's why I brought you here."

Wolf! Jay!

When Booth leaned back and stared at her, she guessed that, despite his bravado, he wasn't certain what to do next.

She hadn't given up, but neither did she want to provoke him. It might spell the difference between life and death if she comprehended what drove him.

"I don't know what Doc was up to."

He growled. "The hell you don't. He confided in you. You're the one person he trusted. What did he discover?"

"Even if he confided in me, why should I tell you? You're going to kill me."

"Kill? You'll disappear. You no longer work for the university. Being awarded the grant is a long shot. People will conclude you've left Potlatch. Gone somewhere far away to lick your wounds. No one will ever see you again. No one will care."

Jay will, she wanted to say but didn't. *Jay, we never had a chance.*

"You've decided that discovering what Doc might or might not have uncovered is worth killing three people? I can't believe you're—"

He rocked back then leaned over her again. "Let me tell you something, Winter. Something you might get because you've probably been toiling in some tiny room, wondering why you went after that fancy degree you'll be paying off for decades to come." He scrubbed his mouth. "I've always given everything to whatever I've done. I pride myself in giving my employers a full day's work for my pay. Long ago, I was convinced that, if I proved to be a dedicated employee, I'd be rewarded. But it didn't happen. Time and time again, I was passed over. Screwed."

She was starting to understand Booth's motives. Maybe she should call them rationalizations. "You decided the only way you'd be recognized was if Doc made you part of his, what…his discovery?"

Booth straightened. Even with the unnatural lighting, she could see his eyes were glittering. "What discovery, Winter?"

"I was just throwing out words. He didn't tell me anything. I came here because I had a few days off, that's all."

His frown said he didn't want to believe her. Maybe couldn't. Her life might end in minutes. She wouldn't have to fight to stay in Olympic after all.

She'd never see Jay again.

Was done trying to comprehend Wolf.

Wolf, are you here? Don't desert me, please.

"You're lying, just like Gilsdorf did." Booth stood and flexed his knees. "We all confide in someone — or want to." He looked down. "For whatever reason, Gilsdorf decided not to confide in me. Before you showed up, I thought he might have confided in Floyd, because, for a while, the two were tight — and secretive."

"You —"

"Kept an eye on Gilsdorf? I had to. He might have been my last chance to make some kind of mark in this world."

With distance between them, she pushed herself into a sitting position. Like earlier, she had to lean forward to keep her balance, but at least she didn't feel quite as vulnerable. "What did you hope to accomplish by killing Doc?"

He stared at the knife. "That hadn't been my intention. I wanted us to be alone, because our conversation wasn't anyone else's business."

You took a knife with you.

"You need to get something. I was served with divorce papers last winter. Fourteen years of marriage down the tubes. My son... He wanted to live with his mother. It was just me. My ex said she was tired of having a part-time husband, but she knew what the job here would require when I took it. All those hours spent poring over those tapes — I told her it was going to amount for something, but she..."

Booth looked around. "You're young. You can't comprehend what failure feels like or how miserable it can be to keep going. The length a person sometimes goes in order to give his life meaning."

In a way, she felt sorry for Booth. She'd just never condone why he'd done what he had.

"I asked Gilsdorf to treat me with respect. That's all I wanted. He said it, whatever *it* was, was bigger than the two of us."

The wolf mask and where it came from.

"When I asked if what I'd been doing played a role in his discovery, he didn't answer. I had no doubt I was right. All those times when I let people take advantage of me, I couldn't let it happen again. Too much was at stake."

"You told Doc that?"

"Yes. I'd backed down for the last time."

"How did he respond?"

Booth stared into the night. She was certain he was replaying Doc's last seconds of life. "The same as earlier, only with more feeling. He said I couldn't grasp what was at stake."

Unable to stop herself, she fought her wrist restraints. So this was what a nightmare felt like. "That's when you killed him?"

He shuddered. "I gave up trying to talk sense into him. I had no choice."

No choice? He could have walked away.

"I grew up on a farm," Booth continued. "I've seen just about every injury that can happen to an animal. What cripples both animals and humans."

"What did you do?" The question made her sick to her stomach. "Incapacitate him the same as you did to me?"

"There were differences, but, essentially, yes. I severed his Achilles tendon so he couldn't walk."

No!

"There was no going back," he whispered. "I've always prided myself on my self-restraint, but something snapped."

Imagining what Doc had endured, she couldn't hold back a whimper.

"I didn't realize what I'd done until it was too late. Then I couldn't stop."

Another whimper pushed past her lips.

"Stop it!" He kicked her in the side, knocking her over. As

she struggled to right herself, he started to walk away only to immediately return. "I'll never get used to this place at night," he muttered. "Bad enough in the day. It swallows me."

Wolf, are you scaring him?

"You can't go on killing people. What about Dr. Wilheim?"

"What about him? He doesn't have the light in his eyes that Gilsdorf did. He doesn't study the forest as if he loves it like you do. Either Gilsdorf told you the essential stuff before you came here, or you have files that weren't on his laptop. You *will* tell me everything. Wilheim will waste time and money blundering around then go home with his tail between his legs. That's when I'll go to work."

Even though she couldn't give Booth's explanation her full attention, she was certain there were holes in his plan. The federal government was responsible for what happened in Olympic. Someone would come across her storage unit contract and find the wolf mask. Bureaucrats and politicians would argue over who should be in charge of a large-scale exploration. Booth would be pushed aside. Doc and Floyd would be dead, she'd be missing. Jay would be left with too many questions.

"Gilsdorf didn't tell me anything." Booth shook his head. "I—damn it, I didn't give him time."

"What about Floyd?"

"He was drunk. At least, I believe he was. I gave him plenty of time to tell me about what he and Gilsdorf had been up to, but he just kept crying."

While you tortured him — same as you intend to do with me.

"He didn't say anything?"

"Nothing I could make sense of. That, in part, is why I came after you."

She struggled not to react.

"I have your laptop. Maybe what I need is in there."

"I don't want to die."

He shrugged. "I can't have you messing things up. You need to disappear, which you will."

Booth was right. Between the lush vegetation, miles and miles of wilderness, and scavengers, in days there wouldn't be anything left of her. No one would realize what had happened to her.

I will, a deep voice whispered inside her.

Chapter Twenty-Nine

For a moment, Winter thought Jay had shown up to save her. Then she realized she'd heard Wolf. Her spirit had done more than just tell her he existed. He'd spoken to her!

Feeling strong, she glared at Booth. "What if your son learns what you've done?"

He slapped her, knocking her over again. "Shut up. I know what you're up to. It isn't going to work." He hauled her upright via her hair. Teeth clenched against the pain, she stared at him. Wolf was out there! Wolf who—what? What could a spirit do?

"I've spent too damn many years doing everything to live up to other peoples' expectations. From now on, I'm in charge."

A howl vibrated through her. Wolf was there, somehow, somewhere.

She was already shaking from fear and the effort of remaining erect, but Wolf's unnecessary warning made it even worse.

Damn you, Doc. Why did you antagonize Booth, if you did?

A yip now, a sound of disapproval.

Wolf was right. She didn't dare let anything distract her from trying to reach Booth. However, she'd barely reminded herself of that when her mind's eye filled with an image of her drifting through the forest. She wasn't walking so much as floating. Remarkable as that was, it paled next to the realization that she wasn't alone.

Wolf was with her. Matching her pace. His essence blending with hers. Accepting her.

"Where are Gilsdorf's files?" Booth demanded. "I

went through everything in that damn cabin. Looked everywhere."

Except inside Doc's slipper. "That's why you took his laptop."

"Of course." He kicked her ankles again, hard enough this time to force a gasp from her. If he hurt her enough, she might tell him about the storage device she'd tucked under her car's rear floor mat. Maybe she'd be unable to hold back from revealing the wolf mask's existence.

"I'd all but given up on getting any kind of recognition before Gilsdorf showed up. When I sensed his excitement, I vowed to be part of it."

"How? By killing people?"

His boot connected with her side. She gasped but managed not to topple over.

"Don't make me mad, Winter. It'll be worse for you."

Reality faded a little, replaced by an image of Wolf gazing at her. Connecting with her. Sharing his courage.

She'd been terrified, but now her courage grew. No matter what happened, she wouldn't beg Booth not to kill her. She'd make Wolf proud of her and be worthy of the ancient mask. "You're the one who's going to have to live with what you've done."

Booth stood on one leg in preparation for kicking her again. She dug her heels into the ground and scooted away. He stalked after her.

Another image — this one of Wolf taking hold of her hand and guiding it behind her, directing her fingers toward something.

Holding her breath, she extended her fingers. They encountered a jagged rock.

"You really are crazy," Booth said as he hauled her back to the tree via the rope around her ankles. Despite the burning in her arms, she managed not to let go of the rock. "What the hell did you think doing that would accomplish?"

Wolf turned her hand until the rock's sharp edge became a weapon.

Sweat ran down her sides as she fingered the rock. One side was so sharp she nicked a finger. Praying Booth couldn't see what she was doing, she jammed the rock against the tree trunk.

"I don't understand why you killed Doc." She barely cared what she was saying, just that she distracted him. "He was a reasonable man. He'd realize that all you wanted was to have your effort recognized."

Booth faced the forest. As she started sawing, she looked in the direction he was, half-expecting to see Wolf.

"You think I haven't worked toward that goal?" His voice dipped. "I have. For years."

"You must have had some successes. You're a historian."

"Right! I got on at a small museum. When the director retired, I thought I'd get a promotion, but I was passed over. I took a job at a larger museum, but that, too, became a dead end."

Wolf again. His shoulder pressing against hers and his strength flowing into her.

Thank you, she told her spirit. As she continued the back-and-forth motions, she pulled up the memory of what Wolf looked like. Magnificent.

"Did you watch both men die?"

Booth again headed toward her. "Don't ask me that. I'd tied Floyd up so he'd have to listen to me. When he died—I told you I let him down."

Did Booth really believe she'd forgive him? With him so close, she didn't dare continue working on the rope. "You obviously love your son, so how can you—"

"I'm backed into a corner. Grasping at my last straw."

That wasn't true, but, the point was, Booth believed it. Unless she could get free and overwhelm him, she was going to die tonight.

Never see Jay again.

Wolf drew back his lips. His fangs glittered.

"I'm out of options. There's only one way to make something of my life."

"By killing three people? How can you face yourself?"

The knife descended, sliced through denim and opened a several-inches-long wound in her right thigh. She screamed.

"Shut the fuck up!" He held the flat side of the knife to his chest with a still-shaking hand.

Wolf's snarl vibrated through her.

"The hell I'll be quiet!"

"What was— No!" His voice squeaked. "Oh no. Can't be."

Liking herself to *her* predator, she watched as Booth scrambled to her left. Using all her strength, she pressed the rope against the rock.

The knife headed for her thigh, a single-minded metal monster bent on inflicting pain and drawing blood.

A howl cut through the night. Low and strong, it drifted around her, relaxed her. Gasping, Booth jerked back. He clutched his weapon in both hands.

Wolf howled again, longer this time, a mystical, magical breath. Much as she longed to simply experience Wolf's gift, she didn't dare let herself be distracted. Gritting her teeth against the throbbing in her thigh, she attacked the rope. Her arms burned, and rope dug into her wrists.

"No, no," Booth whimpered.

Let him fight his monsters. She had work to do. To prove herself.

"What was that? Did you do it?"

Surely Booth knew how insane his question was, but maybe he was too unnerved.

He started to wipe his forehead only to hit himself between his eyes with the knife base.

He rubbed himself there. "That's a wolf."

"Are you sure?"

"Hell, yes." Careful this time, he wiped his forehead. "What's it doing here?"

"You're asking me?"

"The smell of blood must have drawn it in. He's coming for you."

She almost laughed, because the sound hadn't come from a flesh-and-blood predator. Another howl circled around them.

"Oh, shit, shit." Booth reached into his coat's front pocket and withdrew a revolver. "Where is it? I'm ready for it."

Instead of telling Booth that Wolf was responsible, she watched as he tried to determine where the howl was coming from. He took care to remain in the fragile light as he stalked its perimeter. She continued working. In an attempt to ease the strain on her shoulders, she scooted a few inches away from the tree. Her shoe struck a branch, causing it to crack.

Booth whirled toward her. "What are you doing?"

Before she could come up with a lie, Wolf let go with a sharp cry. Booth whimpered. He looked from the pistol in one hand to the knife in the other.

"Don't want to risk a shot if I don't have to." He seemed to be talking to himself. "The wolf's coming. It's the blood."

"That's your doing."

Instead of responding, Booth continued his jerky movements. Then he stopped as if he'd run into a barrier and focused his full attention on her.

"Blood. Lots of blood. Coming in for the kill."

Muttering something she couldn't hear, he slipped the pistol back in his pocket, gripped the knife in both hands and started closing the distance between them.

Wolf! Feel me. Sense my need. Even as she prayed, she sawed.

Predator strength again pressed against her.

Booth stepped to her side, grabbed her hair and jerked her head back. Ignoring her screaming shoulders and arms, she strained to separate her hands. Sweat stained her body. She bared her teeth.

"I'll do — do…"

She sensed more than felt the knife touch her throat. Maybe had less than a second to live. Would die the same way Doc and Floyd had.

Her hands sprang apart. Pain seared her upper body, but she ignored the sensation as she brought her arms forward and struck his cheek with the rock. Cursing, he released her hair. Enraged, she tucked her bound legs under her and struggled to her knees. Growled.

"No! You couldn't—"

She dropped the rock and launched herself as best she could, grabbing him around his hips with one arm and struggling to push him back. She held up her other arm to keep the knife from striking her vital organs. A fist struck her eye. Despite her blurred vision, she saw the knife coming at her from the side.

She ducked and drove her head into his belly. He lurched backward, breaking free of her hold. Off balance, she fell forward.

"How'd—"

Booth danced to her side and kicked her. The force behind the blow made her gasp. He aimed for her head. Despite being stunned, she managed to cover it with her hands.

Pain swelled in her throat. This time, instead of screaming, she howled. The sound strengthened her, and she forced her arms and legs under her. Booth had backed away, retrieved his pistol, and was staring at her as if he'd just seen something inhuman.

She howled again, keeping the sound going until her lungs burned. "Untie my legs," she demanded. "Make the battle an equal one."

"Not supposed to happen like this, not supposed..." Watching Booth fight to hold onto his weapons despite his trembling, she again almost felt sorry for him.

A howl spun him away from her. "Where's the bastard? You can't be calling him in, you can't. What are you, insane?"

Maybe they both were, not that it mattered.

"You aren't going to get away with killing me," she said. "They'll look for me, find—you'll leave clues—"

"Not if that damn wolf gets hold of you. Besides, no one

here cares what happens to you. You've made enemies."

Not with Jay, she hadn't. She refused to believe that. She struggled to stand but couldn't. Sitting on her rump, she bent her legs and reached for the ankle rope.

Her mind-wolf showed his fangs.

Booth shook the knife and pistol at her. "Last chance to live, Winter. Tell me where the damn files are, now."

"Wolf!" she cried. "Please show yourself. Make him face what he's doing."

Booth stared down at her as if he'd never seen her before. Her fingers clawed at the ropes.

"Not a bullet," he muttered. "If there's anything left of you once the wolf's done, they might find it. A knife. Yes. Lots of blood."

Even with her hands free, she was still at Booth's mercy. Her mind stalled over the question of whether Wolf had enough substance to save her. She wanted to live! Needed to experience life!

To love.

Booth wasn't far away, and yet it seemed to take him forever to close the distance between them. She was done trying to talk to him, had become more animal than human.

As her enemy widened his stance, she filled her lungs. Her howl echoed.

"Shit! Stop it!"

Booth rocked from side to side, looking for his advantage. She rocked with him, continuing to howl as she did.

"Don't, don't, don't!" he screamed.

The instant he jabbed with the knife, she threw her body to the right. Her elbow and hip struck the ground. Before she could straighten, he shoved her onto her side with his boot. Snarling, she stared up at her killer.

No way would she plead for her life.

"Get the hell away from her!"

Chapter Thirty

Jay's command pulled Winter back from the brink of madness. It didn't matter how he'd gotten there, just that he was. Jay was little more than a man-sized shadow surrounded by night, and yet, suddenly, she could breathe more easily.

"Who—" Booth started. "Damn it, no!"

"You heard me." Jay's words were like drumbeats. "Get away from her."

Instead of obeying, Booth dropped the knife. The pistol, looking like death, rose. Before Booth could shoot, Jay launched himself. His strength knocked Booth off his feet. The two landed on the ground, feet from her. Grunts and curses filled the air as they wrestled. Wolf's familiar howl was accompanied by cries from a new voice.

Jay, be careful! She wanted to scream but didn't dare distract him. Jay was the stronger of the two, but Booth's desperation might tip the balance. Besides, Booth had the weapon.

Muted thuds told her blows were landing. For several seconds, she remained in place while pain sang through her. Then her mind cleared. Hissing from the effort, she crawled toward the knife. Staring at the combatants, she scooped it up and began slicing the ropes around her ankles.

One of the men cried out. More blows, accompanied by profanity. They embraced, broke free, punched and kicked, again clung to each other. She didn't see how Booth could keep hold of the pistol, but if it was trapped between them—

The gun went off.

"Jay!" she bellowed.

The darkness intensified, and she couldn't remember how to make her hand work. She buried herself in the silence. Became part of it. Felt the wilderness embrace her.

"I'm sorry, I'm sorry," Booth babbled.

"No!" Her throat burned.

One of the men stood.

Jay. The pistol was in his right hand.

"You bastard!" Jay yelled. "You murdering bastard."

Because she'd briefly stopped being a human and had become animal-like, she recognized the same in Jay. If he shot Booth, she'd testify on his behalf.

Wolf wailed. More of the shrill cries she'd heard a few minutes ago joined Wolf's message.

"What's that?" she asked.

"Raven," Jay answered.

As she continued listening to the strident caws, she realized that, on some level, she'd accepted what had been responsible for the sound. Now, she understood something else — Raven was speaking to Jay.

"Get up," Jay ordered.

Booth staggered to his feet. The way he stood bent over put her in mind of a fighter at the end of a long match. His breathing sounded tortured, and his head hung. Thank god the bullet had missed.

"It's over," Jay said.

"I know."

Booth started crying.

Incapable of speaking, she finished freeing her ankles and planted her legs under her. She felt strong. Free. Wild.

"Give me the rope." Jay didn't take his attention off Booth.

She did as he commanded. Her mind replayed what had taken place right before Jay showed up. Without his intervention, she'd be dead, or wishing she were.

Jay handed her the pistol, spun Booth so his back was to them and tied Booth's hands behind him. That done, he ordered Booth to sit. The man who'd been her captor obeyed without protest. He sagged so far over that his head nearly touched the ground.

Jay extended a hand toward her. She started to give the pistol back to him. Then suddenly, somehow, his arms were around her, and her free one was around him. She wasn't going to cry! Not she who didn't know how. Who'd become part wolf.

"I wanted to kill him," Jay said. "I would have if Raven hadn't— Are you all right?"

Jay smelled of sweat and forest. He held her so tight she couldn't move. "I'm fine. What about Raven?" she asked.

"He convinced me not to."

Hard as it was to back away from this man who meant so much to her, she pushed against his chest. His fingers slid down her arms and settled over her wrists. She didn't care what Booth saw or heard. Booth didn't matter. Only Jay and what he'd just told her did.

"You believe Raven..." She couldn't finish.

Jay eased the pistol out of her hand and tucked it in his coat pocket. Then he laced his fingers through hers.

"He brought me to you."

In her mind's eye, she saw Jay's spirit helper and Wolf together. She intended to tell Jay about Wolf's role tonight, but that could wait. Wolf had given her courage while Raven had been Jay's eyes in the dark.

Saved her.

Tears burned. Started to fall. For the first time in many, many years, she didn't will them away as she lifted her head in silent invitation. Jay bracketed her face with his hands and kissed her. Long. Gentle.

"You're crying," he said at length. "Where'd he hurt you?"

"It doesn't matter."

"I heard you scream." His fingers slid to her throat. "I was so damn scared. If I'd been too late—"

"You weren't. Raven wouldn't let you be. Between him and Wolf—"

"Give me time to get used to having a spirit."

She nodded. "You'll love it."

He sighed. "Yes, I will."

Now her fingers were in his hair so she could drag his head down toward her. Her throbbing thigh warned her not to attempt standing on her toes, but she ignored it.

Only Jay mattered.

Jay, with his heritage and ties to this land, with his commitment to the people who shared it with him.

Jay, who'd followed his spirit into the forest to her.

She kissed him. Touched his cheeks and neck. Held onto his shoulders and pressed her breasts and pelvis against him. Moaned when his tongue slipped between her lips. Stopped breathing when he whispered, "I love you."

"You forgive me for not telling you about the mask?" she asked when she trusted herself to speak.

"I know why you did it. Yes, I forgive you."

"Thank you."

"I just wish that hadn't come between us."

"It's in the past, now," she whispered.

"Yes, it is."

As the night breeze slipped through the trees, she had no doubt that Wolf and Raven were out there, watching and listening to them. "Jay?"

"What?"

Her hold on him tightened. "I love you."

Epilogue

A week later…

"Is it what you expected?" Jay asked.

Much as she wanted to answer, Winter couldn't speak. Even though he'd refused to tell her what Grandparents Cave looked like, she'd thought she'd be prepared. It would resemble a bear's den, larger of course and protected from the elements, but nothing awe-inspiring.

How wrong she'd been.

The flashlights she and Jay carried illuminated a stone room nearly seven feet tall and twice as large as the cabin they now shared. They'd had to walk bent over, after he'd pushed aside the boulder that served to hide and protect the entrance. Then the space had opened up.

A natural stone shelf along two walls served as the display area for at least twenty ceremonial masks similar to the one she carried. The painstakingly detailed masks stared at her as if taking their measure of her. Two depicting bull elks must have been part of a heretofore unknown elk renewal ceremony she'd come across in one of the oral histories.

A large, exquisitely decorated wood chest rested on a deerskin rug on the floor. When she trained her flashlight on it, light from hundreds of embedded abalone shells glittered back at her. Next to the chest stood an elongated mask she recognized as being from the Nootka tribe. A dozen carved and painted salmon figures had been secured to the mask's neck to represent the salmon's vital role in early Native survival. She noted an ornate Tlingit pipe that was in far better condition than the one she'd seen at a museum.

Three totem poles at least twenty feet long lay next to each other on the ground. The bases had started to decay due to having once been set in the ground. In contrast, what ancient craftsmen had carved into the poles looked new. The three-dimensional depictions of animals, birds, fish, even humans were so lifelike they spooked her a little.

"Haida," she whispered, indicating the totems.

"Good guess."

"Not really. I know my tribes."

"*Your* tribes. I love hearing you say that."

They'd discussed her place in the Native American world since Jay saved her life, including what Wolf had told her about her right to touch the mask. They'd spent even more time speaking with law enforcement, particularly Christian, who obviously realized they weren't telling him everything but didn't see the point in pressuring them.

Winter had heard from the grants people that they'd rejected Wilheim's request to have the grant transferred to him based in large part on his abrasive personality. They'd told her to contact them when and if she was ready to continue Doc's work. Later the same day, Carolyn had called to tell her rumors were rampant that Wilheim was being pressured to take early retirement.

Michael was still working for the park but was sending out résumés because, as he put it, his talents weren't being appreciated there. The truth was that representatives from the various Northwest Native American tribes had sent a formal statement to several key politicians detailing their objections to his attempts to exploit them. Jay had signed his name to the document.

He'd also put in for a week's vacation next month so he could accompany Winter when she went to visit Doc's son and grandchildren. They'd decided to go well in advance of Booth's murder and attempted murder trial.

Winter had been concerned that Booth's defense attorney would question why Booth had killed Doc and Floyd and she'd be forced to explain more than she wanted to, but the D.A.'s office assured her they'd keep the focus on Booth's attempt to kill her. Hopes were he'd plead guilty.

"No wonder the Natives don't want outsiders to see this," she said. The cave was cool and dark but without the humidity that permeated the rest of the forest. As Jay had explained, the stone walls, ceiling and floor kept moisture out.

"How do you feel?"

They'd come here, just the two of them, so she could return the wolf mask to where it belonged.

"I'm in awe."

"Is that all?"

Jay had changed since she'd first met him—no, not changed so much as evolved. Deeper and more spiritual. He was still a forest ranger and a loving nephew, but it seemed to her that he had a greater appreciation for his surroundings. Maybe that's what he was getting at with his question.

Leaving him, she walked over to the ledge and placed the mask next to one that represented a bear. "You're home," she whispered. "Where you belong."

She faced Jay. "That's what you wanted me to say, isn't it? To realize that not everything about the past is fodder for anthropologists and historians. Not everything should be studied and evaluated and then relegated to professional journals or textbooks."

"In part."

What more did he want? Weighed down by the question, she moved about the cave while he watched her. She touched an ivory and abalone shell double-headed sea lion's head. As she trailed her fingers over the exquisite workmanship, she envisioned the craftsman who'd created what a shaman had once used to capture departing souls.

Next to the soul catcher was a colorful Tlingit rattle some long-dead shaman had depended on to call up his guardian spirit. The wooden rattle showed an intertwined fox and man. Undoubtedly the turquoises, reds and blacks were as vibrant now as when the instrument had been created.

She faced Jay. "This place is all about belief. Endurance. Reverence. That's what Doc didn't understand. When your uncle said Yakanon to me, he was trying to tell me that my mentor didn't have a soul." She sighed. "Yakanon is right, but I still mourn Doc."

"Doc wasn't all bad." Arms at his sides, Jay joined her. "Just as my brother wasn't." He indicated the new tattoo on his forearm that was a likeness of a smiling Floyd. "Even Booth accomplished some good."

A good she hoped to learn more about as soon as she began her new job as park librarian. Smiling, she wrapped her arms around Jay's neck and rose onto her toes. Thanks to the healing salve Talio had given her, her thigh barely protested.

"I'm so glad you brought me here. I want to thank everyone who safeguards this for trusting me enough to make this possible. They'll never understand how much it means to me."

"Yes, they do."

She didn't ask what he meant, and he didn't elaborate, because kissing and holding on took priority. By then, she was half crazy with wanting the man she'd had sex with every night since he'd rescued her from Booth.

He pushed her back from him but held on. "The Native council will continue their efforts to keep Dr. Wilheim and others like him as far from the land around Ghost Totem as possible."

"I'm glad. I agree with their decision in ways I never would have been able to before."

"Which is why they want you to have this."

He reached under his shirt and withdrew an eagle feather on a leather strip. His features gentle, he handed it to her.

One hand went to her mouth while the other reached for what only Native Americans had a right to.

"You belong here," Jay whispered. "My uncle and the

other elders accept and embrace you almost as much as I do."

Unable to speak, she slipped the necklace over her head and settled the feather against her skin, inches from her tattoo. Then she was back on her toes with her arms around Jay. Their lips sealed.

Despite the thick walls, a wolf's howl and a raven's cry reached them. She emotionally embraced Wolf and had no doubt Jay was doing the same with his spirit.

More books from
Totally Bound Publishing

The world has its empty places, and so does the heart.

IN A WORLD AT WAR, SHE WILL DO ANYTHING TO GET WHAT SHE WANTS

A LOVE TO
KILL FOR

HEAT

CONOR CORDEROY

*For Murdoch, women are bad news. Trying to stay alive
in war-torn Andalusia, tracking a vanishing femme fatal,
hunted by The Brotherhood, the last thing he needs is
love…*

FINDING HIM AGAIN

E.R. FALLON

WHEN FRIGHTENING INCIDENTS START TO HAPPEN,
SHE MUST UNRAVEL THE MYSTERY OF HER CHILDHOOD

*She came home to find the one romance she always
regretted not having…*

How can she face the danger when she can't hear it coming?

About the Author

Vella Munn

Vella Munn writes because the voices in her head demand it. She has had upward of 60 titles published both under her own name and several pen names. A dedicated hermit and shopping loather, she's married with two sons and four grandchildren. She's owned by two rescue dogs.

Vella Munn loves to hear from readers. You can find contact information, website details and an author profile page at https://www.totallybound.com/

Home of Erotic Romance